SUDDENLY, BRENNAN WANTED MORE

He took her face in his warm palms, covering her lips hungrily with his. He moved his mouth over hers, devouring its softness. She tasted of lemonade, a hint of garlic, chocolate, and something distinctly Krista.

Shocked, Brennan released her. *What am I doing?* he wondered.

Ready to apologize, Brennan gazed into Krista's eyes. She appeared as dazed as he felt. Maybe that was a good sign.

Moving away, Brennan opened the car door. "Get home safe."

"I will," she answered, climbing into the boat of a car.

"See you tomorrow."

He waited as Krista started the engine and pulled out of the parking space. Seconds later the car disappeared, and he returned to the Saab.

Liz had called it right. He did like Krista. A lot. But that bet between him and Flynn Parr could blow up in his face and destroy any chance they might have for a relationship.

THE WAY YOU AREN'T

KAREN WHITE-OWENS

Kensington Publishing Corp.
http://www.kensingtonbooks.com

I'd like to dedicate *The Way You Aren't* to Althea Johnson. She is my inspiration for Aunt Helen. Mrs. Johnson provided guidance, support, and shelter through many of my life's bitter moments, as well as, a hearty dose of encouragement or boot to the rear when the situation called for it. Thank you, Mrs. Johnson, for being such an intriguing part of my life.

DAFINA BOOKS are published by

Kensington Publishing Corp.
850 Third Avenue
New York, NY 10022

All Kensington Titles, Imprints, and Distributed Lines are available at special quantity discounts for bulk purchases for sales promotions, premiums, fund-raising, and educational or institutional use. Special book excerpts or customized printings can also be created to fit specific needs. For details, write or phone the office of the Kensington special sales manager: Kensington Publishing Corp., 850 Third Avenue, New York, NY 10022, attn: Special Sales Department, Phone: 1-800-221-2647.

Dafina and the Dafina logo Reg. U.S. Pat. & TM Off.

ISBN-13: 978-0-7582-1879-7
ISBN-10: 0-7582-1879-6

First mass market printing: October 2007

10 9 8 7 6 5 4 3 2 1

Printed in the United States of America

Chapter 1

"I hate company functions," Krista muttered, glancing at the green and white exit sign for Kensington Metropark. A low moan escaped her lips as a wave of anxiety and nausea swept through her. Swallowing hard, she focused on the drive, ignoring the little voice in her head that was urging her to make this year different.

Krista hit the turn signal and merged into the I-96 exit lane. She turned right at the stop sign and followed the brown wooden signs with white lettering and a gold, triangular Metropark symbol to the park's entrance.

Dexter Kee's annual picnic was the highlight of the summer. After the employees had returned from the Fourth of July holiday, plans for the picnic had shifted into high gear. Flyers had circulated, announcing the date for the outing, and potluck sign-up forms had appeared on the lunchroom refrigerator. Krista's supervisor had made it clear to her staff that *all* employees were expected to attend the event because it would occur during work hours.

Honestly, if the picnic had occurred at any other time, Krista would have never attended it. She had plenty of other projects to occupy her time. The big, rambling house she shared with her aunt Helen in the Boston-Edison area of

Detroit always needed something. Since Uncle Nick had died, his chores had fallen to her.

There never seemed to be enough hours in the day to complete all her household tasks and finish the projects she brought home from the job. The September 1 completion date for beta testing the Joining Networks advertising software belonged at the top of her list.

Driving up to the gate, she slowed and then stopped the car at the guard's shack. Waiting, she hummed along to Najee's "Joy" as a man dressed in a mud-colored uniform poked his head out of the structure, stepped out of the entrance, and stood next to the vehicle.

"Three dollars, please," he announced, with an authoritarian tone and an outstretched hand.

Nodding, Krista dug in her purse and flashed her Dexter Kee employee badge. The red-haired man gave the plastic card a cursory glance before waving her through the gate. Smiling, Krista returned her badge to her purse. The agency's managing directors had prepaid the entrance fee for the staff and their families. For access, the employees needed to show their badges.

"Have a nice day," Krista called, inching the car forward and following the blue, red, and yellow balloons leading the way to the picnic site. She slowly cruised along the tree-lined road until she came upon a white banner with the company's logo strung high around the upper branches of two large ash trees.

The engine idled as she searched the sea of cars. A familiar sage green Cadillac Escalade, owned by the agency's president, sat among them. *This is the place,* she thought as her hands fluttered nervously around the steering wheel. Her stomach knotted with apprehension.

Krista eased Uncle Nick's silver '98 Chevrolet Caprice into an empty space and switched off the engine. The car sputtered and shook for a few seconds before going silent. Ashamed, Krista glanced around the park area, hoping her coworkers hadn't noticed how terrible her old junker sounded. Not for the first time, she wished she could get rid of this boat and buy a car that would save on gas and was built in the 2000s. Her aunt refused to consider a smaller vehicle. So Krista was stuck with the Chevy.

She made a mental note to change the radio station back to the one Aunt Helen loved before she got home. The old girl would have a stroke if she heard music other than her church music when she turned on the radio.

Three large pavilions filled with people, wooden tables and benches, and barbecue grills sat in the center of the area. Decked out in helmets and arm and knee pads, several Rollerbladers dodged in and out of the people lining the black, tarred bike trail. Squealing children crept to the lake's edge, dipping their toes in the water and tossing rocks into it.

A growl rose from the pit of Krista's belly when she focused on Erin Saunders standing among a few of her cohorts. The day they were introduced, Erin had turned her cold gaze upon Krista and had flashed her dislike for the new IT specialist. From that day on, Erin had made it one of her career goals to terrorize Krista on a daily basis. Although they were peers, Erin persisted in ordering Krista around and treating her like her employee. Krista knew she should say something, but it took so much effort to fight those battles. She found it far easier to go with the flow and do the work.

Krista gazed at the group of people gathered together, taking note of their clothing. Most wore comfortable tops, shorts, and sneakers or sandals. She looked down at the calf-length denim skirt and white oxford shirt her aunt had insisted she wear. A pair of white canvas shoes and socks completed her outfit. Sighing softly, Krista shook her head. As usual, she was inappropriately dressed. Although she'd tried to get out of the house with a pair of pants and a short-sleeved top, her aunt had vetoed the idea, telling her how a proper young woman never appeared in public in pants.

Sometimes Auntie made her feel more like a high school teenager than a twenty-five-year-old woman.

There wasn't much she could do to change her appearance. All she could do was make the best of the situation.

Krista flipped down the visor, checking her image in the mirror. She smoothed the wild tresses of hair with her hand. Milk chocolate skin, almond-shaped brown eyes, and thick dark hair pulled into a brush of a ponytail at the back of her head reflected back at her.

She ran damp palms across the soft denim of her skirt before getting out of the car and strolled across the grassy area, hating the way her belly twisted into knots. She took a second to admire the crystal blue lake, while pulling herself together. Smoke smelling of a hint of hickory, charcoal, and lighter fluid billowed from a line of grills loaded with hot dogs, chicken, and ribs.

This year I'll have fun, Krista chanted silently. *I'll have fun. No more mishaps. Yeah, right. You wear the crown for screwup. For the past three years, you have shown up, and something stupid has happened to you. Don't think about it,* she decided, trying to ignore those thoughts.

Finding a deserted spot under one of the pavilions, Krista searched the picnic grounds for members of her department. She spotted her supervisor and several of her coworkers gathered around a tub filled with ice and brown bottles. Everyone held Miller, Michelob, or Samuel Adams beers in their hands.

Rachel Ulrich glanced her way. Krista tentatively raised a hand to wave but immediately dropped it when her supervisor's gaze skated past Krista and focused on someone or something beyond her. Embarrassed, Krista cupped her hands in her lap and studied the grass.

Krista wished she felt more comfortable among her peers. The only places she felt confident and safe were at her desk and at home. But she couldn't hide from the world. She had to work. Her job required interaction with her coworkers.

She spotted Connor Dexter strolling toward Brennan Thomas. For a second, Krista wondered what that was about. She'd heard rumors of some possible changes in the company. Did some of those changes involve Brennan?

She hoped so. He was a good guy. Grounded. He never acted like he was too good to share a word with anyone at the agency.

Plus, he was drop-dead gorgeous and tall, with smooth dark chocolate skin and soft brown eyes that sparkled with a hint of gold. Business casual or suits, Brennan always dressed with an elegant flair. Today he wore a pair of charcoal cargo shorts and a cream short-sleeved T-shirt.

Erin talked about Brennan all the time. She told her friends how she wanted to get with him. As far as Krista knew, Brennan hadn't shown the slightest interest in Erin.

Brennan stood near the lake, with a bottle of Sam Adams, watching the kids play in the water. He smiled as a little blond tyke rushed to the water's edge and tossed in a pebble. As the ripples spread, the kid stamped his feet and giggled in delight. The boy's mother scooped him up in a big bear hug and kissed his sun-baked red cheeks before carrying him away.

Krista Hamilton slowly inched toward the water. Fascinated, Brennan watched the young woman. As she got closer to the water, she spoke with several children frolicking at it's edge. Waving, she smiled as one little girl waded through the water.

Brennan's heart nearly stopped in his chest. Krista's face was transformed from the closed, weary expression that always greeted him. For a moment, he stood transfixed. Despite the bushy eyebrows, unflattering clothes, and hair going in every direction, Krista looked almost pretty. Shaking off this thought, he dismissed the woman and all the baggage that came with her.

Swallowing the last of his beer, Brennan headed to the bin labeled EMPTIES. Connor Dexter appeared at his side and slapped him on the back. "Brennan, how are things going? Are you enjoying yourself?"

Shrugging, Brennan answered, "Yeah. I am. Thanks."

With an arm around his shoulders, Dexter Kee's president steered Brennan away from the crowd and along the bike trail. "Got a minute?"

Obviously so, Brennan thought, glancing into his boss's face. Pale blue eyes gazed back at him. He never turned the boss down. "Sure."

Mr. Dexter pointed a finger at the bike path. "Let's walk."

The pair strolled along the trail. Connor Dexter was a striking man, tall, with a commanding presence and a full head of white hair. At approximately six foot three, he towered over many of his employees, although Brennan and he stood eye to eye.

Connor Dexter had arrived in the United States via Montreal, Canada. After graduating from the University of Windsor, he accepted a position in the advertising department of the Ford Motor Company. Once he mastered the intricate details of the business, Connor took those skills and started Dexter Kee.

Over the past thirty years, the company had grown, developing a great reputation for unique and innovative advertising, which kept it at the forefront of the advertising market. Recently, Dexter Kee had been named one of the top one hundred businesses by *Fortune* magazine. Brennan admired Connor Dexter's ability to carve out a name for himself from nothing.

"What can I do for you?" Brennan asked after waiting several minutes for Mr. Dexter to speak.

"What do you know about Gautier International Motors?"

Halting in the center of the path, Brennan shut his eyes, seeing a newspaper story about the French automaker on his computer monitor. "I read an article a few weeks ago. They're making a stab at the U.S. market."

"Correct."

"Have they contacted us?" Brennan opened his eyes and examined his boss. "I haven't heard anything."

"They've approached us."

Brennan digested this info before speaking. "Interesting. Where do I come in?"

Connor Dexter stiffened next to him. Surprised, Brennan watched his boss.

"I don't like this part, but I don't have a choice," replied Mr. Dexter, embarrassed. His neck grew red. "The senior management and the board of directors voted to handle things this way. I'm assuming you've heard the rumor that we're planning to increase the management team. Am I right?"

The lightning switch in topics caught Brennan off guard. Frowning, he hesitated, giving himself a minute to travel down the twist in the road Connor Dexter intended to take him. "I've heard a word or two."

Chuckling, the older man said, "Our rumor mill knows their business. Two out of three times they have things correct."

Why had Connor Dexter brought this up? What did he want from Brennan? Was he in the running for this position? Of course, he wanted it, but he didn't want to appear too eager.

"You've been with us for a little over five years. In that time you've done a superb job," said Mr. Dexter.

Acknowledging the compliment with a bow of his head, Brennan said, "Thank you."

"It's not about thanks. I've always believed in rewarding excellence." Connor Dexter stopped on the bike trail. Empty of picnickers, this stretch of the area was quiet. "We've narrowed the field of candidates to two. You."

Maintaining his calm exterior, Brennan silently yelled; *Yes!*

"And Flynn Parr," added Mr. Dexter.

Flynn and Brennan didn't always see eye to eye. But he had

to admit the other man was a great choice. Flynn worked hard, and his team brought a lot of business into the agency. Brennan understood how and why senior management had come to the decision to select Flynn.

Connor Dexter cleared his throat. "Let's get back to Gautier International Motors. Senior management has decided the person who bags a contract with the auto company will be the front-runner for the partner position."

"So Flynn and I are in competition?"

"Actually, yes and no. You'll both be working on the same campaign. We decided to give Gautier an opportunity to choose between more than one approach to selling cars. Whatever your team comes up with will be presented to the automaker on the same day as Parr's material."

"Hmm," Brennan grunted, working out the situation in his head. "I see."

"I'm sorry about this. I would prefer it if one person had a clear shot at winning the account. Unfortunately, Gautier is too important. We want our best men to dazzle their people."

"I can understand that."

Connor Dexter turned to Brennan and placed a hand on the younger man's shoulder. "Anything you need, I want to know about it. I'm counting on one of you guys to get us that contract."

"Thanks for this opportunity. I won't let you down."

"I know you won't. That's why you're my candidate." Connor Dexter snapped his fingers and then pointed at Brennan. "Make it happen." The older man held out his hand, and Brennan took it. The two men shook hands before Mr. Dexter walked away.

Brennan moved back down the trail to the water. He stood at the shore as he reviewed what he'd just heard.

Smiling, he folded his arms across his chest. A chance to make partner was huge. All the energy he had put into building his career was finally paying off.

The tip of his tongue settled in the corner of his mouth as he plotted out a program. First thing tomorrow morning, he'd have the agency's librarian pull every scrap of information she could find about Gautier. Maybe add in some data on the owner and board.

Until the deal was wrapped up, he'd put all of his efforts into securing this contract. Brennan's hand balled into a fist as he sensed victory within his grasp. Winning this contract would put him one step closer to making partner. And nothing would get in his way.

Chapter 2

"Doggone it!" Krista exclaimed as a dollop of mustard hit the front of her white blouse. She crammed the last bite of her hot dog into her mouth while rubbing ineffectively at the yellow condiment with a white napkin. Instead of cleaning the spot, the napkin left tiny flakes of paper above her breast.

Uneasiness spread through her veins. *I don't want to walk around with a mustard stain on the front of my clothes. The staff laughs at me enough without adding this. Maybe a little soap and water will do the trick.* Krista rose from the bench, left the pavilion, and started across the grassy area to the restroom.

Five minutes later, Krista emerged with a huge, damp circle on her chest and glanced around the picnic area, searching for members of her group. Old fears and uncertainties surfaced. She didn't want anyone to see her this way. Embarrassed, she laid a hand across the wetness.

Krista headed to the lake, hoping to stay away from the prying eyes of her coworkers until her blouse dried. Her gaze focused on the lake, which was luring her to its blue crystal waves. The water always calmed and soothed her. She found a quiet spot at the water's edge, sank onto the warm sand, removed her shoes and socks, and dipped her toes into the cool blue wetness.

Krista stretched out and leaned back on her elbows. Eyes shut, she soaked up the sun's rays. Tension slowly oozed from her body, replaced by a sense of peace. The minutes passed quietly; then she heard a faint sound at her side. A toddler stood watching her.

Kids were her greatest love. They were so open and trusting. It was one of the reasons she taught Sunday school classes at her church. Talking and working with children filled her heart with joy and pleasure.

"Hi," Krista whispered, scanning the area for a parent. She caught sight of a young woman standing several feet away. Krista pointed at the boy and then at the woman. She nodded.

"He's mine," she mouthed.

Nodding, Krista patted the spot next to her. "Come sit with me."

The little one watched her solemnly. After a moment, he took a step closer but remained standing. After an added minute of indecision, he flopped down next to her, pulled off his sneakers, and dug his feet into the sand. Giggling, he buried his toes in the sand.

"I'm Krista. What's your name?"

"Toby."

"How old are you?"

He wiggled four sand-covered fingers in her direction. Krista glanced at his mother. Chuckling, the woman shook her head and then displayed three fingers. Nodding, Krista folded one of Toby's fingers down and suggested, "How about three?"

The little boy nodded and then added more sand to the pile he was making. After a while they ventured to the water's edge. The little boy placed his small hand in Krista's, and they strolled into the water, washing their feet. He picked up a small stone and tossed it into the water. Toby squealed and practically danced as he watched the ripples. Krista's heart danced with delight.

A howl of laughter blared from behind her. Krista turned her head and found a crowd of spectators watching a volleyball game between Brennan Thomas's and Flynn Parr's teams. Among the spectators stood Toby's mother.

Grimacing, Krista turned away from Flynn's knowing gaze. Whenever he came near her, he was all touchy-feely, which made her feel as if she needed a shower. Flynn had such an air of entitlement about him. Whenever she did any work for him, he never said thank you.

Her gaze settled on Brennan Thomas. Tall, lean, and attractive, the sales director shared duties with Flynn Parr. Whereas Flynn acted like a pain in the rear, Brennan was an angel. He always greeted her when he saw her and asked how she was doing. When his sales staff messed up their computers and he needed to call her, Brennan always apologized for their mistakes.

Krista glanced down, turning her attention to Toby. A soft gasp escaped her. The little boy was gone. Where was he? Frantic, she shifted this way and that, searching the area, and found him wading toward the center of the lake.

Fear gnawed its way to her heart. *No, baby, No.* she screamed silently, rushing into the deeper end of the lake.

As Krista waded through the water, her denim skirt twisted around her legs. She made it to the child and lifted him into her arms. Sighing with relief, she hugged him close. "What are you doing out here?"

Toby pointed at a red object floating in the water. "Ball."

"Yes, it is. Here. Let me get it for you," she offered, swinging him onto her hip and grabbing the ball in her hand. She fought her way back to land and placed the child on the sand and handed him the toy. With a gentle nudge, she pointed a finger at the volleyball court. "Go to your mommy."

He trotted off in that direction, with the red ball in his hand.

Relieved, Krista returned to the water's edge, squeezing the water out of her wet skirt. She heard the slap of leather hitting the sand behind her. Without warning, determined hands gave her a hard, sharp shove in the back, causing her to fall head first into the lake. Stunned, Krista floundered.

Laughter followed. Filled with dismay, she sat in the lake, fighting to get control. Her clothes and hair were soaked. Close to tears, she tried to stand. Unfortunately, she cut her foot on the sharp edge of a rock and fell into the lake a second time.

Instantly, her humiliation turned to raw fury. But the culprit had gotten away, and there was no one to direct her anger at.

"Time," Brennan yelled, forming the letter *T* with his hands.

"Oh, come on," shouted a member of Flynn Parr's team. "At the rate we're going, we'll still be playing this game when my kids go to college."

Ignoring the complaint, Brennan gestured for his team to come together. Eight men from his sales staff huddled in a circle, discussing strategies for winning the game.

"Can we do it?" the team captain, Brennan, asked.

"Yeah!" the team players yelled.

"Are you sure?" Brennan asked, pumping them up for the final plays.

"Yeah!" the players shouted.

"All right." Brennan smacked the guy standing next to him on the back. "Let's do this."

The men scattered in every direction, forming the proper volleyball formation, and then the game continued. Positioned at the back row, Brennan served the ball. It soared over the net and dropped between two players.

Suddenly, one player pushed between the two men closest to the net and hit the ball, sending it back the way it had come. Brennan moved forward and spiked the ball, slamming it down.

Flynn dived for the ball, punching it too lightly to get it over the net. The ball flew high in the air and then landed on the sand, with a soft thump, at his feet. Hands balled into fists, Flynn cursed, "Damn!"

Brennan's team roared, bouncing up and down. The guys rushed him, slapping their captain on the back and congratulating him on a great play. Smiling, Brennan nodded before ducking around the edge of the net, with an outstretched hand. "Flynn, good game."

Flynn turned a glacier blue gaze on Brennan. For a beat, Brennan read the indecision in Flynn's eyes as he debated whether he wanted to shake Brennan's hand. Good sportsmanship won out, and Flynn grasped the other man's hand in a firm grip.

"You did good," Brennan said.

"Thanks. So did you," replied Flynn, returning the compliment.

"You want to go again?" Brennan dropped the other man's hand and picked up the ball. He balanced it in his palm as a far too familiar and unwanted hand stroked his back from shoulder to shoulder before resting in the center of his back. He stiffened defensively.

"I doubt Flynn would want to lose a fourth game to you," Erin cooed close to Brennan's ear.

"Thanks for keeping score, Erin." Sarcasm peppered Flynn's words. "It's just what I wanted to hear."

Erin pushed a lock of shoulder-length auburn hair behind her ear and answered, with saccharine sweetness, "You're welcome."

"Flynn, you're a great player," said Brennan as he slapped him on the back. "We should collaborate on putting together a team for the agency. I read somewhere it's a great way to build team spirit."

"Maybe," Flynn offered in a noncommittal tone.

Brennan was about to add another statistic on team spirit when he heard a loud splash, followed by the roar of laughter from Flynn's teammates. Curious, Brennan scanned the area until his gaze landed on Krista Hamilton. Fully clothed and drenched from head to toe, the young woman sat in the lake, struggling to get to her feet.

One of Flynn's salesmen nudged the man standing next to him and held out his hand. "Where's my money? Told you she'd do it."

The guy pulled his wallet from his back pocket, opened it, and removed a twenty-dollar bill. "Ah hell. I figured by now she'd had sat her butt down somewhere and stayed out of trouble."

Pocketing the money, the salesman added, "She can't help it. Krista is such a geek. She knows her job but has the social graces of a bear."

Brennan frowned at the cruelty of their words. What kind of people did he work with? Where was their compassion for another human being? Krista worked with them. Why would they laugh at her misfortune?

Without another thought, Brennan hurried across the picnic area. Disregarding his own clothes and the chill of the water, he waded into the lake, to Krista. Soaked from head to toe, she stumbled.

"I got you," he said over the roar of laughter he heard from the volleyball court. Brennan slipped his hands under Krista's arms, set her on her feet, and started for land. It was a slow go, wading through the water with her heavy denim skirt. "Here. Let me help you."

She could barely put one foot in front of the other. After she made a couple of attempts to walk, Brennan lifted her into his arms and carried her from the lake.

At the water's edge, Brennan set Krista on her feet in front of him. He immediately examined her from the top of her wild head to her bare toes. There weren't any obvious injuries. She seemed unhurt, except for the embarrassment flashing from her pain-filled brown eyes. Tears of frustration and pain ran down her cheeks.

A twinge of sorrow and sympathy filled him. *She is such a delicate waif,* he thought as anger began to consume him. This wasn't right. Why were the folks laughing at an accident?

"What happened?" Brennan asked, holding her steady with a light hand at her elbow. Krista's teeth began to chatter as she shivered.

"N-no-nothing." She lifted a wet hand and wiped the tears from her cheeks. "Thanks for helping," she muttered softly, scooping up her shoes and socks.

"You all right?" he asked.

Unable to meet his gaze, she lowered her head, studied her feet, and then nodded.

He steered her away from the picnic area. "Do you need help getting home?"

"No. I can m-ma-make it," she answered.

"I'm sure you can. I'll walk you to your car. Wait a sec." He stopped at a navy Saab and hit the remote. The lights flashed, and the door locks snapped open with a thump. Brennan rummaged inside the trunk, producing a beige blanket. He tossed it around Krista's shoulders and pulled the edges together. "This will help you keep warm." He glanced around the parking area. "Where's your car?"

If it was possible, she became even more embarrassed. Krista pointed at a gray Chevrolet Caprice. Brennan removed the keys from her hands and opened the door. He studied her for several silent moments. "Can you drive? Because if you can't, I'll get you home and have one of my guys follow us."

"No!" she answered frantically, removing the blanket from her shoulders and shoving it in his direction. "T-th-there's no n-ne-need. I'm fine."

Brennan shook his head and returned the fleece garment

to her shoulders. "Keep it. You're freezing. Bring it to work Monday."

"Thank you."

He helped her into the front seat and handed her the keys. "No problem. Get home safe."

"I will," Krista promised, shutting the door and switching on the ignition. Seconds later, she pulled out of her parking space and headed out of the picnic area.

If it weren't for the seriousness of the situation, he would have laughed at the sight of this tiny little woman behind the steering wheel of this huge monster of a car.

Hands on his hips, Brennan stood in the middle of the parking lot, watching the Caprice's taillights slowly fade. Once the lights disappeared, Brennan turned back to the picnic area. Sighing, he started toward the pavilion. There were a few choice words about compassion and understanding he needed to share with his colleagues and coworkers.

Chapter 3

An image of Krista's tear-stained face flashed in his head, tearing at his heart and toughening his resolve to give the staff a tongue-lashing regarding their attitude toward the IT expert. Brennan drew in a deep breath and let it out slowly. His gaze cut across the landscape, focusing on the pavilion filled with Dexter Kee sales staff.

No one on his team would be allowed to treat a coworker like an outcast. More times than he could count, Krista had come through for him. Whenever his sales execs crashed their system, the young woman showed up without hesitation and worked steadily until she found a solution. She deserved better, respectful treatment from the people she assisted.

With that thought firmly planted in his brain, Brennan squared his shoulders and marched across the grassy terrain toward the pavilion. Brennan stopped at a picnic table loaded with Dexter Kee sales staff, waiting for a break in the conversation.

"Give it up," Joe Wright demanded.

"Yeah! Yeah! Yeah!" Rob Albert answered grudgingly, dropping several twenties on the table.

Grinning broadly, Joe scooped up the cash and slipped the

bills into his wallet. "Hey, Rob. I'm taking bets on what Krista's going to do next year."

Rob shook his head and slipped his wallet into the back pocket of his denim shorts and then sat on the bench. "No thanks. I think you and I are done, Joe. She's cost me enough money for one day."

Joe's hands dropped to his waist. He flapped his arms back and forth, making a clucking sound like a barn animal. "Chicken. Chicken. Chicken."

The group roared with laughter.

Eyes narrowing, Rob said, "Make all the noise you want. I'm keeping what's left of my hard-earned change in my pocket."

"You should never have taken the bet," George Edwards added. "Krista has a reputation we can count on."

Rob snorted in disgust. "Well, I didn't work for Dexter Kee last year, so I didn't know."

Laughing, Joe hunched his shoulders. "Too bad. So sad."

"What else has she done?" said Rob as he picked up his Miller Lite and took a long swig.

Someone from the opposite end of the table chimed in. "Last year she fell into the dessert table and sent everything flying in different directions. Most of the good stuff landed in the dirt."

Bill Jones came forward, wagging a finger in the air. "Hey, I remember that. She had cake and pie all over her. Whipped cream ended up everywhere, on her face and in her hair. She looked like a clown."

A hearty round of laughter followed Bill's remark.

"How in the hell did she knock over the table?" Rob asked.

Bill Jones shrugged. "She must have tripped over her own feet."

"Krista is one of the clumsiest people I've ever met," Joe added.

"What about the year before that?" Flynn reached for his

beer. "Didn't she try to play baseball or something and get hit in the mouth?"

Laughing, Joe nudged Rob. "There's always an upside to things. At least you don't have to be bothered with her outside the office. Can you imagine being on a date with her? I don't know which is worse, the clumsiness or the clothes. She dresses like one of those old sisters sitting in the front pew of the church. Krista can't be more than twenty-five. I swear her clothes make her look fifty."

Erin Saunders sauntered up to the group and slid into a place at the table. "Are you guys talking about Kristawolf?"

The crowd laughed uncontrollably.

Amusement gleaming from his eyes, Flynn questioned, "Kristawolf?"

Erin nodded. "That's what we called her in high school."

"Why?" Rob asked.

"Duh! The hair. It's everywhere," replied Erin.

Laughter erupted.

"It looks as if she put her hand in an electrical outlet," Erin explained further.

"Kristawolf. Kristawolf." Joe chanted the name as if he were savoring a fine wine. "I like it."

"I got it," shouted one of the guys. "There's something growing in her hair. You know, like an alien. It's going to burst through her skull, run down the hall, and get out to impregnate the human race."

Shaking his head, Joe added, "Krista is a mess."

"That she is," Rob agreed.

That's enough, Brennan thought. *I've let this go on too long.* "You guys should be ashamed of yourselves."

Rob folded his arms across his chest and eyed Brennan from across the table as if he'd found a snake slithering through his living room. "Why?"

"There's not a person here who hasn't used Krista's skills

with computers and networks," said Brennan. "Treat her with the respect she deserves."

"That's her job," replied Rob.

A surge of anger took hold of Brennan. With his hand clenched into a fist, he held on to his temper. He beat down his feelings until he felt calm enough to speak. "You know as well as I do that she goes beyond the call of duty to help us. Rob, didn't you get a nasty virus on your computer?"

"So?" Rob answered belligerently.

"Didn't I hear something about Krista swapping out her laptop for yours?" asked Brennan. "She inconvenienced herself so that you wouldn't be computerless while she cleared up your hard drive."

Scowling at Brennan, Rob dropped his head and stared at the wooden tabletop.

"Nothing to say?" Brennan taunted.

Flynn Parr stepped in, giving Rob a comforting pat on the shoulder, and said, "Brennan, it's not his fault Krista is one clumsy broad."

"Woman! Not broad!" Brennan corrected, exasperated. What would it take to make these guys behave better?

"Whatever," Rob muttered.

"Are you perfect?" Brennan asked the employees at the table. "Does anyone here have it all together?"

"What are you? Jesus Christ reborn?" George asked. "Ready to defend the rights of the less fortunate and goofy or to champion the cause of geeks and losers. Why are you so concerned?"

Brennan's insides churned. Whatever his reasons, it wasn't their business. "Listen. And listen well. I don't expect to hear any of you talking about Krista like that again." He gazed around the area, establishing eye contact with each person at the table.

Flynn patted the rough table surface. "Calm down, man.

You're taking this way too seriously. We're just having a little fun."

"Not like this. And not at Krista's expense," said Brennan.

"She's a loser. Nobody here made her that way," said Flynn as he picked up his bottle of Sam Adams and turned it up to his lips.

"Treating her like an outcast doesn't help her situation," Brennan reminded.

Joe spoke up. "Why do you care? I can't imagine you're after that piece of tail. She just doesn't seem like your type."

Anger rose in Brennan like a fierce lion ready to pounce. "Don't talk about Krista that way."

"Wow! Hit a nerve," Joe smirked, giving Flynn a significant look.

Brennan took a minute, regained his composure, and then brought it down a notch. "This is exactly what I'm talking about. The agency wouldn't look kindly on a comment like that."

"What are you?" asked Flynn as he looked down his nose, with disdain. "Krista's fairy godfather?"

Joe taunted, "If you are, please do something about that woman's hair. Buy her a comb."

Everyone at the table laughed, except Brennan. Boiling with frustration, his hands balled into fists at his sides. This crowd had ignored every damn word he'd said. It bugged him to see how they treated a person who gave so unselfishly to the people she worked with.

"Hey, my man," said Rob, tossing a twenty on the table. "Take her shopping and buy her a few pieces that don't look as if my grandmother made a trip to the local resale shop."

"You might suggest your girlfriend get a makeover," Joe added.

"Krista's not my girlfriend," Brennan replied.

"Whatever. Take her to Somerset Collection, and have them revamp her from head to toe," said Flynn as he lifted a finger and pointed at Brennan. "Trust me. That'll help in the respect department."

"If I had my way, somebody would teach her how to talk to people," Rob suggested. "Teach Krista how to put a sentence together without stammering like an idiot."

Laughing, someone at the table added, "You are so right. Every time she tries to explain something to me, she shuffles and stutters so much that I laugh at her. I can't help it."

Murmurs of agreement wafted around the table.

"I know," Flynn said. "Let's enter Krista in one of those movie and a makeover programs that the cable stations carry. Lord knows, she could use the help."

Joe waved a dismissing hand in Flynn's direction. "Don't waste your time. Krista's hopeless."

"I've heard enough," Brennan warned in an ominous tone. "All of your comments, jokes, and tricks go against the corporate value of respect. In case you have forgotten, before our first day of work, we all had to take classes regarding the agency's ideas on respect for your fellow coworker and what's considered harassment. If you don't remember, take a look at your employee handbook and read up on that section."

Thoroughly chastised, the group looked away and grumbled under their breath.

"Here's my final word on the subject, and you better listen. Leave Krista alone," Brennan stated clearly, enunciating each word. "If anything gets back to me that you guys have teased or mistreated her again, I promise you, you'll hear from me and the agency's human resources department."

Seething with anger and frustration, Brennan marched purposefully across the grassy area packed with Dexter Kee employees and their families, feeling that his efforts had been for nothing. Those jokers didn't give a damn about anything but their next quarterly bonuses.

Brennan's belly churned and tied into knots as he remembered his friend Juan's earnest expression. Grunting, he shook the image from his head. After all these years, he still felt the same level of shame and wondered how he had allowed himself to be drawn into the cruel and mean-spirited pranks of his high school football team. His only excuse was that after living without roots as a foster child, Brennan had wanted to fit in and be part of the group. So he'd dropped his old friends and hung with the football team, ignoring the people that had been there for him.

Brennan grimaced, remembering how they'd tortured kids that didn't fit the football team's image of cool. Trying to stay on the good side of his teammates, he'd done some pretty awful and cruel things, including hurting his best friend, Juan. That was part of the reason he refused to sit back and allow the sales executives to talk about Krista so maliciously. It sent the wrong message throughout the agency.

The first time he noticed that expression in Krista's eyes, he was immediately transported back to his teens. He felt bad for her and the terrible things he'd done in the past. The wrenching guilt chilled him like a blanket of snow, and he found it almost impossible to be around her when the others treated her so badly.

No one would hurt her the way they had hurt Juan. No one. They didn't have the excuse of being young and foolish, and he planned to make certain that the sales staff maintained the agency's values and objectives.

As he fished his keys from the pocket of his shorts, he heard a familiar and unwanted voice.

"Brennan!"

"Yeah?" said Brennan. Leaning against the car door, his mood soured even more as he watched Flynn Parr jog up to him.

"You were pretty harsh back there. Don't get too upset with the guys. They aren't a bad lot." Flynn gave Brennan one of his thousand-watt smiles, which didn't move Brennan at all. "You've got to admit Krista's fair game for everyone."

"It's got to stop. You should get your people under control instead of laughing it up with them."

Taken aback, Flynn frowned. "What is your deal?"

"I don't have a deal," Brennan countered. "It's not right to do Krista this way."

Flynn shoved his hands inside the pockets of his denim shorts. "You act like you're better than everyone else. News flash! You're not."

"This is not about better or worse." Brennan took a step closer to Flynn, getting in his face. "It's about fairness and how you treat others and expect them to treat you."

Like a curious animal, Flynn tilted his head to the side. His eyes changed, glittering with a hard, dangerous gleam. "If you're so concerned, help her. Make her do better."

What type of crap is Parr babbling about now? Brennan wondered. "How am I supposed to do that?"

Flynn jabbed his thumb toward the picnic table where the sales force still sat. "Do what they suggested."

Confused, Brennan asked, "What?"

"Do a makeover."

"That's not my job."

Sensing he might have a fish on the line, Flynn shifted into salesman mode to bring him in. He glanced around the park before saying, "I'll tell you what. Between you and me, I'll make a bet with you. If you go along with the bet, I'll guarantee my team will back off Krista. Leave her alone and let the woman get on with her business. Is that fair enough?"

For a minute, Brennan considered it but then dismissed the notion. "No."

"Wait a minute. Let me sweeten the pot a little. I'll add some cash." Flynn pulled his checkbook from his back pocket and filled the blank spaces on a check before handing the slip of paper to the other man. Flynn had made the check out to Brennan for fifteen hundred dollars.

"Have you lost your mind?" Brennan hissed softly, thrusting the scrap of paper back at Flynn.

Grinning, Flynn shoved the check into Brennan's hand. "No. I'm willing to put my money where my mouth is. What about you? You're the one preaching to the choir. Are you man enough to back up your words with action?"

Brennan glared at Flynn. The malicious gleam in Flynn's eyes held a message. If Brennan rejected the challenge, Krista would suffer greatly, and he refused to allow that to happen.

Brennan studied his coworker, debating the issue. The two men had never been friends. As codirectors, there had always been a level of competition between them. It always boiled down to who got the most sales each month and how many accounts they brought to the agency.

Flynn exhibited some of the same behavior and traits Brennan remembered from his high school buddies. They lived in the glory days of their youth, doing the same things they had done before entering college.

Thinking fast and furious, Brennan stood next to his car, with the keys dangling between his fingers. He opened his mouth to speak and shut it as he eyed the check in his hand. Fifteen hundred dollars! That was a nice piece of change.

Instantly, his thoughts turned to his sister. Here was another conundrum. Liz had been living with him for months while saving up to buy her own home and waiting for her husband, Steve, to complete his final days in Iraq.

On more than one occasion, he'd offered her the cash she needed. Liz always refused to accept a gift this large from him since she didn't have the resources to pay him back right away.

That extra money would give her the down payment on the town house she wanted. He might be able to convince her to accept a lump sum if she felt as if she'd earned it.

Lips pursed, Brennan looked past Flynn to the employees

of Dexter Kee. He would love to beat the other man and wipe
that permanent smirk off his face.

Could he truly help Krista? Would Liz be able to teach the
young woman anything about fashion and style? Was she a
makeover candidate? All good questions with no answers.

"Come on, Superman. Save the damsel in distress," Flynn
taunted. "Be the hero. I mean, all you have to do is show her
how to dress and comb her hair."

It was just enough of a taunt to push Brennan over the
edge. *Bastard,* he thought, taking a step closer to Flynn. *You
don't think I can do this. It's time I teach you a thing or two.*
"Let's get the ground rules straight."

Flynn nodded. "Works for me. Without some type of limits
in place, you can say Krista's a work in progress till the end
of time."

Brennan grunted. "What's your suggestion?"

"Two months. By the time the Gautier campaign is finished, she's got to be able to hold her own. Walk and talk at
the same time. Have an intelligent conversation with her
coworkers and dress like a regular person. No more granny
clothes."

A million thoughts flew through Brennan's brain as he
stroked the bridge of his nose. Would two months be enough
time? "Can I have someone help me?"

Flynn gnawed on his bottom lip as he considered the idea.
"Like who?"

"My sister. It's not a fair bet if I have to do it all alone. Besides, do you really think I know what a woman should wear
or what's stylish?"

"You know what you like. That should be enough." Parr
lifted his hand and stuck out a finger. "One person. No more."

"That'll work. One more thing."

"What?"

"This is between you and me. Nobody else. I don't want to

hear about this from any of your people. And if I do, the bet is over."

"No problem. I don't want this getting back to the brass," Flynn muttered. "As you've already said, it is about agency values."

That's for sure, Brennan thought. He'd been preaching about company ideas and values. Now he was about to break every one of them. "Okay. I'm in." He extended his hand. The sales director took it, and the two men exchanged a firm handshake.

"It's on." Flynn gave him a smug grin.

Brennan held on to Flynn's hand. "Let me make sure you understand. You leave Krista alone. No more accidents. Got it?"

"Yeah. But, hell, she's an accident waiting to happen all the time. Don't put it on my guys."

"I won't." Brennan dropped Flynn's hand.

"Cool!" Flynn said as he strolled away from the parking lot.

Brennan hit the remote, the car chirped, lights flashed, and the doors unlocked. As he climbed behind the steering wheel, his gaze found Erin Saunders slowly trailing Flynn back to the picnic table.

What was she doing? Frowning, he watched her closely, trying to think of a reason for her to be so close to them. Had she eavesdropped on their conversation? Although Brennan didn't trust her, he did know Erin wasn't stupid enough to run her mouth. If she heard anything, she'd keep it to herself until she needed to use it to pull herself out of a jam.

Dismissing the woman, Brennan started the car and backed out of the parking space. Erin was the least of his concerns. He needed to figure out a way to get Krista near him so the transformation from geek to princess could begin.

Chapter 4

Krista parked the car in front of the house and climbed out. As she shut the car door, her gaze landed on the blanket Brennan had tossed over her shoulders before she left the park. She should wash it before returning it to him. Unlocking the car, Krista grabbed the square fabric, relocked the door, and dragged herself up the long, narrow driveway to the side door of the house.

As usual, the door was unlocked. Krista stepped inside and halted on the landing, debating whether to head for her room or go downstairs and put everything in the washer.

Feeling grubby, Krista decided to get out of her clothes and erase any reminders of the afternoon's fiasco. If she hurried, she'd get out of her soggy clothes and get them in the washer before Auntie got a look at her and started a game of twenty questions.

At the bottom of the stairs, Krista reached for a string connected to an overhead bulb. Instantly, light flooded the small room.

This had been Uncle Nick's apartment. He'd lived here until February.

Her gaze focused on an old fleece robe tossed carelessly across the back of the sofa. Loneliness coupled with pain stabbed at her heart. Uncle Nick had been wearing this when the emergency crew arrived at the house. The medical team had rushed him to Henry Ford Hospital on West Grand Boulevard, and he'd never made it home.

Krista picked up the faded blue garment and brought it to her nose, smelling the faintest hint of Uncle Nick and his favorite cologne, Aramis. Memories of him formed in her head.

"I miss you," she muttered softly, stroking the threadbare fabric. Tears wet her cheeks. After a moment, she folded the robe and returned it to the sofa, glancing around the apartment.

How many times had she sat down here, talking to the only male role model she'd had in her life, discussing everything from homework to boys. Whenever she needed a friend, he'd been there for her. All she had to do was come down the stairs and visit. On days when Auntie Helen drove everyone crazy, preaching the gospel and criticizing them for everything, from waking up late to taking too long to get dressed, Uncle Nick always intervened on Krista's behalf, bringing a soothing balm to her life.

Once she graduated from college and started working, it didn't matter what time she got home. The side door remained unlocked. Uncle Nick would stand at the bottom of the stairs, welcoming her, with a smile and a question. "Have you had dinner, love?"

When she shook her head, he would turn toward the kitchen, saying, "I fried an old, dead chicken I found in my freezer. I saved you the wings. There's mashed potatoes, green beans, and corn. Come on down." With that invitation, she would make her way to his apartment and would sit on the sofa while he warmed up her meal and served it to her.

Everything he owned was stored in this tiny apartment. Krista glanced around the small basement. Another image took root in her mind: Uncle Nick relaxing in his favorite chair, swallowing the last drops of beer from a red, white, and blue can. He'd lean back, waving a hand in the air at the television while explaining the intricate plays being made by the Detroit Lions quarterback.

Krista sighed, hurrying into the laundry room to start the washing machine. She glanced at the pile of dirty clothes sitting on the dryer.

As the surviving member of her three-sibling family, Aunt Helen refused to make any decisions regarding her brother's belongings. Each time Krista gently mentioned cleaning up the place or donating his clothes to the church's homeless program, Auntie vetoed the idea and refused to discuss it.

"Krista?" Aunt Helen called.

Speak of the devil, she thought and then answered, "Yes."

The floor creaked as Auntie crossed the tiled kitchen above and stood at the top of the stairs leading to the basement. "Gurl, what you doin' down there?"

Krista sighed. "Putting some stuff in the washer."

"You all right?"

"Yeah, I'm fine."

"How was the picnic?"

"Okay," Krista answered from the basement.

There was a pause as Aunt Helen turned over Krista's comment. "What happened?"

Krista shut her right eye against the first stabbing pain of a headache. "I had a little accident."

"Come up here and let me look at you," Aunt Helen demanded.

"There's nothing to worry about, Auntie. I'm okay."

The old girl's three-pronged metal cane struck the floor with a hard thump, making Krista jump. "You don't tell me no, gurl. Come here, Krista."

With no reason to delay, Krista started up the stairs and stopped on the landing, waiting. The tiny little woman stood no more than five feet but had the commanding presence of a six-foot, five-star general. Normally, her auntie's voice never rose above a whisper, but everyone understood her.

When she needed to get a point across, her soft tone took on an imposing edge that refused to be ignored. Aunt Helen didn't waste her breath. When she spoke, everyone listened.

The old girl had a soft side. Krista owed her life to her aunt and uncle. After Krista's mother died, they took her in and raised her. She barely remembered the woman who gave birth to her and knew nothing about her father. What she did know was that Aunt Helen and Uncle Nick had done everything within their power to give Krista a good start in life. Although there were days when Krista wished her life was different, she'd never go against the two people who had put her well-being ahead of their own. They gave her a home and a shot at being a productive adult.

That's why she'd buried her plans to find her own apartment and move out before Uncle Nick died. She couldn't leave her auntie alone in this big house. After all, Auntie had always been available for Krista when she needed her.

The old woman examined Krista from the top of her head to the tips of her damp canvas sneakers. Moaning softly, Aunt Helen shook her head and asked, "Gurl, what happened to you?"

No point in making up a story. "I fell in the lake," Krista answered.

"You need to stay away from those people. They don't mean you no good." Aunt Helen wagged a long, bony finger at her niece. "Told you not to go. Every time you come home from one of those company things, something's happened to you. If you'd gone to church like I said, none of this would have happened."

A humorless chuckle slipped from Krista's lips. "Trust me. I wanted to stay home. I've got enough work to keep me busy right here. The picnic was mandatory. All employees had to put in an appearance, including me."

The older woman snorted. "So. Can't you get sick or something? Maybe have car trouble?"

I wish, Krista thought.

"Well, we can't do nothin' about that situation. Put it behind you. It's over. Move on past it." Aunt Helen glanced at her niece, frowning. "Krista, your hair is a mess."

Embarrassed, Krista raised her hand to the side of her head. She tried to smooth the wild, tangled mane into some order. "It got a little wet when I fell."

Aunt Helen pointed a finger at Krista's head. "Better do something with it before we go to church tonight."

"I will," Krista promised, wishing she could get sick so that she wouldn't have to go to church this evening.

Brennan pulled his Saab into the garage and cut the engine. Groaning, he stretched before leaving the car and strolled toward the door leading to his Harbortown tri-level town house. Located minutes from downtown Detroit, the town house suited Brennan's lifestyle. Work was minutes away. The Fox Theatre, a collection of restaurants, and the GM Renaissance Center were straight down Jefferson Avenue whenever he needed to make a quick run.

After disarming the alarm system, Brennan quietly entered the kitchen. The aroma of cinnamon and apples filled his nostrils. Smiling, he glanced around the kitchen and found an apple pie sitting on the countertop, minus a slice. Liz must have had one of her cravings.

In search of his sister, he made his way through the quiet house and found her asleep on the sofa in the living room. A muted Carmen Harlan, from WDIV news, gazed solemnly into the camera as she delivered the details of the day on the 50-inch television. Brennan removed a light blanket from the back of a chair and tossed it over Liz's slight form.

The gesture disturbed her, and her eyes fluttered open. "Heeey!" Liz shifted on the couch.

"Hi."

Liz pushed herself into a sitting position and tossed her bare feet over the edge of the sofa. She took the blanket and folded it into a neat square before placing it on the back of the couch. "How was the picnic?"

"Usual fare." His forehead wrinkled into a frown as he thought about Connor Dexter, Flynn Parr, and especially Krista Hamilton. "Although there were a few surprises this year."

"Like what?" Liz asked, brushing her bangs out of her eyes.

Flopping down on the sofa next to her, Brennan squeezed her shoulder. "We'll talk about that in a minute. How are you feeling? What's my nephew doing tonight? Are you treating him right?"

Liz glanced down at her protruding belly and rubbed a hand across the swollen bump. "Your nephew has been playing basketball inside me."

"Yes! That's my boy!"

She laughed. "Yeah. But I don't get any rest when he's so busy."

"What do you expect from our future NBA player?" He considered her belly for a moment and then said, "He needs more room."

"Tell me about it. I think this kid is ready to be born. But I want him to wait until his daddy gets home."

Chuckling, Brennan linked his fingers with hers. "Lizzie, babies come when they get ready. Not when you want them to."

"I know. But hope springs eternal. I don't want to have my baby without Steve."

Brennan opened his mouth to speak, but Liz raised a hand, halting him before a word left his lips.

"I know. I know," she said. "It's a distinct possibility." Sadness flashed across her face. With a determined resolve, she rearranged her features and smiled at Brennan. Liz relaxed against the back cushions and faced her brother. "What happened at the picnic?"

"Connor Dexter informed me that I'm on the short list for the new managing VP job."

"Wow!" She practically jumped up and down on the leather couch. "Excellent! Congratulations!"

"Yeah, it's very cool."

Silence followed for several moments.

One eyebrow rose curiously over her eye. "Then why aren't you jumping up and down with me?"

"Mm." He stalled, studying the toes of his sneakers. "I don't like the way things are being handled. There's this competition I'm in with Flynn Parr. Whoever wins this new contract gets the pat on the head and thumbs-up from senior management."

"This is bad because . . . ?"

Brennan considered the question while running a finger along his nose. Was he upset? Pissed off? Honestly, he didn't have a clue. "Actually, I'm not sure."

"Well, big brother, you better figure it out before you start your campaign to become VP." Liz scooted to the edge of the sofa and rocked back and forth, preparing to get up.

Brennan placed his hand in the center of her back and pushed, helping her off the sofa. With a hand comfortably on her back, he supported her weight until he felt certain she was steady on her feet. "That's just one of the things going on. I've got something I need to talk about with you."

She turned, examining her older brother's face. "Hold that thought. Let me go to the bathroom, and then we can talk."

Nodding, he watched her disappear down the hall. While he waited, Brennan considered and discarded several ways to broach the subject.

Minutes later, Liz reentered the room. "What's up?"

Brennan patted the cushion next to him. "Come sit back down."

Subdued by the expression in his eyes, Liz returned to her

previous position. "Okay. You've got my attention. What's going on?"

"I know you won't take money from me." He raised a hand to stop Liz before she got going. "But I've got a proposition that will get you a nice piece of change to help you get that place you want."

"I'm listening."

"I love having you here. I also understand you want your own home."

"True." Liz stroked her stomach. "What do you have in mind?"

"Help me help somebody else."

"Who? How? And do what?" she asked in quick succession.

Brennan ran his tongue across his dry lips. Liz might raise hell at him for this. But it could be beneficial for them both. "We're going to do a makeover. You know, like the kind they do on those reality television shows."

"Makeover?" She got quiet for a moment. "Tell me more."

"Flynn Parr and I got into this big debate over one of the employees at the agency. He called her a loser and told me that she wasn't worth helping. I disagreed."

Liz leaned into the soft leather and nibbled on her bottom lip. "You think doing a makeover will make this woman a better person?"

"I don't know," Brennan admitted, with a shrug.

"Who is she? And what are this woman's issues?"

"Don't know all her issues. But her name is Krista Hamilton. She's an IT specialist at the agency. Actually, she's the best."

"Big brother, from what you've told me so far, I'm inclined to say no. You're not giving me enough info to make a fair decision. You're skating around the details." Liz elbowed him in the side. "Talk."

Grunting playfully, he said, "Hear me out, Lizzie girl. Before you decide, let me explain."

She moaned, shaking her head. "I don't think I'm going to like this."

"Here's the deal." He took Liz's hand. "If we can make Krista over from geek to princess, we'll win fifteen hundred dollars."

Her eyes grew round with surprise. "Wow!"

I've got your full attention now, he thought. Nodding, Brennan said, "Exactly. I'm willing to give you half of the money because I can't do this alone. I need a woman's touch."

"Yeah. You truly do." Liz giggled softly. "I can't imagine you going into Victoria's Secret to purchase a push-up bra."

Brennan used his finger to tap the end of her nose. "Cute."

Her forehead crinkled. "That's an awful lot of money. How did you get a pot that big?"

"Arrogance. With this whole 'who gets the contract first' mess, I think Parr wanted to rattle my cage. So he offered up his own money."

"Thank you, Mr. Parr." Liz saluted the air.

He pointed a finger at her. "If we win."

"Parr could lose a lot of money."

Brennan snorted. "His problem. Not mine."

"What started all of this?"

"Here's the way it went down. Krista fell in the lake, and I went to help her. After I got her on her way, Parr's salesmen started laughing at her, and I told them it wasn't funny. I talked about the company's ideals and how we might look to our clients. After that the situation spiraled out of control."

Liz placed her hand on top of Brennan's head and patted it. "My brother, the protector of geeks and little furry animals."

"Go away, girl."

Giggling, Liz asked a question of her own. "Is she cute, big bro?"

He laughed out loud. "Who could tell? Krista's covered with wooly, thick hair, and she dresses like a grandmother with fifteen grandkids. She's a lost soul." His tone turned somber. "Still, she doesn't deserve to be treated so badly. Krista's helpful and good-hearted. Deep down, I think she's incredibly shy and has trouble relating to others. I think of her as one of those people who's one beat different from everyone else. They hear and see the world differently."

Liz's face lit up. "You like her."

"No, I don't. Not like that."

"Oh, come on. You're playing Prince Charming and saving Cinderella."

"Go away, little girl. You're mixing up your fairy tales. It's more like *My Fair Lady*."

"Whatever," Liz muttered.

"She's not my type."

"Obviously, this Krista isn't perfect. That's why she's a target for your office bullies. But she sounds like she needs saving. She needs your help, and somewhere deep in you, you're responding to that need."

Quickly rising from the couch, he stared down at his sister. "That's ridiculous."

"I don't think so. You keep telling me that you're waiting for the perfect woman. I'm here to tell you, there's no such thing. And, if you wait for that gem to come along, you'll miss the unique stone who'll make you truly happy. Look at me." Liz waved a hand over her protruding stomach. "If I had waited for the right time to have a baby, this bundle of joy wouldn't be here. Steve's in Iraq and I'm here." Her voice broke over her next words. "What if something happens to him while he's fighting for his country? If something happens to Steve, I'll have a part of him with me. A baby to love. Getting pregnant is worth the risks."

"Nothing is going to happen to Steve," Brennan declared, praying that his words were true. "He loves you too much, and he's going to take care of himself so that he can come home to you and the basketball star."

"I hope so. But if Steve doesn't I would have lost not only

my husband, but the chance to have his baby. I was scared at first, but I'm glad I did it. Remember that while you're helping your little geek."

"Liz, listen to me." He returned to his spot next to her, took her chin in his hand, and turned her to face him. "I'm not interested in this woman. At least not that way. I feel sorry for her, and I want to help her. That's all."

With a knowing smile, she replied, "Sure, you do."

Exasperated, Brennan waved away her comments. "Let's get back to the situation. Are you going to help me? Financially, you can't beat it. You'll come out ahead. All you have to do is do what you love, shop and get cute. But help Krista get cute, too."

"Before I make a decision, I want to meet her. You and I need to get the ground rules completely straight. Makeover? Clothes?"

He nodded.

"Hair?"

"Yep."

"Once I meet her, and if I think I can help her, I'm in." Liz took her bottom lip between her teeth. "I'm assuming Krista doesn't know about this little bet you guys have going."

"Correct."

"How are we going to convince her that she needs a makeover? Will she take our suggestions to heart?"

"Leave that to me, Liz. I'm working on an angle."

Liz struggled to her feet and made her way across the room to the hallway. "Well, this has been an interesting evening. I can't wait to meet Ms. Krista Hamilton."

Chapter 5

Silent as Santa on Christmas Eve, Krista crept into her cubicle and sank into her chair. Filled with anguish, she covered her face with her hands. She'd suffered through a brutal morning.

Krista hated being the source of entertainment and the center of attention for the people she worked for and with. But short of going back in time and reliving the moments at the park, her options were slim. Yeah! That was going to happen.

From the security guard in the lobby to the people on her floor, everyone had heard about her mishap at the picnic. The stupid grins and snickers were an ugly reminder of how badly she'd mucked up this time. Krista prayed for a new calamity to befall some other hapless soul and take the pressure off her.

The aroma of freshly brewed coffee filled the air, and Krista lifted her head, craving a mug of green tea with a twist of lemon to sooth her frazzled nerves. She dared not leave her cubicle unless she absolutely had to. Her workstation provided a safe haven from the harassment of her coworkers. Work provided the most consuming distraction from the unpleasantness of others.

Krista switched on her iPod, stuck the earpieces in her ears, and was instantly enchanted by the saxophone of Najee. Getting down to the business of work, she turned on her computer and read through her snail mail while waiting for the system to boot up. After logging into the server's e-mail system and deleting some spam, her gaze landed on a message from her boss, marked urgent. Curiosity and apprehension warred within her as she opened the e-mail and found a request for her to go to Rachel's office, with a list of her current projects, the moment she received this message.

Not liking the sound of this request, Krista took a minute to jot down her assignments and then rose from her chair. Generally, when Rachel wanted to see her work assignments, she had a little something extra she wanted to incorporate into Krista's workload. At the corner cubicle, Krista tapped on the wall and received a curt "Come in" for her trouble.

Krista stepped inside the brightly lit workstation and stood. Rachel Ulrich sat at her desk, with a pile of work request forms in front of her.

Here comes more work. Krista felt her stomach twist into knots. "You wanted to see me?"

The IT manager glanced at Krista, pointing a finger at the empty chair in front of her desk. "Yes. Have a seat." Rachel returned to the pile of forms on her desk. "I'll be with you in a minute."

Following her boss's instructions, Krista slipped into the chair and linked her fingers in her lap. She watched Rachel work her way through the pile of work requests. After signing off on the forms, she sorted them into three piles, then bundled the piles together with a rubber band.

The gray-eyed, red-haired IT manager loved to play games with her staff. Rachel made sure everyone understood that she ran the IT department. She often scheduled staff meetings and then turned up late, forcing the members of the team to wait for her arrival. Today wasn't any different. Krista sat patiently until her boss decided she was ready to talk.

Rachel set the forms aside. "How are you doing this morning?"

"Fine," Krista answered, wondering what fresh hell the IT manager had in store for her.

The redhead shifted in her chair and said, "I need to know what you are working on currently."

Krista handed her boss her list of assignments. "I didn't list the new software for the September release. I'm doing most of that work at home, anyway. And a couple of the account execs from Flynn Parr's team have crashed their systems. I'm going to swap out and then try to salvage the hard drives. That kind of stuff I do in between the big projects."

Nodding, Rachel read through the list as she picked up her phone and dialed. "Got a minute?" she said into the receiver. "Good. I need you in my office now."

Frowning, Krista listened to the exchange, wondering who Rachel was calling and why.

"There have been some changes to our staffing," Rachel began.

Apprehension filled her. Great! *I'm going to get dumped on with more work.*

"First thing this morning, I met with Connor Dexter and Brennan Thomas."

Shocked, Krista opened her eyes wide. "Brennan Thomas!"

"Yep."

What did Brennan Thomas want with her? Her heart rate accelerated. He was not like the others. Brennan always treated her with respect. He'd been very kind when she fell in the lake, going so far as to help her out before offering her a blanket to keep her warm. Could his opinion have changed after Saturday's mishap? What was going on? And why was she in the center of this?

"Mr. Dexter wants you assigned to Brennan Thomas," Rachel added.

Confused, Krista asked, "Why?"

"As you already know, the agency is pursuing the Gautier International Motors account, and Brennan feels he needs someone with your software and hardware experience to help him whip his presentation into shape," Rachel explained, with a note of disdain in her voice.

"This doesn't make any sense," Krista responded. "The agency has never done anything like this before. Why now?"

"From what I understand, Gautier is very important to the company. Mr. Dexter is pulling out all the stops in pursuit of this account. Brennan Thomas wanted someone to help with the presentation. He asked for you." Grinning, Rachel added, "What can I say? We're a dictatorship. You go where the boss tells you."

"What about my other assignments?"

Rachel scanned the list of projects Krista had given her. "We'll reassign anything that's urgent. The rest can wait until you return."

That meant nothing would get done until she returned.

Krista tried a different approach. "How long will I be away?"

"Until the automaker makes a decision on an advertising agency. Hopefully, Dexter Kee. I suspect you'll be away a couple of months, maybe a little longer for the clear up after Gautier makes its decision."

Brennan Thomas. Krista's heart sank as a mental image of the man came to mind. *Why would he think I'm the one he needs?* Krista could see him wanting someone like Erin Saunders on his team. Erin practically drooled all over Brennan, and she'd do anything he wanted her to do. *Why not send Erin over to his team permanently and give the IT department a break?*

Erin sashayed into the workstation after the briefest of knocks. She glanced Krista's way and scoffed, immediately dismissing the woman before strolling across the floor and taking the empty chair next to Krista's.

Whenever Krista suffered one of her mishaps, somehow Erin was always nearby. Although Krista couldn't swear to it, she was almost positive Erin had pushed her into the lake.

"Hey, Rach. What's up?" said Erin as she plucked a Hershey's Kiss from the candy dish.

Rachel turned to Erin. "I was just telling Krista, effective immediately, she's being reassigned to Brennan Thomas."

"What!" said Erin, scoffing at the idea, then frowning at the woman next to her. "Krista? Why don't you send me instead?"

"I agree with Erin," Krista added. "Why can't you send her? She'll fit in much better than I will."

"No can do. This came from the boss," Rachel emphasized. "We don't have a choice."

"It doesn't make any sense," replied Erin pouting.

"Erin, you'll pick up anything that comes along for the next few months," Rachel explained. "Other than the September go live, we'll let your projects ride until you return to us, Krista. Bring Erin up to speed on what you're working on."

"Erin, I'll do a summary of everything I'm working on and will e-mail it to you," said Krista. Standing, Krista turned to Rachel. "When does Brennan want me?"

"Never!" Erin hissed too low for their boss to hear.

"Now," replied Rachel as she handed Krista's handwritten sheet to Erin. "He's expecting you this morning."

Nodding, Krista left Rachel and Erin and returned to her desk. Dazed, she sank into her chair and stared at her computer monitor.

Something didn't feel right about this change of assignments. She couldn't put her finger on it, but there was definitely a foul odor associated with the move.

What was going on? Many of the IT people in her department, including Erin, were qualified to work with Brennan Thomas. Why had Mr. Dexter insisted on Krista? Until today, she would have sworn Mr. Dexter didn't know who she was.

She took a few minutes to type up instructions and notes and then e-mailed the files and info to Erin.

Time to go, Krista thought, checking the time at the bottom of her monitor. Her gaze fell on the blanket Brennan had loaned her at the picnic. She folded the fleece fabric over her arm, grabbed her purse and briefcase, and headed through the maze of cubicles.

There were so many questions, and no one seemed to have any answers. After all, there were several IT employees with work experience and backgrounds similar to hers. Why did Brennan and Connor Dexter want her on this campaign, especially after seeing her at her worst? Her cheeks burned when she remembered how Brennan had fished her out of the lake and helped get her to the Caprice.

Krista entered the elevator and punched the button for the executive floor. One thing she did know. There wouldn't be any answers until she reported to her new assignment and talked to the man in charge.

Where was she? Brennan stared out the window. Krista should have been here an hour ago. How long did it take for Rachel Ulrich to pass along the news? Generally, when Connor Dexter got involved with a problem, a solution was found pretty damn fast.

Turning away from the images of Cobo Hall and the Detroit River, Brennan glanced toward the office bull pen. Large glass windows framed the door, giving him an excellent view of his staff and the surrounding desks.

Antsy, Brennan rose from his chair and began to pace the office. He should call Rachel and find out when Krista would be available. As he reached for the telephone, the elevator doors opened, and Krista stepped out. She looked a hot mess.

Jesus, who dressed this woman? And who wore that kind of getup in this day and age? Most women liked to show off their body piercings and tattoos. Krista dressed like a nun. The multicolored jacket and skirt had a white background. Large stripes of blue, red, and yellow filled most of the fabric.

An oxford shirt peeked from the jacket opening, and the skirt brushed her ankles as she walked.

And that head of hair! Damn! Didn't anyone in her house own a comb or brush? The ponytail she wore had more hair outside the band than inside.

Brennan shook his head; looking at Krista made him question his sanity in agreeing to this bet. This woman required serious help. Overwhelmed by the task facing him and Liz, he wondered if they could truly accomplish the job.

Impatiently, he waited for Krista to navigate her way to his office. After several seconds, she tentatively knocked on the door.

Brennan hurried across the carpeted floor and opened the door before Krista turned the knob. He put on his best and most friendly smile. "Hi."

"Hi," Krista mumbled, brushing a quick hand over her wild mane of hair.

He stepped away from the door and waved her inside the room. "Come in."

With her eyes glued to the carpet, she stepped inside, waiting quietly while Brennan shut the door. He cupped her elbow and guided her to a guest chair across from his desk before returning to his chair. "I'm really happy to have you on my team," he said.

Krista nodded but remained silent, staring at a spot beyond his shoulder.

How am I supposed to talk with this little mannequin? She can barely look at me, thought Brennan. He searched for a way to make her feel comfortable.

"I know you must have questions," he said. "Once you get settled in your office, feel free to come back here. We'll talk about what I need from you." He stroked the bridge of his nose. "There's a lot of work that has to be done before we make our presentation to Gautier. Your help will be invaluable."

"Mr. Thomas?" Krista said.

Finally, words were coming out of her mouth. "Yes?" Brennan replied.

"W-wh-why did you choose m-m-me?" she asked, looking him directly in the eyes for the first time since entering the room.

That was an easy question. However, there were several answers he could give. Something about her direct, nervous expression made him want to put her fears to rest. The simple truth seemed to be the best way to go.

"Gautier International Motors is being wooed by every ad agency in the state. You're the best at what you do. I want your knowledge and skills on this campaign. And there's nothing you don't know about putting together presentations on the computer."

His answer must have struck a cord with Krista, because she relaxed a fraction. The tension twisting his muscles did the same. Good. Maybe he'd found the key to making her feel comfortable. "Fair enough?" he said.

"Yes." Krista smiled a sort of Mona Lisa smile. It came and went so quickly that he almost missed it. His insides began to quiver like jelly in response.

What just happened? he wondered, finding himself charmed by her small gesture. The silly urge to do or say something that would make her smile again filled Brennan.

Shaking off those feelings, he stood and waited while Krista gathered her belongings. "Let me show you your new office. While you're in this department, do whatever you like to it. I want you to feel at home. Once you're settled in, come back, and I'll give you the tour of the place. Introduce you to everyone."

Suddenly, her features took on a somber expression. She handed the blanket to him. "Here. T-th-thank yo-you for letting me use it."

"No problem. Glad to help." He tossed the piece of fabric over the chair and headed for the door, with Krista in tow.

They left Brennan's office and stopped at the closed door next to his. He reached inside his pocket and removed a silver ring. "Here's your keys. Since we might be working long, un-predictable hours, I'd thought you'd like a key to the floor."

As he spoke, he unlocked the door and threw it open. "Welcome."

There hadn't been time to do anything special. A desk, chair, file cabinet, and computer were the only items in the room. Embarrassed, Brennan shifted into persuasive mode. "We can fix anything. Let me know. Whatever you want."

My God! I sound like a used car salesman trying to palm off a lemon on a little old lady. He took a deep breath and started again. "What I mean is, we didn't have much time. I hope this will work until we can do better."

Krista stepped farther inside the office and moved around the desk. She sat in the chair and leaned back. "It's fine." She didn't seem to know what to do with her hands. They fluttered around her purse for a moment before she came to a decision. "Well, I-I-I b-be-better get started."

"Yeah." He retraced his steps to the door. "Come see me when you're ready."

She nodded.

Brennan left her to get settled and returned to his office. He dropped into his chair, locked his fingers together, and placed them behind his head. He swiveled the chair in the direction of the Detroit River.

As he watched a steamer move slowly down the river, he contemplated his plan. Step one had been accomplished. Krista had arrived and was close at hand. Step two: facilitate a meeting between Liz and Krista. Step three: have Liz do her thing and get this little geek a new look that would change her world.

Chapter 6

Well, I can't sit here forever, Krista decided, rising from the desk and starting across the office. First stop, the supply closet. She raided the place for supplies, returned to her office, and dumped all of the stuff on her desk. Krista plucked a yellow pad and a pen from the mess on her desk before heading out of the office.

Seconds later, she stood at Brennan Thomas's door, tapping lightly.

"Come in," came a commanding male voice.

She pushed the door open and found Brennan at his desk, going through what looked like a stack of expense reports. He glanced up and smiled. "Hi."

Krista's mind went blank, and she stopped dead in the entrance. *Oh my, this man is gorgeous.* "U-um-umm," she stammered like an idiot child, trying to pull her thoughts together.

Brennan rose and strolled across the office, meeting her at the door. With a firm grip, he cupped her elbow and led her to a chair facing the desk. "Did you find everything okay?"

She nodded. Her skin grew warm at the spots where his fingers touched her.

"You all settled in?"

"P-pr-retty much. I'll n-ne-need a few things. But I'll get th-those later," Krista answered as her heart pounded.

"Let me know if there is anything I can do to help you feel more comfortable," Brennan said in an odd, yet gentle tone. Krista got the impression that he was trying to keep from frightening her.

She brushed a nervous hand over her hair, hoping the wild mess didn't make her look too crazy. This was an awkward moment. What should she call him? How did he like to be addressed?

For the present, he's my boss. Give him the respect that position deserves. Start formal, she decided. *If he wants you to call him anything different, he'll let you know.* "Mr. Thomas, I'm ready to get started."

"Whoa! Stop!" He placed a hand on her shoulder, squeezing it reassuringly.

"What?" Confused, Krista twisted in the chair, facing him, while her stomach twisted into knots. Had she offended him? *Great! You've been in the man's office less than ten minutes, and already you've caused a problem.*

"First of all, my name is Brennan." He dropped his hand, returned to his place behind the desk, and sank into his chair. "We're not that formal in this department. No one on my staff is mister anything. Okay?"

"Okay." As her stomach muscles began to relax, Krista rolled the name around in her head, liking the sound of it. "Brennan," she muttered shyly, giving herself an extra minute to process the information she'd just received.

Jacketless, he wore a pale blue shirt, a multicolored tie with geometric figures on it, and charcoal gray trousers. Brennan looked awesome.

Krista's pulse fluttered and then sped up. She brushed her wet palms against her skirt. Why was he affecting her this way? He was a man. *Think back, Krista. You've never had very good luck with men. Remember Jamal from Michigan*

State? Besides, Brennan certainly wasn't interested in an oddball like her. Her expertise in the computer kingdom fueled any relationship they might share.

Focus on the work, her brain screamed. "We need to d-di-discuss what your goals and expectations are for m-m-me. I understand this is all about the Gautier project," she mumbled hastily. "Tell me what you want me to do."

Brennan leaned forward and folded his arms on the desk. "I know squat about computers. I can fumble my way around our Intranet, find a few sites on the Internet, and work through a couple of software programs, like Word or Excel. I'm far from being a pro."

Krista smiled to herself. "Your j-jo-job doesn't require a lot of c-co-computer usage."

"Exactly. But for this campaign, I want to dazzle Mr. Gautier with something unique. And I think the Internet may be the key."

Somewhat intrigued, she pulled her chair closer to the desk and sat her pad on the edge, ready to scribble notes if he said anything she needed to remember. "You could be right. T-te-tell me more."

"I want to impress Gautier with our cost-effective form of advertising. The goal is to penetrate the largest market we can. A simultaneous ad campaign on the Internet, on television, in the movies, and in print will saturate the market. If things work out the way I envision, this might be a launch base for other customers and their products. What do you think?"

Nibbling on the edge of the blue cap of her ink pen, Krista responded. The words flowed a lot easier once she got started. "You've hit on something. More and more people are u-us-using the Internet for advertising and marketing. Gautier will see us as an innovative agency using cutting-edge technology. It's a g-go-good move."

He grinned back at her. That smile did interesting things to her insides. "Glad to hear you're on board with my idea. How do I get from the concept to the reality?"

"T-there are a few issues we're going to have to a-ad-address before we tackle the idea of a commercial."

"Like what?" Brennan asked, turning his white-lined pad to a fresh page.

Now Krista was in her element. Her uncertain tone took on a confident edge. "How long a commercial? Are we going to link them? Will it have music and real actors? Different commercials for the Internet or the same one on both? Are you going to make it like a video game? We're going to have to do some statistical stuff so that we have our facts right and target the proper audience."

Brennan waved a hand in her direction. "That's why you're here. You have the logical mind to work out the details." He patted Krista's hand.

For a moment, Krista studied the place where he'd touched her. Her skin felt hot and tingly.

"I'm the idea man," he explained. "You're the woman that's going to make it happen."

She smiled nervously. "I hope so. You know there's a lot of work to be done before we even get to the actual commercial itself."

"True." His smile widened.

"Can I order some graphics-intensive computer software?" she asked, making note of several packages she wanted.

"Whatever you need." He pointed to the people outside his office. "Talk to my administrative assistant, Tanisha. She'll place your orders. Or you can buy what you need and give me the receipt."

"I need an extremely powerful laptop with buckets of memory and top-quality graphics."

"You've got it. Pick it out or pick it up. Your choice." Brennan added a note to his list. "I have three sales execs working with me on this campaign. I want you to meet them and get their input."

Krista nodded.

"While you're waiting for the new hardware and software to arrive, I'd like to get started on the statistical data. The more we know about Gautier, the tighter our proposal will be."

"All right." Pursing her lips, Krista studied her notes for a moment. "When and w-wh-where will the actual p-pre-pres-entation be held?"

"First week of September is as close a date as I've been given." He jabbed his pen in her direction. "We'll shoot for an August twentieth completion date. That will give us a couple of weeks to tweak the project as needed."

"Sounds good."

A knock on the door cut off further discussion.

"Come in," Brennan called.

The knob turned, and the door opened a fraction. A young woman poked her head inside the office. "Hey."

"Hey, yourself," he responded, with a grin.

The woman's gaze settled on Krista. "Oh! Sorry. Tanisha was away from her desk. I didn't know you were in a meeting. I'll talk to you later."

"No." Brennan hopped out of his chair, hurried across the room, and took the woman's hand, leading her into the office. "We're almost done here. Come in. Let me introduce you to a new member of my team."

Was this Brennan's wife? Krista wondered, impressed by the tender way he addressed the woman. No. She'd never heard anyone mention that he was married. Maybe this was his girlfriend. A very pregnant girlfriend.

"Krista Hamilton, this is my baby sister, Liz Gillis," said Brennan. "Liz, Krista Hamilton. She's working with me on the Gautier contract."

Smiling, the young woman offered her hand in a firm handshake. "It's nice to meet you. I'm sorry for disturbing you guys. But I wanted to see if I could con my older brother into taking me to lunch."

Brennan glanced at his watch. "You're right. It is lunchtime. Where do you want to go?"

"Southern Fires," Liz answered promptly.

He groaned, shaking his head as if he were in pain. "Not again."

Liz smiled and patted her plump belly. "I can't help it. Junior and I need catfish."

Brennan glanced at Krista and winked. "Yeah. Yeah. Yeah. When don't you want fish?"

"Do you have lunch plans, Krista?" Liz asked.

Oh no! She didn't want to be caught between these siblings. Besides, things always went very wrong when she tried to mingle with other people. It was best for her to mind her own business and have lunch alone in her new office. "No. I-I-I don't want to intrude."

Brennan's sister rolled her eyes. "Please, come with us. Save me from my brother and his incessant talk about work. If you go to lunch with us, I'll have an opportunity to talk about something other than advertising."

Torn, Krista felt a wave of anxiety sweep through her, pinching her stomach into a thousand knots. Krista's gaze shifted from brother to sister and back again. People seldom invited her anywhere. She wanted to go. She opened her mouth to say, "No thanks." What came out was, "If you're sure I'm not getting in the way."

Liz slipped her arm into the crook of Krista's and guided her to the door. "Let's go. It's time to eat." She lowered her voice and whispered into Krista's ear. "Just between you and me, I plan to stick my brother with the bill."

Southern Fires was their destination. Brennan drove down Jefferson Avenue, silently maneuvering through the noontime traffic. Liz sat in the front passenger's seat, chatting with Krista from between the bucket seats.

At the restaurant, Brennan pulled the Saab up to the valet booth, jumped out, and helped his sister from the car before offering a hand to Krista. An attendant rushed from the shack and quickly took charge of the vehicle, pulling away from the curb as the trio climbed the stairs and entered the restaurant. They were immediately seated. Together, Liz and Krista sat on a wooden bench, facing Brennan.

A woman dressed in a white long-sleeve blouse and navy trousers took their orders and hurried away. Krista gazed out the window at a parking lot adjacent to a series of lofts facing Jefferson Avenue.

"So," said Liz as she shook out a white cloth napkin and placed it over her protruding belly. "How long have you been working for my brother?"

Instantly, Krista became tongue-tied. Her words tripped over each other. "A-a-a-about t-t-two hours."

Leaning back, Liz opened her eyes wide. "Oh. I thought you'd been with the company for a while."

"I-I-I have," replied Krista.

During this time, their server returned and placed their drinks in front of them. Liz's hand drew patterns in the frost on her glass of lemonade.

Brennan touched Liz's arm, drawing her attention to him. "What Krista is trying to tell you delicately is she started in my department this morning," he said.

Surprised, Liz lifted her eyebrows. "This morning! Wow!"

"Krista's on loan to my department until we bag this Gautier contract," Brennan explained. "So give the woman a break and let her eat her meal in peace."

"I wasn't bothering her," Liz stated loftily as she sat straight in her chair. "I was making conversation. If I offended you, I'm sorry."

"N-n-no. Yo-yo-you didn't," replied Krista. "I-I-I-m n-ner-nervous about this assignment."

"Don't be," said Liz as she squeezed Krista's hand. "We're all friends here."

The soothing tone of Liz's voice and the touch of her hand reached something deep within Krista, and she felt herself relaxing. When she spoke, the words came easier. She whispered, "Thank you."

"No problem. Are you from Detroit?" Liz asked.

Nodding, Krista searched for something to say. *You're just such a great conversationalist.* "You?"

"We were born in River Rouge but ended up in Detroit," Liz explained, sipping on her lemonade.

"Did your parents move here?" asked Krista.

Liz went silent. Brennan picked up the thread of their conversation. "Our parents are dead. They were killed in a car accident when we were kids. With no other family, we went into foster care and were placed with a family in Detroit."

Krista understood completely. They shared similar childhoods. Her mother died when she was an infant. The big difference was her relatives had taken her in and raised her. "I'm sorry."

"Don't be. We're fine," said Liz as she reached across the table and squeezed her brother's hand. "Besides, we had each other."

"Yeah, we did," Brennan agreed. "The county kept us together."

They chatted together amicably until the server arrived with their meals. Liz rubbed her hands together before digging into her fish. "I've craved catfish all day long."

Brennan turned to Krista. "I swear she lives off the stuff. That poor baby is going to come out asking for a catfish dinner. Mark my words. When I get home this evening, dinner will consist of either salmon, pickerel, perch, or catfish. She'll plead her case by telling me she couldn't help herself."

"Y-yo-you live together?" Krista asked.

Liz nodded, buttering a slice of corn bread. "Yes. My dearly beloved brother took me in when my husband got shipped off to Iraq."

Poor thing, Krista thought. *Pregnant, with her husband off fighting a war in another country.* "When is your b-b-baby due?"

"August thirty-first. And I can't wait," Liz confided, popping a green bean into her mouth.

Smiling uncertainly, Krista added, "I'm sure he can't wait to meet you."

"Actually, it'll be great to see my feet again. Plus, my husband, Steve, is supposed to come home on leave," replied Liz. Her eyes lit up when she mentioned her husband. Envious, Krista wished she had someone special to look forward to seeing. She glanced at Brennan, wondering about his personal life. Did he have a friend? Someone to spend time with? A special someone in his life?

"What h-ha-happens if-if-if your husband doesn't m-ma-make it home in time for the baby?"

"Then big brother here will get to play my coach during labor," said Liz as she snatched a french fry from her brother's plate.

Groaning, Brennan picked up his glass and took a long swallow of tea. "I'm praying Steve makes it back in time. I do *not* want to go where few older brothers have gone before. Labor scares me more then trying to sell to the worst client in the world."

Krista laughed out loud. "I hope S-S-Steve m-ma-makes it home."

"Me too," Brennan admitted.

This banter continued throughout their meal. Krista had never enjoyed herself so much. She liked this set of siblings, who loved each other so openly.

As Liz chewed the last bite of catfish, the server returned to their table. "How was everything?" she asked, removing used plates and cutlery.

"Good!" Brennan said.

"Great!" Krista added.

Liz said, "I enjoyed it all."

"There's a surprise," Brennan muttered sarcastically, pointing at Liz, with a fake expression of shock on his face.

"Brennan!" Liz yelped. "I'm going to get you for that."

"Would you like to check out our dessert menu?" the server asked.

Liz shook her head and wiggled in her seat. "No. I don't need it. I'll have the strawberry shortcake with a double helping of strawberries and ice cream. What about you, Krista?"

"N-n-no thanks. Nothing."

Liz turned to her brother. "Brennan?"

"I don't need anything. You've ordered enough for the three of us. I'm going to wait until you turn your head and steal strawberries off your plate."

Krista removed her napkin from her lap and folded it into a neat square, laying it on the table. She looked down at her skirt and noticed a white glob of mashed potatoes.

Fear and anxiety knotted inside her. Her blood pounded; her face grew hot with humiliation. She didn't want anyone to see how sloppy she was, especially not Liz and Brennan. They had been so nice to her.

Krista glanced at the pair, happy to find them deep in a friendly discussion. She took her napkin and scooped away the mess, feeling a bit of relief as she balled up the napkin and placed it on the table. Her relief was short-lived. Unfortunately, a white spot remained. A wave of apprehension swept through her.

Great! Now she had to go back to work with a stain on her clothes and listen to another round of jokes about her. That was why she didn't go out with her coworkers. She always had problems. Mercifully, neither sibling noticed Krista's distress.

A light tap on her arm drew Krista's attention to Liz. Liz handed a small packet to Krista under the table. When Krista glanced at her, Liz appeared absorbed in a conversation with her brother. Krista took the packet and turned it over, reading the directions. It was one of those damp towelettes. She tore it open, removed the sheet, and dabbed lightly at the spot on her skirt. After a couple of wipes, the spot came clean, and all of Krista's anxieties faded as the fabric dried. During the whole time, Liz kept her brother occupied, distracting him.

Lunch ended with Krista and Brennan helping Liz polish off her strawberry shortcake. The trio left the restaurant and waited on the porch for the car to arrive. Krista got her chance to express her gratitude to Liz when Brennan went to pay the valet. She whispered, "Thank you."

Liz smiled and patted Krista's arm. "No problem. Like I said, we're all friends here."

Krista couldn't remember the last time anyone had done something so nice for her. Generally, she hid in her cubicle, hoping people found a new victim to torture. For once, she wouldn't have to be the recipient of the staff's tricks.

She studied Liz for a beat. Growing up, she'd found it difficult to make and keep friends. The few she had acquired during high school had quickly faded away once they graduated. While at college, she'd kept to herself and avoided a lot of the pranks and drama that went on in the dorm.

Brennan and Liz were wonderful people who accepted Krista for who she was. It warmed her heart and made her feel good to think that people could be nice. For a day that had started out so bad, it was shaping up to be pretty good.

Chapter 7

"What ya doin'?"

Arms loaded with books, Brennan glanced up from his desk and found his sister standing in the doorway. "Hi, Lizzie girl." He moved across the room to the bookshelves. "I'm trying to make this place look presentable. Krista Hamilton is coming over to set up my network connection to the server at work."

Nodding, Liz strolled across the room and stopped next to the desk. She stacked a pile of books together on the edge of the wooden surface. With a twinkle in her eyes, she said, "Thank goodness you decided to clean up this junk hole. We might never see that girl if she comes in here without a road map."

Brennan balled up a wad of paper and threw it at his sister. "Ha! Ha! You're just so funny."

Giggling softly, she caught the crumbled sheet and tossed it in the wire trash bin. Liz turned somber. "Seriously, I'm glad you mentioned Krista. I want to talk to you about her and the bet."

He shoved an armload of books into every empty spot on the shelf and then faced Liz. The frown crinkling her forehead caused Brennan a moment of apprehension. Something was wrong. "What's rolling around in your head?"

She glanced at him and then quickly looked away, trying to mask her guilty expression. "I'm not sure I want to do the makeover thing."

That shocked him. Brennan wasn't expecting that. He returned to the desk and stood in front of her, then placed his hands on her shoulders. Normally, once Liz agreed to a course of action, she kept her end of the bargain. "Why?" he asked.

Liz swallowed loudly and then brushed a lock of hair away from her eyes. "Krista seems like a really nice lady. She's shy, painfully so. That's why it's so difficult for her to talk with people. It's hard to have a conversation with anyone when you can't look them in the face. Other than that, Krista's very sweet."

"What's that got to do with anything?" he asked.

"Everything!" Liz shot back, then moved around the desk, dropped into his executive chair, and swiveled around to face him. "You are such a sensitive soul."

He shrugged, not sure what to make of Liz's 180-degree turn. "What am I supposed to say?"

Exasperated, Liz struggled to her feet and put her hands on her hips. "How about you understand how I feel."

"I don't," he admitted. "Explain it to me. Make me understand."

"I feel this whole situation might backfire on us. We could end up causing a lot of unnecessary pain and suffering for Krista. I don't want to do that. Maybe we need to take an extra moment, calm down, pump the brake, and regroup before we get ourselves into something we can't step away from."

"Lizzie, we're not going to hurt Krista. Or beat her into submission." Brennan stepped around the desk and took his sister's hand. "The worst that will happen to her is she'll look better, get her hair combed, and have a little more confidence. Help me with this project and I promise I'll never ask you to do anything like this again."

"There you go again." Lizzie's hands balled into fists. "Krista is not a project. She's a person with feelings."

"I know." Brennan took her hand and uncurled her fingers. "Sorry. I used the wrong words."

Liz gave Brennan a hard, unhappy glare. "You see Krista in the same way you see the Gautier campaign. She's a project to finish before you go on to the next one."

"That's not true," he denied, frowning down at his sister. Did he act that shallow and unconcerned? "Why would you say that? Granted, this isn't a traditional situation. But I do want to help Krista. Give her confidence level a boost. Make her feel better about herself."

"And make money off of her at the same time," Liz reminded.

"Yes. There is that part of things," Brennan admitted, feeling heat burn his cheeks.

"She may be shy beyond belief, but she's not a fool."

"I agree. Krista's very bright."

"Exactly. Her heart is good. If she learns that we used her for a bet and money, it could destroy her trust in people."

"She won't find out." Brennan straightened the manila folders in his in-box, scooped up a batch of miscellaneous pens and pencils, and shoved them inside the middle desk drawer.

She laughed loudly and heartily. "Famous last words."

Brennan perched on the edge of the desk, near Liz. "Let's take a look at this logically. This is all under the table. Nobody wants to get into trouble. Flynn Parr doesn't want the management team to know about our bet. Think of it this way. It's a win-win situation. Krista gets a little help with clothes, hair, and make-up, which will help her cope with the idiots at the agency."

"I don't think it's that simple. Stuff always has a way of coming back to haunt us."

He continued, ignoring Liz's comment. "You get the money that will help you and Steve buy the house you want."

Leaning back in the chair, Liz asked, "How do you figure that?"

"Think about it, Lizzie. Krista has never felt comfortable with others. She's happy with computers and networks. Being with us will help her get over some of those rough patches. If the situation works out, Krista will develop more confidence. She'll be able to hold her own against her coworkers and stand up to the bullies that keep bothering her."

Liz sighed. "I don't know."

Brennan rubbed a finger along the bridge of his nose. "How can I make you feel better about this?"

"You can't," Liz answered softly, studying the hardwood floor.

"Lizzie girl, come on. You can do this. It won't be so bad. Please. I can't do this without you." Sensing her distress, Brennan touched her hand. His sister played an intricate part in the equation. He needed a way to convince her to stay in the game.

"All I see is a very nice person being exploited by the people she works with, including you and me." Liz gave him a significant stare.

He felt bad about Krista. Maybe Liz was right. They should stop this madness before someone got hurt. That someone would most likely be Krista. In the week that he'd worked with her, Brennan had found her to be intelligent, informed, but very, very shy. She worked efficiently and quickly, needing little or no direction. On some level, he felt that she understood him better than anyone he'd ever worked with.

"What about the money, Liz? Are you willing to give that up? It's easy cash, and you're being helpful."

She ran her hand through her short hair. "Part of me keeps going back to that. Yeah, I want the money. It would make my life easier, especially when Steve gets home and we have to think about finding our own place. There's part of me that knows this will hurt this young woman, and I don't want to do that."

"Me neither."

"Then why are we, Brennan?"

His tone turned persuasive. "I think we can also help her. You know as well as I do that the squeaky wheel always gets the oil. Krista's like fish bait for the sharks in our office. Don't bail on me. Appearances count when it comes to promotions."

"I won't," Liz promised. "But I am feeling pretty bad about what we're doing."

With a sigh of relief, Brennan pulled Liz to her feet. "Help me get this room straight. Krista should be here by seven."

"Be here! Aren't you going to pick her up?"

"No. Why?"

Liz stopped in the center of the room and planted her hands on her hips. "You're going to let her run around at night by herself? That's not right, Brennan. What if something happens to her on the way here or home?"

"What am I supposed to do?"

"Go get her. After she does the work, take her home. She shouldn't be out and about alone, especially when it's for you."

"Yeah. You're right," he admitted begrudgingly. "What about this place?"

Liz shooed him away with a wave of her hand. "I'll take care of this. Go. Get Krista."

He shook his head, warning, "I don't want you lifting anything."

Liz snorted. "Don't worry. I don't plan to hurt myself."

Brennan shoved a handful of folders in the beige file cabinet. "Okay. I'll be back within an hour."

"Bye," she stated. "Take care of your business."

With a wave of his hand, Brennan left the house.

* * *

Krista worked steadily, storing the leftovers from dinner in the refrigerator, washing dishes, and putting them away. Once she finished cleaning up the kitchen, she hurried up the two flights of stairs to her attic apartment and changed into a loose-fitting dress and sandals. After changing, Krista returned to the den, where her aunt sat channel surfing.

Krista entered the room and sat on the brown corduroy love seat opposite her aunt. When a commercial flashed on the television, she said, "Auntie."

"Yes," Aunt Helen responded, never taking her eyes off the TV.

"I'm headed back to work."

The old girl glanced at the clock on the cream wall and dropped the remote in her lap. "Work? You just got home. Why'd you come home if you weren't done? You should have stayed until you were finished."

Ignoring her aunt's comments, Krista added, "It'll probably be a couple of hours before I'm done. When I leave, I'll lock the side door and set the alarm."

Auntie glanced at the television screen and then said, "I'll sit up and wait. Don't want you coming in by yourself."

"Don't do that," Krista vetoed. "You know you need your rest. Besides, this is a new project, and I'm not sure how much work is involved."

"This don't sound right. What's going on?" Auntie reached for the remote to turn down the theme music for the news. She turned and gave Krista the look that usually made Krista quiver in her shoes. Even at twenty-five years of age, Krista found it difficult to hold her own against that penetrating glare.

After a minute, Krista lost the battle and answered, "I'm going to Brennan Thomas's house to work on his computer."

Frowning, Aunt Helen moaned softly and shook her head. "Mmm. His house? This don't sound good to me. Are you sure this is on the up-and-up? Will there be anyone else there?"

Ready to explain, Krista opened her mouth but was interrupted by the doorbell. Surprised, she pursed her lips. She wasn't expecting anyone.

"Who's that?" Auntie asked, getting to her feet.

Krista waved her aunt back to the sofa and rose. She went to the front door and peeked out. A man stood on the porch. "Who is it?" called Krista.

"Brennan."

Brennan? What was he doing here? Krista had expected to be at his house within the hour. She flung open the door.

Brennan smiled. "Hey."

Frowning, Krista stared at the man. "W-wh-what are you d-do-doing here?"

"It's late. I don't want you riding around town by yourself."

"There's no problem. I-I-I'm fine. I work all kinds of hours."

He shook his head. "Not tonight. You're doing me a favor, and I won't allow you to drive around alone."

"Who's that?" Auntie called.

"My boss," said Krista.

"Well, let him in," replied Auntie.

Grinning, Brennan said, "Yeah, let me in."

Krista whispered, "You're g-go-going to regret this."

Lowering his voice, Brennan answered, "I'm a big boy. I can handle it."

"That's what you think. Come in. Let me get my keys," Krista said, shutting the door after him. She led him through the house to the den. "Aunt Helen, this is Brennan Thomas. I'm going to his house to work on his computer. Brennan, this is my aunt, Mrs. Johnson."

He nodded at the woman sitting on the sofa. "It's nice to meet you, ma'am."

Krista waved a hand at the sofa. "Have a seat. I'll be right back."

When she returned, Auntie and Brennan were sitting quietly, watching *Jeopardy*. Although both adults were silent, tension filled the air. "I'm ready," said Krista.

Brennan rose from the sofa, reached out, and took her aunt's hand. "It was nice meeting you."

"You, too," Auntie answered.

Krista led the way out the side door. She armed the alarm and locked the side door before making her way to the car parked in the driveway. Brennan drove through the neighborhood on his way downtown. He popped in a Brian Culbertson CD, and the music kept them occupied until they reached Harbortown.

Even at night, Krista could tell that Brennan had a beautiful home befitting one of the sales directors. From the outside, the tri-level town house appeared immaculately cared for and tastefully decorated.

When she entered the house through the redbrick attached garage, she halted inside the kitchen door. It was a gorgeous room filled with every modern appliance.

"Liz," Brennan called, leading her across the ceramic tile floor.

The aroma of fried chicken and fresh green beans filled the air. "It smells good in here," Krista muttered softly.

Brennan nodded. "Sure does. And for once, it doesn't smell like fish."

Krista giggled.

"Lizzie girl, we're home," he called, shutting the door connecting the garage to the kitchen. Although the fried chicken sat on the stove, there was no sign of the cook.

Charles Gibson's voice floated from the front of the house to the kitchen. Brennan hung his keys on a dark wooden wall rack and started out of the kitchen.

His sister emerged from one of the rooms at the front of the house. "Hi. I was watching the news. I know you guys have work to do. Go ahead and get started, and I'll call you when dinner is ready. Krista, I hope you haven't eaten yet."

"Yes," replied Krista.

Liz slowly made her way to the kitchen.

Brennan took Krista's arm, leading her down a hallway. "Come on. Let me show you my office. I'm telling you in advance, I'm not a very organized man. The room is not exactly as neat as it could be."

Krista smiled. "That's okay. I've seen some interesting filing systems. I'm sure yours won't be too hard to handle."

Chapter 8

The following Wednesday afternoon, Krista sat in Brennan's office, facing him, as they went over the statistical information she'd pulled from the Internet. His alluring aftershave, coupled with his unique scent, filled her nostrils, making her extremely conscious of his virile presence. Krista shifted in her chair and stole a quick glance in his direction.

The more time she spent with him, the more she liked him. Eyelids lowered over her eyes, Krista studied Brennan's lean, dark face. He wasn't exactly handsome, but he had a commanding aura about him, which drew people into his circle. She fully understood why Erin Saunders found Brennan so appealing and fascinating—and why the other woman found excuses to wander into the salesmen's bull pen.

Her respect for Brennan went beyond the way he came to her rescue that horrible day at the park. He was kind and gentle, yet firm when necessary. Under his direction, her creative side had flourished, and she'd found a place at Dexter Kee where she felt comfortable and received credit for her work.

Brennan glanced up from the papers on his desk, catching Krista examining him. His unreadable expression shifted to surprise. "You okay?"

Nodding, she quickly dropped her gaze to her laptop. Her heart raced, and butterflies fluttered in the pit of her stomach.

Had he caught her staring at him? *Oh my! I hope not. Get your brain in gear,* Krista chastised herself silently, refocusing on the numbers dancing before her eyes.

A knock on the door filled the silence. Brennan looked up and Krista turned toward the door as Connor Dexter poked his head inside the office.

"Got a minute?" This was Connor Dexter's polite code for "We need to talk."

Nodding, Brennan rose and beckoned the agency president into the room. "Come in. Krista and I are working on stuff for the Gautier campaign."

Krista gathered her spreadsheets and data into one neat pile, preparing to leave. With an armload of paperwork, she stood and headed for the door. "Hello, Mr. Dexter," she asked. "H-ho-how are you t-to-today?" She turned to Brennan. "I'm g-go-going back t-to my office. Call me w-wh-when your ready."

Mr. Dexter stopped her, with a gentle hand on her shoulder. Surprised, she faced him, with a question in her eyes. "Please stay. This involves both of you," said Mr. Dexter.

Frowning, she gazed toward Brennan. He hunched his shoulders, returning to his desk.

This must be about Gautier, Krista decided, returning to her seat.

The white-haired man crossed the floor and took the chair next to her. He laid one Italian leather–covered foot over the opposite knee and tugged gently on the hem of his trouser leg. "The management team and I want to make the Gautier team feel as if our company is their company. So we've decided to have a reception. It's sort of a meet and greet cocktail party for everyone."

Biting her lip, Krista looked away, wishing she could disappear. She didn't want to attend another agency function. Nothing ever worked out for her.

"Sounds good," said Brennan. He picked up a pencil and drew a yellow pad closer. "When and where?"

"First week of September," replied Mr. Dexter. "I want their people to feel comfortable with our people." He plucked an imaginary speck of lint from his dark gray trousers.

Brennan jotted notes on his pad. "Where will it be held?"

"Sweet Georgia Brown. Hors d'oeuvres and cocktails will be served," Connor Dexter added.

The younger man leaned back in his chair and nodded approvingly. "I like it! Nice!"

"We hope so. Everything related to Gautier should be done just so," said Mr. Dexter. For the first time Connor Dexter's pale blue eyes focused on Krista, making her squirm. "I expect everyone involved in this project to be present. The management team wants to show Gautier a united, dedicated group of professionals."

That means me, Krista thought, wishing she knew of a way out of this. Mr. Dexter's expectant gaze remained on her.

She felt as if she were back in high school, when the teacher would ask a question to which none of the students knew the answer. Everyone would shift in their seats, hoping the teacher didn't see or call on them. She couldn't hide. Mr. Dexter required an answer.

Swallowing loudly, Krista managed to say, "I'll be there."

"Excellent!" came Mr. Dexter's booming reply. "I look forward to seeing you. Brennan?"

The sales director replied, "We'll both be there."

"Glad to hear it." Mr. Dexter rose and headed for the door. Placing his hand on the knob, he faced the pair. "By the way, how is your presentation going?"

"Good," replied Brennan. "We're crunching numbers right now and putting together a couple of proposals."

"I'm looking forward to seeing them." Pursing his lips, Mr. Dexter nodded before slipping out the door.

Krista remained at the desk, studying the hem of her skirt. Functions like the one Mr. Dexter had described always made her feel awkward and out of place. Just like with the picnic, Krista didn't have a choice. The boss had spoken and had made it extremely clear she better show up for the meet and greet.

Krista rubbed a hand back and forth across her forehead. Tired of her role as the company misfit, she shuddered inwardly. She knew what the people around Dexter Kee thought of her, and she was sick of it. From the top of her head to the tips of her toes, she was a constant joke.

Gnawing on her bottom lip, Krista did a quick inventory of her wardrobe and came up empty. She didn't have anything appropriate in her closet. Unlike most women who made this statement, it was true for her. Plus, there was the tiny issue of her not knowing what to buy. Aunt Helen picked her clothes because Krista had long ago lost interest in how she looked. But now things were different.

If she could find a gentle hand to guide her, that would do the trick. But who? Aunt Helen was not that person. The old lady would choose something that would make Krista look even less appealing than her normal garb. And, yes, she wanted to look and feel attractive. Hopefully, an added bonus would be an end to the derogatory remarks and snickers she always heard behind her back.

If she went to the mall, stopped at Saks or Nordstrom, pled ignorance, and persuaded a sympathetic salesperson to help, she might find the right outfit. Krista's heart sank at the reminder of how inept she truly felt about choosing clothes.

Instead of going to the mall with her few friends, Krista had always followed her aunt's orders to come straight home. She'd never had a chance to experiment with clothes and make-up. Eventually, Krista had made herself believe that her looks didn't matter. Unfortunately, that was a lie. They did matter, and they always had. How did she get to be twenty-five years old and remain so clueless about her appearance?

There had to be a way out of this mess. An answer was just out of her reach. Krista needed to sit down and think everything through and come up with a solution.

Soon after Connor Dexter left Brennan's office, Krista excused herself and made her way to the restroom. The ladies' lounge catered to the fashion-conscious women of the agency, with a make-up mirror mounted above the wall of mirrors and a vanity. As she approached the vanity, she got a good look at herself from every angle.

Krista's hair stuck out of her sand-colored ponytail holder. Using the palm of her hand, she brushed down the hot mess on her head. That didn't help. Hair was everywhere. *I need a haircut,* she thought.

Her sepia brown skin was blemish free. A little blush and lipstick would go a long way toward making her look better. Plus, they would add color to her face.

What am I going to do? she wondered, taking a cold, hard look at her thick, bushy eyebrows.

For once she planned to go to an event and look presentable. Maybe even turn heads and receive a few accolades from her coworkers.

After washing up, Krista returned to her office, sank into her chair, and dropped her head in her hands. She felt crushed by the cruelty of her coworkers.

The phone rang. She picked up the receiver and unconsciously recited the company greeting. "Krista Hamilton speaking. How may I help you?"

A slight pause followed and then she heard, "Krista?"

"Yes?"

"Hi. It's Liz Gillis."

Liz! Krista drew the phone away from her ear and stared at

it. This was a surprise. What had prompted this call? "Hi. What can I do for you?"

Laughing nervously, Liz answered, "I'm calling for a favor."

This conversation kept getting more intriguing. *Favor? Second surprise. Why me?* Krista wondered. "Go on."

"I need to go to Frankenmuth this weekend, and I was wondering if you'd like to ride shotgun for me."

Shocked, Krista sat with the phone to her ear. Why would Liz want her to go anywhere with her? Didn't Liz have friends? Heck, Krista could barely string a sentence together. "Umm. Shotgun?"

"Yeah. Be my front seat driver."

"A-ar-are y-yo-you sure you d-di-dialed the r-ri-right number?"

Liz giggled. "You're silly. Of course, I did. Are you free Saturday?"

"Sure," Krista answered slowly, all the while considering how Liz's request might feed into her clothing dilemma.

"All right. The truth is my big brother worries about my driving that far alone," Liz explained. "Normally, I'd con him into coming with me. Brennan's busy this weekend. I promised him I would find someone to ride along with me."

But why me? Krista questioned silently. Frankenmuth. She would have to hold up her end of the conversation for more than an hour. Could she handle it? Krista caught her lower lip between her teeth. Liz looked so nice the few times Krista had seen her. Maybe she could get up enough nerve to ask for Liz's help in buying a dress for the reception. She remembered the beautiful clothes in the other woman's closet. It was obvious Liz had very good taste. During the ride, Krista might glean more information about fashion and clothes.

"W-wh-what time Saturday?" asked Krista.

"Noonish," Liz answered. "We can have lunch or an early dinner before we head back to Detroit. What do you say?"

"Okay," Krista confirmed, crossing her fingers and silently praying that everything would work out.

"Great! This will make Brennan very happy."

Krista smiled, thinking of the bantering siblings. They argued, teased one another, but neither seemed to get upset with the other.

Liz continued. "I'll pick you up at your place. Brennan told me you live close to the Lodge. We can take the Davison Freeway and pick up I-75 to Frankenmuth."

"T-ta-take down my-my address and phone number," Krista suggested. "If you can, c-ca-call me before you leave home, and I'll be ready when you get to my house."

"No problem."

"I'll s-se-see you Saturday," Krista said.

"Will do. Krista?"

"Yeah?"

"Thanks. I really appreciate the help."

"You're welcome."

Smiling, Krista hung up the telephone. Maybe this was a blessing. She could talk with Liz without the watchful eye of her brother and get some advice and direction about how to dress.

Chapter 9

Saturday at noon, Krista stood at the front door, with her purse in her hands, waiting for Liz to arrive. A navy Ford Five Hundred pulled up to the curb in front of the house and blew the horn. She hurried through the house and stopped in the den doorway. "Auntie, I'm gone. I'll probably be back around six or a little later."

"You be careful on the road," her aunt said.

"We will."

"Don't let nobody talk you into doin' nothing you know is wrong," Aunt Helen warned, wagging a finger at Krista.

"We won't."

"Remember your religion. It'll keep you on the right road."

Krista shook her head. Since she was a child, Aunt Helen had gone through this drill each time Krista went anywhere other than church and work. When she moved to Lansing for college at Michigan State, her aunt had called every few weeks with the same lecture.

"Auntie, Liz is almost eight months pregnant. And I'm not exactly the belle of the ball. Our getting in trouble days are pretty limited."

"How'd she get that way? Does she have a husband?"

"Yes." Krista searched inside her purse for her keys and

started out of the den. She reached the landing. A gush of warm air rushed past her when she opened the side door.

"Where is he?"

"Army. Shipped to Iraq."

"Oh." That stopped her for a moment. But not for long. Within seconds Aunt Helen began her third tirade. "Don't know why you've got to go so far, anyway."

Enough! Krista shouted in her head. "See you later. Bye." She shut and locked the door at her aunt's disapproving words. Today she planned to have a good time and ask for some help. She refused to let her aunt's pessimism destroy the beauty of the outing. Krista drew in a deep breath, letting it out and leaving the negativity at the door. She hurried down the driveway to the car and opened the door. "Hi."

"Hey, yourself. Thanks for coming with me," Liz said as Krista climbed into the passenger seat.

"You're w-we-welcome," Krista answered, placing her purse on the floor and buckling her seat belt.

"Your coming along put Brennan's mind at ease."

"No p-pr-problem."

Liz reached across the transmission gear and squeezed Krista's hand. "Calm down. Take your time. We're all friends here."

The tension tightening Krista's shoulders eased. Krista took a deep breath and let it out. "Thank you."

"Don't worry about it. I really appreciate your help today." Liz waved a hand in the air, advising, "Never have an older brother."

Blinking at the lightning change of topics, Krista smiled softly. That wasn't very likely, since her mother had died when she was a baby, and no one knew who her father was.

"Brennan went all protective when I mentioned I wanted to make this trip. So I had to assure him I would be fine."

Images of her temporary boss filled her head. Krista could see him pacing in front of her, all the while giving her instructions. He loved Liz very much, and the feelings were returned. Krista sensed that Brennan would always worry about those he loved. But he had to understand, Liz was a grown woman, with a life of her own.

"Why?" asked Krisata.

"He feels it's too close to my due date, and he's worried something might happen."

Krista ran her tongue across her dry lips and said, "Brennan's trying to p-pr-protect you and the b-ba-baby."

"I know. Most times he doesn't mind traveling with me. And I love him for it. Today he had stuff to do for your Gautier campaign." Liz's hand swung in a circle. "But I still need to make this trip and do my thang."

Krista nodded. Brennan had plenty to do. Instead of a plate, he had a platter of items to complete before the presentation. Casting the local actors for the commercial and choosing the studio were high on his list of projects. Yeah, Brennan was very busy today. "I've never"—she paused, feeling like a hick in her own town—"been to Frankenmuth."

Liz hit the turn signal, waited for a passing car, pulled away from the curb, and then merged into the light Saturday afternoon traffic. "It's lots of fun. When my husband and I were dating, Steve took me to Frankenmuth one afternoon. We rambled around, went to Bronner's, bought Christmas ornaments, and ate chicken dinners at Zehnder's. It's one of my favorite memories. We gorged ourselves on entirely too much food. But, of course, you and I would never do a thing like that, would we?"

"Oh no. Never," Krista teased.

They settled into a comfortable silence as Liz merged onto the Lodge Freeway, exited onto the Davison to I-75, and headed north. The compact disc player hummed and started to play "Your Secret Love" from a selection of Luther Vandross hits as they cruised along the highway.

Krista sat quietly, watching the scenery zip by and plotting how to approach Liz about buying a dress. Once they reached town, she planned to ask Liz for her help. "Is there a r-re-reason we're going to Frankenmuth?" asked Krista.

"Fudge."

Puzzled, Krista stared at the pregnant woman as if she'd lost her mind. "What?"

"Steve loves Frankenmuth fudge, and I promised I would buy some for him."

"Isn't there an easier way to do this?"

"Mm-hmm. Couple of them. But, my dearly beloved husband can taste the difference between Frankenmuth fudge and other places. I've learned over the years to get him what he wants. Normally, I'd order it online and then have it shipped overseas. I don't want to take the chance that Steve might end up home before the mail gets to him. If I pick it up and have the package shipped express, he'll have it within a few days."

"An-any word on when he'll be home?"

Liz accelerated past a huge tour bus. "No official date yet. I'm still expecting him home before the baby comes."

A question nagged at Krista, and she had to ask it. "Why did you ask me to come along, Liz?"

"Most of the people I grew up with are married. They have husbands, kids, and they just don't have the time for me like they used to. I'm not complaining," she rushed to add. "It's just our lives have changed, and family comes first. And I understand that. It's the way things should be. You grow up and apart. Do you know what I mean?"

"I think so."

"Here's the other part of it. A lot of my friends don't know what to say to me, so they avoid me. I see them hesitating as they debate whether to ask about Steve. They feel uncomfortable, so they say nothing and stay away. It's not pleasant for either one of us."

We're both outcasts, Krista thought, looking at the other

woman from a different perspective. *Although it's for different reasons, it has the same results.*

"I'm sorry."

Liz brushed away Krista's sympathy with a wave of her hand, although Krista suspected it hurt more than Liz felt willing to admit. "It's not your fault. It's not even my fault. Besides, you didn't treat me any different. Sometimes I run into couples that Steve and I used to hang out with. When I tell them that Steve is in Iraq, they do this head thing."

"Head thing?"

"Their heads tilt to one side like this." Liz demonstrated, tilting her head to the left. "And then they say, 'Oh! I'm so sorry.' I absolutely, one hundred percent hate that. Unfortunately, there's nothing I can do about it. So you were elected to accompany me on this road trip."

"I'm honored."

Liz giggled. "I'll tell you a secret if you promise not to say anything to my big brother."

Intrigued about any information about Brennan, Krista leaned closer and said solemnly, "Sure. I promise."

Liz took her eyes off the road for a second and glanced in Krista's direction. "My brother trusts you. When I told him I was going to ask you to come along, he grunted approvingly. He's told me more than once that you have a level head and he can depend on you. That's high praise coming from Brennan. He doesn't trust very easily."

Her comment warmed Krista's insides and boosted her confidence. "Thank you."

Hours later, Liz stored butter pecan and chocolate walnut fudge in a cool spot in the car. After strolling along Main Street in downtown Frankenmuth, checking out bakeries, novelties, and Bronner's Christmas store, Liz announced baby Gillis wanted dinner at Zehnder's.

After more courses than she could eat, Krista got out of the restaurant without any major mishaps, although she had noticed a bed of bread crumbs in her lap. She'd inconspicuously brushed them to the floor when she rose from her chair and then had trailed after Liz.

As they left the white building and started for the car, Liz touched Krista's arm and asked, "Do you mind if we stop at Birch Run for a little bit?"

"No. That's fine," Krista answered, debating how to bring up her need for help as she buckled her seat belt.

"Great! Jones New York has an outlet store there," Liz explained, pulling into Main Street traffic. "I love their designs, and I want to check out what's new for the fall lineup."

Eyebrows raised, Krista ran a questioning eye over Liz's protruding belly.

"Okay. I know I can't get into anything right now," added Liz. "There's no harm in looking. I won't be pregnant forever. Although some days it feels that way."

Krista didn't feel Liz wanted a response.

"I love to shop. Sue me," Liz stated, with a wiggle of her head. Liz sped past Bronner's Christmas store and turned right onto South Gera Road and sailed across the I-75 freeway to the entrance to the mall.

"Here we are. Ohh! Look!" said Liz as she pulled into an empty spot, put the car in park, and switched off the engine. "They've added some new stores. Come on. Let's check them out." With some difficulty, she climbed out of the car and reached for her purse in the backseat.

Krista stayed in the passenger seat for a moment, watching this busy woman.

As fast as her plump body allowed, Liz ducked in between cars and rushed to the door of a store, with Krista on her tail. A bell jingled as Krista stepped inside the building, searching the store for Liz. Women of all ages, body types, and ethnic backgrounds filled the store.

Liz stood at a beige, wooden spinning rack peppered with jewelry. She turned, spied Krista, and waved her over excitedly. "Come here. Look at these."

Curious, Krista hurried to her side. "What you got?"

Liz shoved a small square of cardboard at Krista. "These are perfect for you."

Face scrunched into a frown, Krista shook her head. "Not for me."

"Sure they are." Liz pushed Krista's wild mane of hair away from her face and positioned one of the earrings near her earlobe. She turned Krista toward the tiny mirror mounted on the side of the rack. It dangled near her earlobe by a thin string of braided silver. At the bottom of the silver, a teardrop held the two pieces of metal together. A lone rose-colored stone filled the center of the teardrop. "With your coloring and the shape of your ears, these are perfect for you. Buy them," Liz insisted, thrusting the jewelry into her hand.

"I don't know." Krista turned her head this way and that, studying herself in the mirror.

"What don't you know?" Liz placed her hand on her waist, or what would have been her waist if she had one.

Krista shrugged.

"If you don't buy them, I will, and then I'll give them to you as a gift. And you will *not* say no."

Saying no was not the way to get Liz to agree to help her, especially when it involved shopping. "Okay. Okay."

Krista could have saved her breath. Liz had moved on to something different. "This is gorgeous." Liz pulled a sunflower-colored two-piece pantsuit from the rack. She draped it in front of her. "I love this color."

Krista fingered the silk jacket. The fabric felt cool to the touch. "I like the feel of silk."

"Me, too."

"Again. Why don't you buy this? You've got the figure. What size do you wear? Four or six?" Liz turned around, sliding the hangers along the rack as she searched for the proper size. "Unlike someone else we both know."

"No. It's not for me."

Frowning, Liz asked, "Why not?"

Flustered, Krista shook her head, stammering. "Too b-br-bright. Too m-mu-much color."

Giving Krista an incredulous look of disbelief, Liz asked, "You're kidding, right?"

"No."

The pregnant woman gave the suit a second, more severe examination. "It's loud. Funky. But you're not a Mormon. Besides, yellow would look great on you."

"Not me. Can't do this."

Liz stood perfectly still, silently studying Krista.

Bracing herself for an argument, Krista was surprised by what came out of Liz's mouth.

"Let's pay for these," Liz suggested, nodding at the earrings in Krista's hand. She headed for the checkout counter.

As she stood in line to pay for her earrings, Krista worried over what Liz thought of her. She didn't know how to explain her feelings. Once they left the store, Liz took her arm and guided her across the parking lot to a bench. Liz pushed Krista onto the seat. "Wait here. I'll be right back."

Liz went to a vending machine and bought two bottles of water. She returned to the bench, sat down next to Krista, and handed one of the bottles to her. "Okay. Talk."

"'Bout what?"

"You are a very pretty girl. Why do you dumb yourself down?"

Voice quivering, Krista admitted, "I've been laughed at all of my life. But t-th-this is who I am. It's all I know."

Shaking her head, Liz muttered softly, "Don't believe that. It isn't true. You're so much more."

"Yes." Krista nodded remorsefully. She held back tears, but

her voice shook just a bit. "Most times I ignore it. But lately, it's been really bad."

"How so?"

"They call me Krista wolf."

A sharp intake of air followed Krista's comment. Liz reached out and grabbed the young woman's hand and held it. "Oh no. That's so mean. I'm so sorry. They're just a bunch of fools. You shouldn't have to take that."

Dabbing at her eyes, Krista said, "You didn't do anything."

"No. But I don't think it's right for the staff to harass you this way. Do you want me to talk to Brennan?"

"No!" Liz's brother might cause more trouble. She'd rather take the ugly comments.

"I don't understand." Frowning, Liz linked her fingers and laid them on her stomach. "Why not? He can put an end to all of it."

And make my life more of a living hell than it already is, Krista thought. Embarrassed, she shook her head. "It'll be worse."

"Not if you stand up for yourself."

Krista scoffed. "L-lo-look at me. I wear my g-gr-grand-mother's rejects. Do you really think a-an-anyone will t-ta-take me seriously?"

"Not like this," Liz stated. "Why don't you go to the mall and buy something different?"

"I don't know how," Krista admitted.

Liz fingered a lock of Krista's hair. "Have you ever had a haircut, manicure, pedicure, anything? What about your eye-brows? Plucked, waxed?"

"No."

Shaking her head, Liz nibbled on her bottom lip. "Has anyone ever created a hairstyle for you?"

Ashamed, Krista bowed her head, twisted off the bottle cap, and took a long swig of the water before confessing,

"My aunt would pull the Bible out and preach for hours if I came home with an outfit like the yellow one."

"How old are you?" Liz shot back.

Krista opened her mouth to respond, and Liz cut her off.

"Never mind. That's not what I meant. You're old enough to make your own decisions."

"You don't understand." Krista spread her hands. "Help me. It's too hard to make those changes."

Liz sat back and swallowed some water. "Here's a question for you. Do you enjoy looking like this? Don't you feel foolish around people who are dressed so differently from you?"

"Sometimes."

"That's what I thought." She touched Krista's hand. "I can help you if you want."

"How?"

"We can work on a better wardrobe. Give you some direction on make-up and hair."

Now that the offer had been made, Krista felt uncertain about whether she wanted to do this. She turned to Liz and held her gaze with her own. "Why? Why would you help me?"

Liz quickly looked away and bit her lip. It took her a minute to answer. "Because I think I understand how you feel. You don't have anyone to help you, and I can. Besides, you've been good to me."

"What do you mean?"

She smiled at Krista. "I'm sure you had more interesting things to do than baby-sit a pregnant lady. Even if you stayed home and watched television, this is your time."

Krista remained silent.

Liz scooted to the edge of the bench, pushed herself up, and reached out a hand to Krista. "Come on."

"W-wh-what are you doing?"

"We're going to do a little something special for you."

"I-I-I'm not ready for that yellow outfit."

Liz smiled. "I know. We're not going to do anything drastic."

"Then what?" Krista asked, standing.

"I've got an idea." She grabbed Krista's hand. "We're going to do a little confidence building."

Krista followed Brennan's sister down the sidewalk to another block of stores. They stopped outside a different store. "I told you I love to shop," said Liz.

Krista opened her mouth to speak, but Liz raised a hand.

"Stop. Nothing big. This is stuff you can live with," Liz assured her.

At a slower pace, she followed Liz across the street. That little pregnant woman was on a mission, and nothing was going to stop her. Krista wanted help, and now she had it, whether she wanted it or not.

Krista hoped she hadn't made a bad situation worse. She prayed softly that she wouldn't look too crazy by the time they left Birch Run and started for home.

Chapter 10

Monday morning Brennan glanced up from his desk and noticed Krista shyly approaching his office. His head dipped as he returned to his work, and then he halted. He lifted his head to conduct a second, more thorough inspection of the woman.

She looks different, he thought, watching her through the glass pane in the window. Was his sister responsible?

When he asked Liz how their trip to Frankenmuth had gone, she'd smiled slyly and muttered, "You'll see."

Now watching Krista, he knew without a shadow of a doubt that Liz had achieved a goal with Krista. But what? Twisting the pen in his hand, he wondered what was going on. Krista looked somehow different today, yet the same. Instantly, he flipped through a short list of reasons but came up empty. The answer rested somewhere beyond his reach. His brain refused to embrace it. Brennan felt certain a significant change had occurred that he should be able to identify.

Euge Groove's "Chillaxin" played on the Bose compact disc player. The smooth tones usually coaxed him into a mellow mood. Not today. His neck and shoulder muscles drew taut. The last thing Brennan wanted to do was chill out or relax.

Krista tapped softly on the wood surface before opening the door and poking her head inside. "Hi, Brennan."

"Hey."

"Got a minute?" She waved a manila folder in the air. "I've worked up some statistical data on our target audience."

Standing eagerly, he ran a hand over his tie and waved her into the room. "Absolutely. Come on in. I've been waiting for that info."

She entered the office and crossed the carpeted floor, stopping in front of the desk. He examined her closely, searching for some unique quality he could attach a name to. Unfortunately, he came up with nothing, nada, zip.

In the weeks she'd worked with him, her wardrobe had never varied. Only a slight change in color and fabric distinguished one ugly outfit from the last.

There wasn't anything special or outstanding about the way Krista was dressed on this day. The same unflattering, too-long skirt and oxford blouse covered her slim frame. She had pulled her thick mane of hair into the same unattractive ponytail at the nape. And soft tentacles of hair still escaped its bonds.

Yet, when Brennan glanced into Krista's face, a spark of something special glared back at him. He felt a lurch of excitement as he watched her. Her eyes appeared brighter, more appealing than he'd ever noticed before. "Have a seat," he said.

"Thanks." She slipped into an the empty chair, and the first whiff of a floral fragrance danced under his nose.

Surprised, Brennan gazed at her, enjoying the olfactory delight. Krista had on perfume. Wow!

He shook his head and admonished himself silently. *This is work. Get your brain right.* "Want a cup of coffee?" he asked, strolling to the granite countertop, with a mug in his hand.

Head down and eyes focused on her work, Krista hadn't noticed his interest in her appearance. "No, thanks."

Brennan poured a cup and added cream. More important than the paperwork in her folder, he needed to figure out why Krista's presence disturbed him so greatly today.

"Did you have a good weekend?" he inquired, sipping on the brew as he returned to his desk.

"Yes, I did. How about you?"

A little surprised, he answered, "Worked all weekend." She always stammered over any personal questions. Today she answered him without a moment's hesitation or a quiver in her voice. Very interesting.

Krista grimaced, and then her eyebrows furrowed over her brown eyes. That was it! The bushy brows were gone. She'd gotten her eyebrows done. They were arched and smooth. Her eyebrows had always detracted from her face. Now he could distinguish the almond shape of her eyes and the soft texture of her brown skin. Both were incredibly appealing.

"Oh, that's right," she said. "You did interviews for the commercial. How did that go?"

"Nightmare!" Brennan sank into his chair. "We should have hired a talent agency."

Her head tilted to the side. He noticed the long, delicate slope of her neck and her tender skin.

"Really! Why?"

For a moment, he was so enthralled by the soft, musical tone of her voice, he forgot to answer her question. He stammered, "Mmm-mmm. I wasn't sure who had talent and who didn't." *This has got to stop. Now I'm mumbling like a fool.*

Nodding, she removed a sheet of paper from her file and pushed it across the desk toward him. "What about the script? Have you finalized the material you want to use?"

"No. Still working on it. But we're close."

"Good."

"How about your weekend? Didn't you go to Frankenmuth with Liz this Saturday?"

Her gaze quickly swung away from his. Krista mumbled an affirming "Mm-hmm."

His lips pursed. Something had happened. But what? "How did that go? Did my sister drive you crazy?"

"Not at all. We had a great time! Liz bought your brother-in-law boxes of fudge, and we stopped for a meal at Zehnder's."

"Liz didn't bore you to death with all her talking, did she?"

Krista lifted her head and smiled at him.

For an instant, Brennan's mind went numb, and logical thought disappeared. He felt as if he had just been hit by an out-of-control runaway Hummer. He shook his head, working to clear the cotton stuffed deep inside his brain. When had Krista begun to affect him so deeply?

Brennan studied her a second longer. Her eyes sparkled, and her lips were lush and kissable. Where in the hell had that thought come from?

He never did things like that and certainly not with this pathetic little geek. *No! No! Get your act together, brother man, and stop acting like the horny teenager.*

"No. She didn't." Krista fidgeted with the teardrop of her earring. "Actually, we had lots of fun. That was the first time I'd been to Frankenmuth."

There it was. He finally realized what the difference was. An aura of confidence surrounded Krista, which he'd never seen before. What had his little sister said or done to boost Krista's confidence this way?

Brennan's thoughts switched to a different idea. Or could it be the work? Krista always showed her best side when she managed a project. The stammering stopped, and the self-consciousness abated. That must be it.

His gaze shifted to her face, and he noticed a pair of earrings dangling from her lobes. Krista never wore jewelry. At least he'd never noticed any in the past. Then his gaze shifted to her lips. There was something unique about her mouth.

Frowning, he stared. Krista's lips were moist and kissable, displaying a hint of plum. There was color on her lips.

Brennan fell back in his chair. He felt like yelling, "Eureka!" That was it! She had on lipstick.

Embarrassed by his obvious interest, Brennan shifted his gaze away from Krista's lips to the door. Erin Saunders stood there, peeping through the glass pane at the pair. *What is she doing here?* he wondered, rising from the chair and smoothing his tie into place. "Excuse me," he said. He crossed the office and opened the door. "Hi, Erin."

Her face turned apple red. "Sorry. I didn't mean to disturb you. Tanisha is away from her desk. I was checking to see if you were in your office."

"No problem," Brennan answered, blocking the doorway. "Is there something I can do for you?"

"Umm. I was looking for Krista," Erin answered, gazing beyond Brennan, into his office.

"She's here. Come on in."

"Thanks," she muttered, slipping inside and making a point of brushing up against his chest. Instantly, he took a step back. He didn't want Erin to get the impression he liked what she was doing.

Krista's expression immediately changed. Wariness replaced the wonderful smile he'd been subjected to for the last twenty minutes. Brennan felt like a child deprived of his favorite piece of candy.

"Hey, Krista," Erin called, with a friendly wave. "Rachel and I need to talk with you about one of your projects."

Warily, Krista glanced at Brennan. "Is it okay?"

"Yeah. Go," replied Brennan. "Leave the folder. I'll look at it while you're gone. Once you're done with Erin and Rachel, get back with me."

"Will do," said Krista as she rose and started across the room. She stopped at the door and smiled at Brennan. "Talk to you later."

For the third time this morning, he felt himself enthralled by Krista's beautiful smile. He caught Erin studying their exchange. This shark was no fool. She had noticed the way he responded to Krista, and from the dangerous, evil daggers Erin shot at Krista's back, he knew she didn't like what she'd just witnessed.

Brennan watched Krista leave like a lamb to the slaughter. He raised his hand, intent on calling her back and getting her away from Erin. Just as quickly, he dropped his hand to his side. He couldn't interfere. That would cause even more problems for Krista. Poor thing. The pit bull was ready to pounce.

Side by side, Erin and Krista silently made a zigzag path through the maze of cubicles to the elevator. Erin gave the elevator button an angry jab as they waited. She glanced at the other woman, growled low in her throat, and then opened her mouth. The elevator doors slid open, and she lost the chance to speak as they stepped inside.

Krista pushed the button for the IT floor and leaned against the wall, with her arms folded protectively in front of her. As usual, Erin's outfit reflected her good taste and style. Her silver blue sheer top outlined her perfect hourglass figure. The short gray skirt encased her hips and flared dramatically around her knees.

The malicious gleam in Erin's eyes startled Krista, and a tiny gasp escaped from her lips. Erin turned to Krista, with a hard stare. For the second time, Erin opened her mouth to speak but was caught off guard when the doors to the elevator opened.

Two sales execs from Brennan's team stepped inside. "Hey, Krista," said Mel as he touched her elbow.

"Hi," replied Krista.

Chris, the second salesman, gave Krista a quick wave. "How you doing today?"

"Good. And you?" Krista asked.

"I woke up. I'm still above ground," replied Chris. He grinned at Krista, revealing a slight gap between his front teeth. "That works for me."

Krista giggled. "Me, too."

Mel tilted his head to the side, examining Krista. "There's something about you today. What is it?"

Krista shrugged, feeling a surge of heat spread through her before settling in her cheeks.

"Yeah. You're right," Chris chimed in, moving closer to take a second, closer look. "You didn't get a new do." His lips pursed as he worked things out in his head. "I don't know what it is. But whatever you've done, keep doing it."

The elevator bell dinged, and the men stepped closer to the door. When the elevator stopped, they stepped off. Mel turned to Krista, and said. "See you."

"Bye," said Krista.

The second the doors shut after the men, Erin attacked. "Krista wolf, don't think a little lip gloss and earrings will make you look any better."

Even though she had expected something unpleasant from Erin, the other woman's verbal assault stunned Krista. Erin hated her, although Krista didn't know why. Closely watching Erin, Krista leaned against the elevator wall and thought, *Let the fool rant, and then be done with her.*

"W-wh-why?" Krista asked.

"W-wh-why?" Erin taunted, giggling at the look of horror on Krista's face. "You're still the same pathetic girl who can barely string two words together. I remember how you fell into the dessert table at the picnic, because you tripped over your own feet. That's who you are. The only thing you're good at is computers because they don't require words, Krista wolf."

Instantly, Krista was transported back to high school,

where she had suffered the humiliation of being called "Krista wolf." She thought she'd outgrown all of that. "Don't call me that!"

Why couldn't Erin leave her alone? Every day Krista encountered new foolishness that she had to wade through and pretend didn't bother her.

Krista shut her eyes and turned toward the front of the elevator. She didn't want this kind of confrontation. All she wanted to do was get her work done and go home.

Krista went on. "Don't start. I know you don't like me. But I don't feel up to you and your theatrics."

"Who cares what you want. I'm just trying to put everything in perspective for you so that you won't get your hopes up."

Frowning, Krista faced Erin. "W-wh-what are you t-ta-talking about?"

"Oh, come on. I can see right through you."

"S-se-see what?"

"Do you really believe a man like Brennan Thomas would ever be interested in a little nobody like you?" Erin snorted. "Trust me. You're not his type. I don't think you're anybody's type."

Krista stared at the floor, willing herself not to cry. That remark really hurt. But she refused to let Erin know how much.

Krista was well aware of how she looked to others. And, yes, Brennan Thomas was well beyond anything she expected. But, she liked him, and he respected her skills as an IT expert. That was way more than some of her colleagues gave her.

Feeling her anger rise, Krista shot back, "W-wh-why are y-yo-you so concerned?"

Instantly, Erin responded, "I'm not."

Without saying a word, Krista raised one eyebrow inquiringly.

Erin repeated, "I'm not."

Allowing a tiny smile to creep across her lips, Krista held the other woman's gaze with her own. "Mmm."

"What's that supposed to mean?" Erin demanded.

Krista hunched her shoulders.

Without another word, Erin twisted toward the front of the elevator, ignoring Krista. Erin stood that way until the doors opened.

Moving along the corridor, with Erin at her side, Krista took another peek in the other woman's direction and stifled a grin. Erin's cheeks were red, and her hands were clenched into fists at her sides.

Good. I hit a nerve, Krista thought as they walked side by side to Rachel's cubicle. *Maybe she'll leave me alone.* Krista did a mental leap in the air. *Got you,* she thought. *You're not that smart. I should do this more often.*

Chapter 11

Just a little while longer and you'll be at your desk, Krista promised herself, crossing the marble lobby of the Roney & Company building on her way to Dexter Kee's offices. Her heart pounded so hard in her chest, she felt positive that the guard watching her heard it across the open area of the lobby. Krista stepped inside the elevator and tapped the button for her floor and then leaned back against the silver wall, shutting her eyes while reaching for calm.

After spending most of the weekend with Liz, Krista had emerged from the pregnant woman's bedroom charged and ready to handle Brennan and the account executives of the agency. It didn't take long for reality to set in. Insecurities reared their head, and Krista admitted she might have projected a little more than she could deliver. Everything inside her screamed, *This isn't you! Go home. Hide!* Unfortunately, when the elevator doors opened, she'd be on her floor.

Liz's words of encouragement seemed so distant and far away. This part belonged to Krista. She had to handle her coworkers alone and without support. Preparing to face her peers, she felt naked and defenseless.

Krista realized something new about herself and shook her head sadly. The way she used to dress had insulated her against the cruelness of her coworkers. Liz had removed that armor, and Krista felt vulnerable.

Brennan's sister's reassuring words gave a silent push to Krista's reluctance. She'd talked the talk. Now it was time to walk the walk.

Krista had deliberately stepped out of the geek zone into the next phase of her metamorphosis from caterpillar to butterfly. Although Liz's plan sounded great on paper, the reality of the situation scared the heck out of Krista.

She opened her eyes when the electronic voice announced that she'd arrived. The elevator doors opened, and she stepped into the madhouse known as the sales bull pen. Dexter Kee employees raced in and out of cubicles, shouting orders. Phones rang. Groups convened, dispersed, and reassembled, discussing their daily call sheets and possible sales leads while printers hummed and produced contracts.

With her briefcase in one hand and her purse tossed over her shoulder, Krista drew in a deep breath and let it out slowly. This was it. She held her head high and strolled purposefully between the cubicles. When she was halfway to her office, Shane Jenkins, an account exec, walked past her. Preoccupied with the paperwork in his hands, he bumped into her. He reached out a hand to steady her and glanced up, with "Excuse me" on his lips. Recognition widened his blue green eyes. He stopped in the center of the aisle and stared. "Krista?"

"Hi, Shane."

Grinning broadly, he nodded approvingly and then gave her the thumbs-up sign. "Lookin' good!"

Immediately, she combed her fingers through her hair before touching her cheek. "Thank you," she replied shyly.

"No. Thank you. You brightened my morning," he responded, walking backward to the elevator, adding, "Keep up the good work."

His compliment boosted Krista's fragile confidence a

notch. Honestly, she hoped to get to her desk without any additional incidents.

Krista continued on her way, feeling the curious gazes from her coworkers. She didn't feel comfortable being the center of this much attention. That wasn't quite true, she amended silently. Sometimes she caused a lot of commotion with horrendous results.

Today was different. So far everyone she'd encountered had had a positive response to the changes in her. It warmed her heart and made her feel like she belonged among these people. Maybe Liz had been right. This was the right thing to do to gain confidence and respect.

Flynn Parr stepped away from his administrative assistant's desk, with a typed page in his hands. His blue eyes swept over her without any signs of recognition. Suddenly, the lightbulb switched on, and his thin lips parted in surprise. "Krista!" he exclaimed.

She sidestepped his outstretched hand. Normally, Flynn ignored her unless he needed something for his team or himself. She didn't mind. Flynn really creeped her out with his sly remarks and busy hands, which always made her skin crawl.

"Look at you!" Flynn moved closer to her. "I love your hair." He reached out and ran a finger across her bangs.

"Thank you." Smiling uncomfortably, she took a step away from the sales director.

Erin Saunders turned the corner and halted. Her eyes narrowed to dangerous slits. She slowly approached the pair, examining Krista. The cruel intent in Erin's eyes made Krista cringe in preparation for some cutting comment. What came out of Erin's mouth shocked Krista.

"Wow! Don't you look nice!" exclaimed Erin.

Confused, Krista stared at the other woman.

Erin slowly and deliberately circled around Krista, taking in her new hairstyle from every angle. "Very nice."

Brennan's door opened, and he strolled out of his office, with a mug of coffee in one hand and a stack of reports in the other.

"My man," Flynn called, holding Krista's hands in his and drawing her into the other man's path. "Check out your IT person. She's looking pretty hot this morning."

Focused on the information in his hand, Brennan glanced Krista's way with a faraway gleam in his eyes. He zeroed in on her face, and his expression went from curious to shocked.

Flinching, Krista stammered through stiff lips, "Hi, B-Br-Brennan."

"Hey," Brennan muttered. His gaze roamed over her sharply, assessing. "You look nice."

"Thank you."

"Nice!" Flynn chuckled, waving a hand up and down the length of her. "Oh, come on, my man. Is that all you've got to say? I mean, look at her."

Her blood pounded at her temples as her cheeks burned with heat. Krista might have changed her appearance—the shoulder-length, layered locks accentuated the shape of her face—but she felt like the same girl under the new do.

Brennan cleared his throat and approached her. "Your hair looks really pretty."

Tugging at her hand, Krista responded, "Thank you." She ducked her head. *Boy, I need to increase my vocabulary. That's the fourth thank-you this morning.*

Flynn let go of Krista's hand. He moved behind Brennan and muttered something far too low for the others gathered in the area to hear. Brennan gave a sharp, equally low retort and then pushed past the other man. Shrugging, Flynn grinned, showing pearly whites that had probably put some dentist's kid through college. "Must not be a morning person," muttered Flynn.

Tired of the whole situation, Krista dismissed both men and hurried past Flynn to her office. She unlocked her door and was turning the knob when she felt someone at her side. She glanced over her shoulder and found Erin at her side.

"Don't think because you got your hair cut that anyone thinks better of you. You're still Krista wolf." Erin smiled sweetly, turned on her heels, and left before Krista could come up with a reply.

Feeling abused by Erin's hateful words, Krista entered her office and shut the door. She sank into her chair and studied the Canadian border from her window. When would all of the negative comments end? It seemed as if the more she struggled to gain some measure of confidence, the more people stood in her way. She needed to find a way to ignore those comments and get on with her work.

Liz paced the kitchen floor, with the telephone attached to her ear. "Come on. Answer the phone."

On the fifth ring, someone picked up the line. "Krista Hamilton. How m-ma-ay I help you?"

"What took you so long?" Liz demanded. "I've been dying here, waiting to hear from you."

"Hello."

Okay. I've completely lost my mind. I don't have any manners, Liz thought. "Sorry. Hi, Kris. How are you?"

"Fine."

"How are things going?"

"Mm." Krista hedged. "Okay."

"And?" Liz prompted impatiently. Sometimes she felt like shaking the words out of Krista. "What did people say?"

"C-co-compliments," Krista answered.

Pleased, Liz balled her hand into a fist and jerked it down. "Yes! See, I told you we were doing a good thing."

"Y-yo-you did."

"What about my brother?" Liz inquired, slipping into one of the chairs at the kitchen table. "Did he like how you looked?"

Static filled the telephone line. Krista swallowed hard and then admitted, "I d-do-don't know."

Liz's forehead crinkled into a frown. "What do you mean, you don't know? You were there, weren't you?"

"Yes."

"Come on. I want all the details," Liz demanded. "What happened?"

"He c-ca-came out of his office and s-st-stared at me like I'd just grown three heads and he couldn't d-de-decide which one to speak to."

Giggling, Liz said, "Stop exaggerating. I'm sure you surprised him with the new do."

"Maybe."

"Don't worry about it. We're going to work on clothes next. By the time I'm done with you, you'll be beating the men off with a stick."

"I h-ho-hope not. I don't w-wa-want to beat them off."

"Ohh!" Liz sang. "You naughty girl."

"Liz!"

"I know what you meant. Can't a girl tease you? I want you to feel good about yourself. Don't let anybody put you down."

"Okay."

"I'm your friend. I'm here to help. If you need me, call." The baby kicked. Liz rubbed her belly. "At least until this little guy makes his grand appearance."

Liz heard a soft sigh from Krista's end of the telephone line. She waited for the young woman to turn her thoughts into words.

It had taken a lot of persuasion and all weekend for Liz to convince Krista to agree to a haircut. Although Krista had doubts about the results, Liz knew the other woman had begun her transformation.

"I know it took a lot for you to walk into that particular den of thieves," said Liz. "But I want you to know how proud I am of you. You've done some amazing things in the past few days. Don't let anyone make you think anything else."

"You're the only one that believes that."

"No. I'm not," Liz refuted. "There's always someone with a personal agenda. Ignore them. You hang in there. I'll talk to you later."

"Bye."

Liz hung up and placed the phone on the table. She went to the refrigerator and poured herself a glass of orange juice. She returned to the table and sipped her drink.

A smile curled on her lips. For the first time since she'd agreed to take part in this bet, Liz felt she'd chosen the right course to help both Krista and her brother. Krista looked different enough to turn a few heads, although she found it difficult to see herself as anything other than a misfit.

Liz picked up the phone and punched in a series of numbers. She waited as the phone rang. Several rings later, she heard, "Brennan Thomas."

"Hey, big brother. What's going on?"

"Work. How about you? You okay?"

She chuckled. "I'm fine. This is not a baby alarm. I'm checking on you."

He snorted. "On me? I'm fine. You're the one with the big belly."

"Well, thank you." She studied her belly, feeling the baby move and then settle into a more comfortable position. "You say the sweetest things."

"What can I do for you, Lizzie?"

"Have you seen Krista this morning?" she asked casually, toying with her empty juice glass.

There was a long pause on the opposite end of the line. "Yes," Brennan expelled in a long drawl.

"How do you think she looks?" Liz asked, giggling softly.

"You did a good job," Brennan replied in a neutral tone.

Pleased, Liz bounced around on the seat cushion. "What about the other people in the office? Were they surprised?"

"Oh yeah," he answered.

Come on, Brennan. Give me something to work with, she thought. Trying to get info from these two felt like more work than being pregnant. Liz couldn't wring a good emotion out of either Krista or Brennan. That was okay. She still had a few tricks.

"Didn't you just love her hair?" said Liz.

"It's nice."

"Oh, come on," Liz whined, dropping her head to the table-top. "Can't you think of anything better to say?"

Brennan cleared his throat. "I have a question for you."

"Go for it," she replied, lifting her head and staring out the window at the children playing near the pool.

"How did you work on her without my noticing?"

Giggling softly, Liz replied, "You were locked up in your office most of the weekend. I don't think you came out to go to the bathroom. Besides, Krista and I were in my room. You wouldn't have come in there unless I yelled for you. Krista looked great, didn't she?"

"How many times are you going to ask me that?"

Liz could hear the exasperation in his voice. "As many as it takes to get you to answer me."

She heard him draw in a deep breath of air and then let it out. "If it will shut you up, then, yes, Krista looked beautiful."

Liz grinned. "That's all I wanted to hear."

"Can I go back to work now, Lizzie?"

"One more question."

"What?"

"Am I doing a good job? Does Krista look more presentable to your coworkers?"

"I think you're getting the job done. And, yes, Krista is looking pretty good."

Laughing, Liz added, "I just wanted to know."

"Bye, Lizzie."

Liz switched off the telephone and leaned back in her chair. She was right. She was moving in the correct direction. Her thoughts turned to the past weekend and the time she'd spent convincing Krista to let her cut her hair. That young woman had given Liz the hardest time. But in the end, she'd agreed to a new look.

Their trip to Frankenmuth had showed Liz a different and painful side of Krista's life. Although Liz had grown up in the foster care system, she'd always had her brother. She knew he loved her and always protected her. It didn't appear that Krista had anyone. She needed a friend, and Liz planned to be that person.

Hair, nails, and eyebrows had been cut and shaped. Clothes were the next item on Liz's list of things to change about Krista. All she needed to do was convince Krista to buy some new clothes, and then Liz needed to sneak into Krista's house and burn her present wardrobe.

Chapter 12

One week after Krista made her appearance with her new hairdo, she stood in the center of the bedroom of her attic apartment. She'd moved into the third-floor apartment of her aunt's house when she returned to Detroit after receiving her bachelor's degree from Michigan State University.

The apartment was perfect for a single person. It had a living room, bedroom, and private bath. Krista shared the kitchen downstairs with her aunt. There was just enough space, so Krista felt as if she had a degree of privacy in her aunt's home. However, she didn't doubt her aunt Helen made a trip or two to the apartment after Krista left the house for work.

Her hands smoothed the silver silk top over the waist of her short navy skirt. Krista felt naked without the heavy covering of her long skirts. She turned right and then left, examining her reflection. Rows of linear pleats molded the pliable fabric of her top against her breasts. The fabric cinched at the waist and floated around her narrow hips.

Krista sighed, finger combing her soft, layered locks. After a week of compliments, she still felt uncomfortable with the attention she'd been receiving. She shuddered. Flynn Parr had been the worst. His false smile, praise, and knowing looks always put her on edge.

Mentally, she shut the door on those thoughts and turned her attention to more immediate problems. When Aunt Helen got a look at her outfit, the old girl would have a whole lot to say, too much to say. The haircut had eased by Auntie without much comment.

There wouldn't be two miracles in one week in this house. When Aunt Helen got a look at her clothes, the verbal battle of the century would commence.

Even during the years Krista spent at Michigan State University, Auntie had filled her care packages with her selection of clothing. This was the first time Krista had chosen an outfit that didn't resemble those of the sisters in the front pew of the church. Granted, Liz had shared in the selection of Krista's new clothes. Krista smirked. Actually, Brennan's sister had bullied Krista into buying some of the more revealing items.

Squaring her shoulders, she grabbed her briefcase and purse and headed down the two flights of stairs. The aroma of freshly brewed coffee permeated the first floor. She halted on the landing leading to the side door and placed her belongings on the black leather bench and then headed for the kitchen.

Aunt Helen sat on a stool at the kitchen island, dressed in her rose-colored satin robe, with a cup of coffee in front of her. The Detroit morning newspaper covered the countertop, while familiar faces from the *Today* show flashed on the white nine-inch television mounted under a dark wood cabinet.

Krista drew in a deep breath and tried to relax.

Silently, Auntie eyed Krista while sipping her coffee. Her gaze followed her niece's movements. Biting her lips, Krista prepared a meal of wheat toast, a poached egg, and orange juice, hiding her nervousness.

The only sound in the room came from Matt Lauer as he discussed the progress of rebuilding in New Orleans a year after Katrina. Tension stretched between the two women. Yet they continued their morning routine as if nothing had changed, until Krista rose from her chair to rinse her dishes.

"When did you get that outfit?" Aunt Helen asked.

Auntie always got the upper hand by catching her off guard. Krista swallowed hard, managing a feeble response. "Saturday."

Nodding, Aunt Helen mumbled, "Mm."

Facing the sink, Krista loaded the dishwasher before returning to the island for her juice glass. Auntie's interrogation had just begun. More was sure to follow. She swallowed the last of the orange juice and then returned to the sink to add the glass to the dishwasher.

"That girl you went to Frankenmuth with helped you buy this stuff, didn't she?" Aunt Helen's cool, disapproving tone put Krista on the defensive.

She folded her arms across her chest and faced her aunt. "Some."

"Mm," Auntie scoffed, tipping her head toward her niece. She focused in on Krista's face and muttered knowingly, "The hair, too."

Self-conscious, Krista ran her fingers instantly through the soft tresses. *I'm not going to let her rattle me,* she promised herself. "Yes."

"I see." The old girl folded her newspaper and laid it aside, giving Krista her full attention.

"What do you see, Auntie?"

The woman's unwavering gaze unnerved Krista. "Hair. Clothes. Gurl, you're forgettin' yourself." Aunt Helen rose from her stool and stepped to the coffeemaker and refilled her cup before returning to her stool at the island.

"What's that supposed to mean?"

Auntie shrugged. "Nothin'."

"S-s-something." Krista slammed the dishwasher door. She hated confrontations, but she refused to back down from this one.

"I'm wonderin' if you've forgotten all the things your uncle Nick and I've taught you over the years. The stuff you learned in church. Are you tossin' your church teachin' aside so that you can act and look like all the fast girls you know?"

"Why do I have to be fast?" Krista folded her arms across her chest. "There's no sin in wanting to look nice."

"It's the road to something you ain't ready to try."

"I'm not planning on going down any particular road."

"Then there's no reason for you to do this, is there?"

Krista licked her dry lips. "Yes, there is. Things are changing at Dexter Kee. I'm in the limelight now. No more cubicle in the back of the office. I have to be in meetings and present info to our management team. It's time I look more professional." *That's not completely true. You want to look better for you and feel less like an idiot in front of your peers,* she admitted silently. *That little gem belongs to me alone.*

"Didn't bother you before. Why now?"

Maybe a few words of truth might calm her auntie's fears. "It's always b-bo-bothered me. I just k-ke-kept it to myself."

"Why didn't you say somethin'?"

Krista shot back, "Because it didn't m-ma-matter before."

"And now?"

Brennan's handsome image popped into Krista's head, causing a surge of warm heat to course through her veins. She didn't plan to tell her aunt everything. All Auntie Helen needed to know was Krista wanted to make a few changes. There was no reason to feel threatened by the transformation.

"The job has made me realize that I want to be seen differently. Be taken more seriously by my coworkers."

Frowning, Auntie wagged a finger at Krista. "This don't sound right to me. You sure there ain't no man involved?"

I'm not going there with her, Krista decided.

Auntie went on. "When your mother was alive—"

Krista groaned and rubbed her fingers back and forth across her forehead, feeling the tug of guilt her aunt laid on

her. Whenever a problem cropped up that Auntie couldn't resolve, she played the guilt card. "This is not about my m-mo-
mother," Krista said, cutting her short.

"You're actin' just like her."

"How can I? I never k-kn-knew her."

Auntie snorted, slipping off the stool. She picked up her
coffee cup and saucer. The delicate pieces of china tinkled as
she approached the sink. She opened the dishwasher, adding
her cup and saucer. "Genes."

"This has nothing to do with my m-mo-mother. I want to
fit in and be c-co-comfortable on my job. That's it." Krista
glanced at her watch and then started for the landing. "I have
to get to work."

"We're not done," Aunt Helen promised.

That's for sure, Krista agreed to herself, picking up her
briefcase and purse and hurrying out of the house and down
the drive to her car.

"That went well," she muttered, with a cynical edge to her
voice, as she climbed behind the steering wheel and started
the car. There must be a way to make her aunt understand how
important it was for her to feel better about herself and get
what she wanted at the same time, and have people look at her
without pity in their eyes.

She couldn't let anyone keep her from the path she'd decided
to go down. Neither Aunt Helen nor Erin Saunders. Krista was
tired of seeing that look of pity in other people's eyes.

At the end of the day, Brennan stood outside Krista's
office, intently peering at her through the windowpane in her
door. She sat at her desk, her arms spread wide as she
stretched.

He couldn't help noticing how the soft fabric molded
around the gentle swell of her breasts. Something intense

flared inside him, stoking a gentle, growing fire. He shook himself.

Get your head in the game. You did not come here to ogle Krista, he thought, turning away. *Lizzie is doing a great job. Krista is looking really hot these days. I'm a better man than this.*

Brennan drew in a deep breath of air, rubbed his hands over his face, twirled on his heels, and rapped on the door before entering. He stood inside the entrance, with a hand on the knob, and smiled at the woman sitting behind the desk. For a moment he watched her organizing her desk in preparation for going home.

"Hey," he greeted, moving farther into the room. "I wanted to catch you before you left for the day and tell you how much I appreciate your work. Krista, you already know this campaign means a lot to me and the agency, and I've pushed you hard because of it. But you've come through on everything I've asked you for. And you've done a great job. Thanks."

A faint trace of red stained her cheeks. Krista drew a lock of hair behind the delicate shell of her ear and stammered, "Y-yo-you're welcome."

He studied the clean desk. "Are you ready to leave?"

She nodded.

Brennan returned to the door. "Let me get my briefcase, and I'll walk out with you."

"Okay."

Minutes later, Krista arrived at the elevator to find Brennan standing with one foot inside it. She hurried between the elevator doors. He removed his foot and allowed the doors to shut.

Grinning, he said, "I didn't know you could move that fast."

She giggled softly. "I'm ready to get out of here. It's been a long day."

"That it has. Got any plans for this evening?"

Krista shook her head. "Home. Television."

Brennan realized that he liked being with her, and over the past few weeks, he had begun to depend on her and treat her as part of his team. This brought on a new curiosity about Krista's private life. Before he realized where his thoughts were taking him, he asked, "How about a sandwich before you head home? My treat for doing a bang-up job for the last few weeks."

An expression of panic flashed across her face before she controlled it. Krista's tongue appeared at the corner of her mouth as she hesitated. She looked adorable and so incredibly appealing. "Sure. W-w-where?"

"Let's head over to Magnolia's. They have a decent menu."

"Sounds good. Maybe I should get my car."

"Leave it. We'll pick it up after we're done." Brennan took her by the arm and led her across the lobby, out of the building, and to the parking lot next to the Roney & Company building. They climbed into his Saab and made the short trip to the restaurant.

After the valet drove off with his car, Brennan followed Krista into the building, and the hostess escorted them to a table near the back of the restaurant. They examined the menu of nontraditional soul food and then opted for dinner instead of sandwiches. Their server brought soft drinks as Brennan and Krista sat watching the minimal, quiet Monday night crowd.

"You look very nice today," Brennan complimented.

She grimaced and combed her fingers through her soft tresses. Confusion dulled the glow in her eyes from under lowered eyelids. "Thank you."

An idea hit him. Krista didn't have a vain bone in her body. He reached across the table and covered her hand with his. "I'm sorry. Did I say something wrong?"

She offered him a shaky smile and asked, "What?"

"Something about my compliment didn't hit the right note. Care to tell me what's going on in your head?"

"It's just that . . ." Krista paused, focusing on a point beyond him.

Brennan waited, hoping she'd elaborate. He really wanted to know what Krista was thinking and feeling.

She seemed to come to a decision and focused directly on him, holding his gaze with hers. "I appreciate the compliments and praise. I really do. It gives me something I've always had a hard time holding on to."

"What's that?"

"Confidence."

"Good." He studied the somber expression on her face and then added, "I think."

"Don't get me wrong. Everything your sister has done for me has been good. It made me feel better about myself than I ever have. But at the same time, I think I understand a little more about me and who I want to be." Krista gnawed on her bottom lip for a few seconds. "Nobody sees beyond the hair and clothes. They don't care about how I feel or my opinions. The real me." She sighed. "That's so sad."

The real woman was sitting across the table from Brennan. No stuttering or stammering, just an honest expression of her feelings. Listening to her made him more aware of the bet with Flynn and how unfair it had been to her. How shallow his thoughts had been. He felt ashamed because he hadn't taken the time to get to know the woman. He had made assumptions without considering how Krista felt or what she truly needed.

She shrugged. "I'm still Krista. The woman I was before this change."

"Is it a bad thing to have people notice you?"

"No. Not at all." She folded and refolded her napkin nervously as she spoke. "I g-gu-guess I'm saying there's m-mo-more to me than how I look. Some of the people with the new attitude toward me were the ones who l-la-laughed at me before. Trust me. That's not something you f-fo-forget very easily."

Krista had a point. How could she trust people that treated her so shabbily and then expected her to help them at work? He felt a twinge of compassion and sympathy for this woman trying to make a place for herself in this very cruel world.

"I think I understand what you're saying," he muttered, reaching across the table to capture her hand.

"Human beings can be so small-minded and thoughtless. All we care about is how the exterior looks. N-no-nobody wants to get to know me for who I truly am. That's so distressing."

"It is," he agreed. It was very sad and lonely.

Their server arrived with their meals and effectively cut off further discussion for several minutes. By the time the man had left their table, Krista appeared to have given herself a mental shake and had come back to the present. "I don't want to be a d-do-downer. So, how's that s-si-sister of yours? It's getting close to her due date. Is she f-fe-feeling okay?"

"So far, she's good. I think Liz has picked up a lot of weight in the last few weeks. I don't know." He removed his hand from hers and stroked the bridge of his nose. "But she looks bigger to me."

"The last month or so, she's going to gain a few pounds. I think that's w-wh-when the baby goes through its biggest growth p-ph-phase before delivery."

He nodded.

"What about her husband? Any news on when he'll be coming home?"

"Nothing so far. I hope soon. I don't want to do the delivery thing," Brennan admitted, feeling a cold shiver slither down his spine.

"Why did you agree?"

He answered simply and truthfully. "Because Lizzie is my sister and she needs me."

Dinner occupied them. They spent the rest of the evening making small talk about the office and the Gautier campaign.

Brennan paid the bill, and they retrieved his car. He drove down Woodward Avenue and cut across the Lodge Freeway to the Joe Louis Arena parking structure. Following Krista's directions, he located her car on the fourth floor and pulled into the space next to hers.

She grabbed her briefcase and purse, opened the door, and swung her legs out of the car. "T-th-thanks for dinner. It was fun."

"You're welcome. It's the least I can do. You've been a great help to me and the department."

"That's my job."

Brennan got out of the Saab and ran around the back end to help her out of the car. He took the keys from her hand and unlocked the driver's door of the car before handing them back to her.

He meant to stroke her cheek and then open her car door. Instead, he cupped her cheek and leaned close, feeling the warmth of her body. Her unique fragrance swirled around him, and before he knew it, he leaned in for the light touch of her lips against his.

Krista responded, wrapping her arms around his neck and holding him close. Her soft and pliable lips made him moan deep in his throat. A ripple of excitement sped through him.

Suddenly, Brennan wanted more. He took her face in his warm palms, covering her lips hungrily with his. He moved his mouth over hers, devouring its softness. She tasted of lemonade, a hint of garlic, chocolate, and something distinctly Krista.

Shocked, Brennan released her. *What am I doing?* he wondered. *If she slaps my face and files a sexual harassment claim against me, I certainly deserve it.*

Ready to apologize, Brennan gazed into Krista's eyes. She appeared as dazed as he felt. Maybe that was a good sign.

Moving away, Brennan opened the car door. "Get home safe."

"I will," she answered, climbing into the boat of a car. "See you tomorrow."

He waited as Krista started the engine and pulled out of the parking space. Seconds later the car disappeared, and he returned to the Saab.

Liz had called it right. He did like Krista. A lot. But that bet between him and Flynn Parr could blow up in his face and destroy any chance they might have for a relationship.

He ran a shaky hand over his face. Until he figured out how to get out of this mess, he'd better cool it with Krista. Keep his distance and play the professional.

Chapter 13

Saturday afternoon, Krista tapped her toes to the compact disc playing and shifted the laptop so Brennan could see the Excel spreadsheet on the monitor. "I'll extract this data from the file, and we'll be able to create a slide-show presentation for Gautier with this statistical data."

Eyes narrowed in concentration, Brennan leaned forward, studying the numbers for a beat and then nodded. "Sounds good."

She turned the computer to face her and used the mouse to save the file. "I'll make everything look pretty and professional, and then you and I can run through the info so that you know what the numbers mean."

"Okay. We've got a plan." Brennan made a few notations on the file in front of him. "Krista, thanks for giving up your Saturday to work with me."

"You're welcome. It was no problem." She logged off the computer and shut the lid.

Brennan's critical eye moved over her. The expression on his face made her feel a tiny bit uncomfortable. Since the night they'd kissed, he'd made a point of keeping his distance and treating her as professionally as possible when they were alone together in and out of the office. No reference had been made to what happened that night and what they shared.

She had to admit she enjoyed those moments with him and wished for more. But it had been a fluke that would probably never be repeated. Her heart felt heavy at that thought. Somehow, Brennan had become very important to her, and she wished she was more attractive or sophisticated and knew how to appeal to a man of his caliber.

"You mean to tell me you didn't have a hundred things to do today?" he teased.

"Not really," she admitted. "Just some h-ho-housework, and I'm testing a piece of software for the agency."

He frowned. "I hope Dexter Kee is paying you for your time."

"No. It has to be done. It's easier to do the work from home than to go into the office. This way I can do other things while the software is running through a series of routines."

Nodding absently, he made an additional note on his file. "I'm going to talk to Rachel about compensating you."

"D-do-don't do that. It'll s-st-stir up too much dust. Let it go." She reached across the desk and touched his hand. "Until this project is completed, I work for your department."

A jolt of awareness went through her, making her heart beat faster. His skin seemed to leap to life under her hand as he focused on her. Longing, hot and sizzling, glared from his eyes. With a blink of an eye, it was quickly extinguished. Brennan withdrew his hand, placing it on top of the file.

"But you don't work for free." Brennan changed the subject, asking, "So what do you have planned for the rest of your weekend?"

Krista blinked. Other than the night they went to dinner and talked so openly, this was the first time Brennan had asked her anything personal. Actually, since the night they kissed, he seemed to have withdrawn from her, maintaining a professional demeanor without any personal contact.

"Home. W-wa-watch TV tonight and go to church Sunday." She started to pack up her paperwork. "W-wh-what about you?"

"Liz and I are going to the Smooth Jazz concert this evening at the Southfield Civic Center."

"Wow! I've been listening to the DJs talk about it. Najee, Euge Groove, and Alexander Zonjic are going to perform there. I'm jealous," she teased, secretly wishing she could go with them. She loved Najee, and to see him live would be a wonderful treat.

He smiled. "I'm looking forward to it."

"Do you sit on the grass?"

Brennan rose from his chair and stored the file in the desk drawer. "You can." He chuckled. "Can you imagine Liz, with her big belly, sitting on the ground?"

Laughing softly, Krista answered, "No!"

Brennan stopped, watching her as if he were in a trance. Embarrassed, she brushed a lock of hair off her forehead and wet her dry lips with her tongue.

He shook himself. "I'm sorry. Don't be upset. I didn't mean to stare. This is the first time I've heard you laugh. It's soft and almost musical." He grinned. "It was pretty, and I liked it."

"Thank you. I think."

"You're welcome."

"What do you do for sitting?" she asked.

"Lawn chairs."

"It sounds nice. Have a good time," she said wistfully. Here was one of the times she wished she had someone to do things with. Go to concerts and shows together. A friend she could share things with.

"We will." The back door slammed shut, and the sound resounded throughout the house. "That would be my sister."

Krista tossed her files in her briefcase and added the laptop. "I'm going to say hi to Liz, and then I'll be on my way. Enjoy your concert."

Krista strolled down the hall toward the kitchen. Slowly limping, Liz emerged from the opposite end of the hallway.

"Liz!" Krista rushed to meet her friend. She dropped the briefcase on the floor, hooked an arm around the pregnant woman, and helped her make her way to the front of the house to the living room.

With a groan, Liz sank onto the leather sofa.

"Are you okay?" asked Krista.

"Yeah."

"What happened?"

"I fell," Liz answered in disgust, tossing one of the pillows at the chair.

"How? Where?" Krista moved the ottoman from the corner of the room and placed it in front of the sofa, lifting Liz's foot onto the stool.

Rolling her eyes, Liz explained. Self-disgust filled her voice. "I missed a step coming out of the bank. Somehow I ended up on the ground."

Taking a seat next to her friend, Krista asked, "Are you all right? Do you need me to call your doctor?"

"No. I'm fine. Just need to rest a while." Liz rubbed her hand up and down her leg.

Liz didn't look fine. Her ankle was swollen. Blood oozed from a scrape on her knee, and her skin had flushed cherry red. Krista rose from the sofa and started out of the room.

"Where are you goin'?" Liz asked.

"I'll be right back." Krista headed down the hall, stopping at Brennan's office. She tapped on the door before entering the room.

With a question in his eyes, Brennan glanced at Krista. "Hey! You ready to head home?"

"No," she answered.

A look of confusion spread across his pleasant expression. "What's wrong?"

"It's Liz," she began.

Brennan dropped the files in his hands and hurried around the edge of the desk. "Is she okay?"

"I think so."

En route to the door, he gazed at her over his shoulder. "What do you mean, 'You think so'?"

"You need to talk to your sister. Liz told me she fell and hurt her leg. She doesn't look too good."

Nodding, he marched out of the office and down the hall. Krista hurried after him. When he reached the living room, Brennan sat on his knees next to the ottoman, holding his sister's hand.

"What about the baby? Everything feel okay there?" he asked.

"He's fine," Liz answered, leaning back on the sofa. "Besides the fact that he's doing the hustle inside my belly."

Brennan eyed her leg, saying, "You don't look fine to me. How did this happen?"

Liz shifted on the sofa, lifting her rear end off the leather surface and then reseating herself. "I wasn't watching where I was going, and I missed a step and took a tumble."

He examined her ankle, noting the bruising and swelling. "I should take you to the emergency room."

She shook her head. "No. I didn't break anything. At the most, it's a sprain. I'll tell you what. I'll call the doctor Monday morning and go in to see him."

As Brennan considered Liz's suggestion, the tip of his tongue appeared in the corner of his mouth. "You promise that you'll go Monday?"

Liz crossed her chest with her finger. "I promise."

"Okay." Brennan got to his feet, looking down at his sister. "I guess that's it for the evening."

"What do you mean?" Liz asked.

"You can't go to the concert like this. And I'm not carrying you."

Liz's forehead crinkled as she considered his words. "I

don't want my ticket to go to waste." She glanced at Krista, who was hovering in the doorway. "What are you doing this evening?"

Surprised, Krista asked, "What?"

"Are you busy tonight?" asked Liz.

"Me? No." Krista shrugged. "Going home."

"Great! Do you like Najee?" said Liz.

Krista's heart skipped a beat. Hope burned a path through her veins. She loved Najee. But she didn't want to impose, and she didn't want to be pushed on Brennan if he didn't want her with him. Just because Liz willingly gave up her ticket didn't mean Brennan wanted to be bothered with her. If the way he'd been treating her lately indicated anything, he wanted to keep their relationship friendly, but professional.

"Hmm," said Krista, hesitating, trying to think of an excuse. "Liz, m-ma-maybe y-yo-your b-br-brother's got plans?"

"Puh-leese," Liz muttered, waving a dismissing hand in Krista's direction. "Big brother, can Krista go to the concert with you?"

He turned. Brennan had the same look that trapped animals exhibited when cornered. For a beat, the room filled with tension as he slowly considered the possibility. After a long pause, he answered, "Sure."

Dejected, Krista felt like the kid that nobody wanted on their baseball team. "I-I-I," said Krista as she latched onto the first thing that came to mind. "I've got nothing to wear." She turned to Brennan. "Y-yo-you sh-sh-should c-ca-call a friend."

"That's ridiculous," Liz huffed, crossing her arms across her chest. "Go upstairs and pull out a pair of my denims. I won't be wearing them for a while, and put that top on that you wore here a few weeks ago. It's perfect with those jeans." She shooed Krista away. "Go!"

With a heavy heart, Krista stomped up the stairs like a child sent to her room for a time-out. She hated being thrust on Brennan like the date nobody wanted.

Krista climbed two steps and halted. *I'm not doing this,* she decided, starting back down the stairs.

Brennan met her at the bottom of the staircase. Concern was etched into his face. When he reached her side, he smiled and took her hand, squeezing it reassuringly. Every time he touched her he made her skin tingle. "I didn't mean to be rude. I'd love to take you with me."

The warmth and sincerity of his smile released the tight knot of misery swirling around in her belly. She smiled back.

"It'll be fun," he added. He ran his finger across the back of her small hand. "I'm going to change, and I'll meet you downstairs in thirty minutes."

Hand in hand, they started up the stairs together. Krista stole a quick peek at Brennan before letting out a gentle puff of air.

They could do this. Go out as friends and enjoy the concert together. Things would be just fine.

Chapter 14

Brennan parked the Saab in the lot across from the South-field Civic Center. A tall white fence with V98.7 written in multiple colors surrounded the concert grounds. He took a quick peek at Krista, lingering over her full, sensual lips while remembering the sweet nectar he'd tasted far too briefly. Climbing out of the car, he strolled to the rear and opened the trunk, removing two lawn chairs, before making his way to the passenger door.

He opened the car door and extended a hand. Tentatively, Krista placed her small hand in his.

"Thank you," she offered in a husky whisper that pierced his heart and headed straight for his groin.

Get yourself under control, he warned, enjoying the sway of Krista's hips in Liz's denims.

A hot puff of air escaped from his lips. This was going to be one long afternoon. She looked hot in those tight denims and that scarlet, lacey top with the tiny camisole underneath. How was he supposed to keep his distance when they were going to spend the next six hours almost in each other's laps?

And he didn't plan to let things get any more intense be-tween them until he talked to Flynn Parr. It scared Brennan

silly to think that Krista might find out about the bet and mis-
interpret his part in the whole sorry mess.

Brennan gave himself a mental shake and focused on the
present. For today, he planned to show Krista a great time.
He'd been waiting all week to see Alexander Zonjic and Euge
Groove. His concert partner might be different, but he wanted
to enjoy the music, food, and afternoon. He cupped her elbow
and guided her across Evergreen Road to the concert entrance. An attendant exchanged their tickets for a stamp on
the back of their hands and then allowed them access to the
grounds.

They entered the park, examining the terrain. Krista turned
to Brennan, asking, "Which way?"

"Over there." Brennan tilted his head to the left and steered
Krista around a group of people to the white picket fence
encircling the stage. The gold circle area was sparsely popu-
lated with blankets and lawn chairs. Brennan and Krista were
able to stake a claim on a spot near the stage.

They set up their chairs. Krista spent the next few minutes
checking out the people in the areas. Brennan rose from his
chair. "I'm going to get something to drink. Do you want anything?"

"Whatever you get will be fine."

He started for the fence entrance. "I'll be right back."

Waving him off, she nodded.

Concession stands were set up around the edge of the park.
Brennan strolled from booth to booth, examining the items
for sale, until he found what he was searching for. Ten minutes later, he returned with a plastic cup in each hand. Surprised, he halted next to Krista's chair. "Who's your friend?"

"This is Chinetha. We call her China," said Krista. She
lifted the toddler so the little girl was face-to-face with Brennan. "This is Mr. Thomas. Can you say hello?"

Watching Brennan with shy eyes, China slowly shook her
head and buried her face in Krista's bosom.

Smiling at the child, Krista explained, "She's a little shy. But China warms up fairly quickly."

"Where did China come from?" he asked, sinking into his lawn chair and taking a sip from his cup.

"China's parents are here for the show. They went to check out the concession stands and asked me to keep an eye on this little bundle for a few minutes."

"Sounds good." He placed the cups on the ground between the chairs and took the little girl's hand. "Nice to meet you."

The child shied away from Brennan, hiding her face in Krista's cleavage. He practically drooled. Lucky little girl.

"Ooh, it's okay. He won't hurt you," Krista cooed, rocking the child back and forth.

"How do you know her?"

"Her parents go to my church." Krista tickled the little girl. The child giggled, tickling Krista back. "She spotted me from across the way."

While Krista gave her explanation, a man and woman approached them. Krista smiled at the pair.

The man held several slices of pizza, while the woman carried bottles of Mountain Dew.

Krista made introductions. "Oscar, Denise, this is Brennan Thomas. Brennan, Oscar and Denise Gaines. They're members of my church and China's parents."

Brennan rose from his chair and shook hands with the man and woman. "Nice to meet you."

"We'd like to stay and talk, but we better get back to our seats before the show starts," said Denise. "We'll try to catch you during the break."

"Come back. We'll be here," Brennan encouraged. He was curious about Krista's friends and wanted to know more about them.

"Will do. Thanks for keeping my boo-boo," said Denise as she handed the soda bottles to her husband and reached for her daughter.

"No problem," said Krista as she smiled broadly. "You k-kn-know I love kids. And China is one of my f-fa-favorites."

Krista gave the toddler a juicy kiss on the cheek and then handed her to her mother. "I'll see you guys tomorrow."

"Take care," Oscar said and waved. The family crossed the grassy area and met up with their friends.

Krista turned to Brennan. "I saw two cups. What did you get?"

"White wine. And now that I think of it, I've never seen you drink anything stronger than a soda. Do you drink alcohol?"

She grimaced. "No. Not really."

"Oh," he muttered.

"But there's always a first time," she admitted shyly. "Besides, we're on an adventure, and having a drink could be a new one."

Brennan's eyebrows rose to his hairline. Krista had never spoken so clearly about anything other than work since he met her.

They sat back in their chairs, sipped their wine, and watched the bands tune their instruments and adjust the acoustics. The sounds began to blend, creating noise, not music. Madison Leigh and Kevin Sanderson, V98.7 morning radio personalities, stepped onto the stage and introduced themselves, discussing today's program and other shows scheduled for Chene Park.

Madison Leigh introduced Kimmie Horne. The songstress dazzled the audience with her arrangement of familiar tunes. Brennan leaned back in his chair and observed Krista. His heart caught in his throat. Krista was so involved with the show, she didn't noticed anything around her. Awe, excitement, and exhilaration were present for him to see.

Unable to resist her, Brennan leaned close and whispered, "Do you know much about Kimmie Horne?"

She shook her head. "I don't know her. But I do like her voice."

He smiled at her. "Me, too."

Euge Groove took over. Instantly, he had the audience out of its chairs and on its feet.

Brennan sat back in his lawn chair, sipped his wine, and watched Krista. Happy to be here, she practically bounced up and down in her seat. The different expressions on her face captivated him. It was exciting and downright sensual to watch the way her hips swayed with the music.

Euge Groove and Alexander Zonjic completed a set together. With each new performer, Krista sank deeper into the music. Occasionally, her movements brought her in contact with Brennan. He savored those slight touches. Fascinated, Brennan watched her out of the corner of his eye. Krista tickled him. Her enthusiasm and childlike innocence and wonder regarding everything felt refreshing in a world of cynicism, and he loved it, almost as much as he loved her.

Whoa! His hand flew to his temple, while his heart nearly stopped in his chest. Where in the hell had that idea come from? Brennan searched deep within himself and allowed those feelings to emerge and blossom. Her shy smile and gentle voice always brought out his protective instincts. Yet, the sensual way she moved and the new clothes brought out the primal male in him. It was a hearty combination.

Yes, he did love her and had for some time. It wasn't just the physical stuff, although Krista stirred his blood.

Brennan chuckled softly, mentally revisiting the conversation he had had with his sister when he first asked for her help. Liz had been right. He had had feelings for Krista all along.

Maybe his feelings had started out as the desire to help Krista and beat Flynn Parr. Now, Krista's well-being was his primary concern. He saw Krista differently. The light in her eyes thrilled him, making him admit that he wanted to be the one to keep the sparkle in her eyes.

After a short break, Madison Leigh introduced Najee.

Krista straightened in her chair and leaned forward. The eagerness on her face was like nothing he'd ever seen before.

Najee approach the stage from the ground level, with a flurry of music and applause. He skipped from one side of the stage to the other, all the while playing the songs from his latest compact disc. The people in the audience roared, clapping and tapping their feet to the music. Some whistled. Her face filled with awe, Krista stood.

After several tunes, Najee kicked things up a notch. He disappeared from the stage, but his band continued to play.

Suddenly, the saxophonist reappeared at the base of the stage, among the audience. Like the Pied Piper of Hamelin, he traveled through the crowd, playing the theme from his first compact disc as the crowd roared.

Thrilled, Krista practically danced, eyes glued to the man as he serenaded his way through the audience. A guard stood several paces away, making certain no one got too close. On his final turn, Najee played his way down their row.

Krista's breath caught in her throat, and her eyes were huge as they focused on the man. Without realizing it, she grabbed Brennan's hand. Najee stopped in front of their lawn chairs, playing the sax for several minutes. Then he did the most incredible and unexpected thing. Najee removed the saxophone mouthpiece from his mouth and leaned close to plant a soft kiss on Krista's cheek.

Jealousy surged through Brennan. But he remained silent, understanding how important this treat was for Krista. Many times they had worked to the saxophone of Najee. Krista had often told him how much she loved Najee's music. She deserved this special moment and many more.

Sliding the mouthpiece back into his mouth, Najee retraced his steps and returned to the front and slipped through a door. This time the saxophone player disappeared and seconds later reappeared on the stage, all the while playing his saxophone. When the song ended, he thanked the audience and announced that he would be taking a short break and would be back to continue the show.

"That was a surprise, wasn't it?" Brennan said.

Krista held her cheek, and her eyes danced. "It was amazing. I've heard that he comes out into the audience and plays. But I never thought I'd see him do this live."

"It was nice."

"No. It was magnificent!"

Ten minutes later, Najee and his band returned to the stage, and the show resumed.

Another thirty minutes and two encores later, the show ended. Brennan and Krista gathered their lawn chairs and started for the exit along with the rest of the crowd. It was slow going, but fifteen minutes later they arrived at the Saab. As he stored the chairs in the trunk, Brennan evaluated his feelings for Krista. He did love her and wanted her in his life. But he still had a few problems to work out before he could talk freely with her about his feelings. *Stay cool, my man. Your time will come,* he cautioned silently.

He slammed the trunk door shut. Krista stood next to the car. A spark of something unreadable flared in her eyes. "You all right?" he asked.

Krista nodded and drew closer. "Oh, Brennan." She threw her arms around him, hugged him, and then touched his cheek with her lips. "Thank you so much for letting me c-co-come here with you."

Surprised, he wrapped his arms around her, savoring the feel of her curvy flesh against his. The butterfly-light peck on his cheek had stirred his blood. All the emotions he'd suppressed and stored away for their possible future surfaced. He wanted more than her sweet, innocent kisses. He wanted to taste her sweet nectar and devour her. Brennan captured her mouth, drinking from her lips. Krista responded, giving as well as receiving.

When they broke apart, both were panting. Brennan recovered

first. He took her arm and helped her into the front seat of the car. As he moved around the hood, he let out a shaky sigh before opening the door and climbing into the Saab.

All of his good intentions had just shot out the window. He chuckled humorlessly. His plan to take things slow and act like Krista's friend until he resolved the bet with Flynn Parr hadn't worked. He could not be this woman's friend. He needed more, and he planned to get it.

There were many issues he needed to address before he could approach Krista regarding a relationship. The mess with Flynn was primary. What if Krista didn't want to be involved with him? He didn't want to cross any lines that could be described as sexual harassment.

No more kisses or anything else, Brennan resolved silently. He glanced at the woman next to him and thought, *At least no more until all of this mess has been completely sorted out.*

Chapter 15

"There. That'll do it." Liz snapped off the black thread with her teeth, stuck the needle into the spool of thread, and then used the edge of the bed for leverage to get to her feet. Grunting, she rubbed the small of her back with her hand. "Come over to the mirror, and let's take another look."

Krista followed her friend to the wooden, full-length cheval mirror. In the background, Everette Harp's saxophone played "You Make Me Feel Brand New." On the dresser a lit red candle peppered the room with the fragrance of cinnamon apple spice.

"I don't mean to be a whiner. But I'm so nervous. I feel as if I'm gonna throw up," Krista confessed as she fought down the rising tide of panic creeping through her veins, heightening her anxiety.

Meeting the Gautier people scared the heck out of her. Plus, her penchant for clumsiness worried Krista to no end. What if she tripped and landed in the middle of the munchies or got food on her clothes? How would that look? There would be no way to explain any of this away. She didn't want to embarrass Brennan or herself. After all, the Thomas family had been good to her.

Krista was petrified. She wanted the evening to go well,

wanted to make a good impression on Brennan and the top brass at Gautier. But her history of mishaps at agency functions kicked her apprehension up several notches. Plus, there was the problem of Erin Saunders. If Krista kept the other woman as far away as possible, she might get through the evening without a major accident or incident.

Liz fluttered around Krista, adjusting her hair and dress. "Calm down. You're fine."

A shiver of fear went through Krista. "I don't know if I can do this."

"Do what?"

Krista waved a nervous hand over her dress before setting her hands on her hips. "This. Me. Going to the party. Everything. I'm afraid."

"You should be." Liz slipped her arm through the crook of Krista's arm and steered her to the bed. "I'd be surprised if you weren't. The people at Dexter Kee haven't always been kind to you, and it's only natural for you to be concerned. This is the first time you've been with your colleagues in a non-business setting since the picnic. Relax. Everything will be fine. You"—Liz paused, taking Krista's hand—"look perfect. Beautiful!"

"Easy for you to say. You don't have a history of calamities that end with you wearing the salad."

"Nonsense." Liz wagged a finger at Krista. "Stop exaggerating. You'll do fine. Don't let anyone tell you differently. Just look at yourself." She turned Krista to the mirror, resting her hands on Krista's shoulders and squeezing reassuringly. "You're gorgeous. And tonight a lot of people will see that."

Krista hoped so. Tonight's reception for Gautier International Motors at Sweet Georgia Brown made her antsy. She swallowed a lump the size of Texas and prayed silently that all would go well tonight.

The black crepe fabric swirled gracefully around Krista with each movement of her body. She wanted to look good for the reception and make the right impression. Liz had assured her that this was the perfect image for her debut. *Is that really me?* she wondered, examining her reflection.

Liz gave Krista a little shake. "Everything is going to be great. Don't let a case of nerves destroy all the hard work you've done."

Snorting, Krista moved to the bed and grabbed her purse. She checked for her house keys and the invitation. Finding everything in order, she shut the purse and sat down on the edge of the mattress. "I'm scared."

"Why?" Liz dropped down on the mattress, next to Krista.

"I don't want to make a fool out of myself," she admitted.

"You won't. Look at you. You're a talented woman with a lot to offer. Don't let the pettiness of a few people complicate what should be a fun evening for you and Brennan."

With a low moan, Liz shifted around and then rubbed her belly.

Concerned, Krista touched Liz's arm. "You all right?"

"Yeah," Liz reassured her. "My back is killing me."

"How so?"

"There's an ache at the base of my spine." Liz smiled, looking lovingly at her protruding belly, and then rubbed her lower back. "It won't go away. It's not bad, just annoying and constant. Makes it hard to sit for very long."

"Do you need to tell Brennan?"

"Nah. I've had this before. It'll go away once I'm off my feet."

"You sure?" Krista persisted, feeling as if she should do something more for her friend.

"Positive. There's only a few weeks to go, and I'm getting anxious about the whole birth thing. Don't worry about me."

"I'm concerned, and I can appreciate how you feel," Krista replied. "I think I'd be a little afraid myself."

"I am. But I do understand that at the end of all the pain,

I'll have this beautiful baby." Liz grinned nervously. "It'll be worth it."

Krista patted her friend's hand. "Promise me you'll rest tonight. Don't do anything that could stir up trouble. Okay?"

Liz laughed. "Like what? Too much sitting on my butt. Come on. I'm not going to do anything that will hurt me or the baby. Now that we've talked about me, let's discuss you and the party. I know there will be cocktails and munchies at this shindig. Will dancing be included?"

With an edge of devilment to her voice, Krista added, "I hope so. A little s-sl-slow dancing would do me just fine."

Giggling, Liz shook her head and bumped her hip against Krista's. "Listen to you, wild woman."

"I don't think so."

Liz turned Krista to face her. "Seriously. Go. Enjoy. Have a good time. Ignore the idiots that always cause trouble. When you feel antsy, take a deep breath, and then show them what you've got. Okay?"

"I'll try," Krista answered hesitantly.

"No! No! No!" Pointing a finger at Krista, Liz insisted, "Do! Have fun!"

"Okay. I will."

"That's the way I want to hear you talk."

They rose from the bed and headed out of the room. Krista followed Liz down the stairs. All the while Krista prayed that her night would be a good one. She hoped that she wouldn't cause any major disasters and would get through the evening with her clothes and dignity intact and without any embarrassing moments.

Brennan sat on the sofa, watching a Detroit Tigers baseball game, dressed in a charcoal suit, a pale yellow shirt, and a tie with black, brown, and yellow stripes. He glanced at his watch. *Krista and Liz better get a move on things.* Connor

Dexter and the management team planned to gather at six for a short powwow. He wanted to sit in before their guests arrived an hour later.

Liz had insisted Krista get dressed under her watchful eye. Brennan didn't have a problem with that. He loved having Krista at his house. Since Liz started offering fashion advice to Krista, he'd seen a marked improvement in Krista's appearance and confidence level. He was happy with that. But her appearance offered a distraction that interfered with his work.

He'd been looking forward to this evening for weeks. Once the reception ended, he planned to confess his feelings to Krista and tell her about the bet. He hoped that her forgiving nature would allow her to see past his stupidity. It put his nerves on edge to imagine what might happen if Krista learned of his duplicity from someone else. He needed to be the one to explain and beg for her forgiveness.

He heard the pair make their way down the stairs. Krista's lighter steps followed his sister's labored movements. Liz stumbled over the bottom step and yelled, "Oops!"

Brennan rose from the sofa and hurried out of the living room, to his sister's side. While examining Liz for obvious problems, he asked, "You okay?"

"Yeah. Fine," said Liz as she rubbed the lower part of her back. "Just a little tired. Once you guys leave, I'm going to get in the bed, watch TV, and let the TV watch me while I rest."

Somewhat convinced, but not completely, Brennan nodded slowly. He studied her for a moment longer. Liz looked worn-out and ready to drop. Maybe doing all this stuff with Krista was taking a toll on his sister. He touched her arm. "You do that."

"Don't worry about me. I'm fine. Take a look at your colleague and date for the evening." Liz waved a hand in the air. "Ta-da!"

Brennan stood near the landing, waiting. Krista reached the landing and stood next to his sister, nervous with hopeful an-

ticipation. Her small hand curved around the wooden staircase railing.

His breath caught in his lungs. The first thing he noticed
was the shapely curve of her legs in black hose and high-heel
pumps. His eyes moved upward to her round hips, covered
by the black full skirt, and then to the delicate curve of her
shoulders. He considered how perfect she looked and the
things he wanted to say and do to her. *Not yet,* he chastised
himself. *After the reception, you'll tell Krista everything and
clear the air.*

Krista looked gorgeous. The sleeveless black dress curled
around her curves. The square top cut across her breasts and
gave Brennan a tantalizing peek at the swell of her breasts
above the bodice. The dark fabric pulled tight against her
narrow waist and flared into a full, tea-length skirt.

Mesmerized, Brennan moved across the hallway to Krista,
like a puppet on a string. A ripple of excitement surged
through him as he took her hand and kissed the palm. The
subtle fragrance of her perfume made his head spin, and he
practically drowned in the soft glow in her brown eyes. "You
look beautiful."

Smiling shyly, she answered, "Thank you. So do you."

Brennan glanced beyond Krista as Liz gave him the
thumbs-up sign. He grinned back at his sister before refocusing on Krista. "Ready to go? I'd like to get to the restaurant a
little early."

Krista nodded and took a step toward the kitchen. Liz followed the couple through the house. She stood inside the
doorway, waving them off. "Have a good time. See you later."

"You get some rest," Brennan commanded, helping Krista
into the car. He rounded the back end of the Saab and opened
the door. "I mean it."

"Okay. Okay. Have fun. See you tomorrow," said Liz as she
shut the kitchen door.

Brennan hit the remote, and the garage door opened. He

switched on the engine and put the car in reverse. "Here we go."

Silently settling into the bucket seat, Krista placed her purse in her lap. She flipped through the compact discs located between the bucket seats until she found what she wanted. Within seconds the sassy saxophone of Kim Waters filled the confined space.

Softly smiling to himself, Brennan realized how far Krista had come within a few short weeks. When Krista first started working with him, she could barely get two words out of her mouth without stammering and stuttering. Lately, her opinions and the words came much easier.

"Is there anything in p-pa-particular you want me to do this evening?" Krista asked, tucking the dress around her.

He considered the question, going through a mental list of things he wanted her to do that had nothing to do with work, before shaking his head. "Have a good time. Don't let anyone upset you."

Facing him, she asked quietly, "What are you saying?"

"Watch out for Erin."

"How did you know?"

"I remember the picnic," he answered.

"Oh." Heat flushed her cheeks red as she repeatedly pleated her dress.

Brennan reached for her hand and squeezed it. "Don't worry. I never thought you were at fault, and I still don't."

"I think Erin pushed me into the lake."

"What makes you say that?"

"Every time I get in trouble or something bad happens to me, Erin's always someplace close, laughing and pointing at me."

A fierce, protective resolve settled on his face. This was going to stop. "I won't let her get close to you tonight. We're going to put an end to her nonsense."

"Thank you, Brennan."

"Don't forget, we're a team." He shifted a tad in the driver's seat so that he could see her face. "Although there's one thing I do expect from you."

Frowning, she asked, "What?"

"I want a dance. You and me. Forget about work and Gautier, and enjoy some good music and dancing."

Her voice turned soft, enticing him. "I'd love to. But I'm warning you. I'm not very g-go-good. I haven't danced since high school. You might end up with broken toes."

He chuckled, and his thoughts flashed back to the way her hips had swayed to Najee's music at the concert. "I'm not worried. You've got a great sense of rhythm."

"I th-th-think I'd like that."

Silence filled the car as Brennan steered it down Jefferson Avenue. Then he spoke, admitting, "Me, too."

Chapter 16

Woodward and Jefferson Avenues were finally calm after the end of the workday traffic. Krista sat quietly while Brennan parked the car across the street from Sweet Georgia Brown. To make everything as convenient as possible, Dexter Kee had prepaid parking for the employees attending the reception.

He turned to her, with a smile on his lips, while caressing her bare arm. Krista's heart leapt in her chest, and she felt the sensation to the tips of her toes. "Ready to go?" he asked.

Her gaze cut across the street, as she examined the brightly lit restaurant. No, she wasn't ready. Unfortunately, it was way too late to get out of the evening. She felt nervous about standing in front of a group of strangers and the employees of Dexter Kee, who had never been her friends. "Yes."

"All right. Let's do this." Brennan got out of the car and ran around the back end to the passenger door. He opened it and reached out a hand to her. Krista took it, swung her legs out of the car, and stood, stumbling over her feet. Instinctively, Brennan's arm went around her waist, holding her against his side. His warm, hard flesh seemed to mold itself against the soft curve of her body.

"I know you're nervous. Just remember, I've got your back,

and I won't let anything happen to you," he promised, keeping a strong, muscular arm around her waist.

Touched by Brennan's thoughtfulness, Krista didn't know what to say. She focused on the colors in his tie and brushed a few locks of hair from her eyes. "Thank you," she uttered in a small, worried voice. The words seemed so inadequate.

With a finger at her chin, he tilted her head so that she looked at him. "I'm here for you." He held out his hand. "Don't ever forget it. We'll do this together."

Nodding, she placed her hand in his. They crossed the street. He opened the door, and Krista stepped inside, with Brennan at her side. Connor Dexter stood just inside the doorway. Tall and handsome, he greeted the couple as they entered the building.

"Brennan," he said, with an outstretched hand. "I'm glad you got here before Gautier." He glanced at Krista. There wasn't a speck of recognition in his eyes, and then his eyes widened. "Krista! Is that you?"

No, it's my neighbor, she thought, but said, "It's me."

Mr. Dexter took her hand, drawing her from the curve of Brennan's arm. "You look wonderful."

She dipped her head slightly and answered softly, "Thank you."

"Come on," said the white-haired man as he placed her hand in the crook of his arm and led her away from her date. "Let's get you something to drink."

Dazed, she allowed the company president to lead her across the restaurant to the bar. Mr. Dexter helped Krista onto a stool, with a warm smile on his lips. "What would you like to drink?"

"A glass of Riesling, please," replied Krista.

"Good choice," Mr. Dexter praised.

Brennan leaned close and whispered into her ear. "I think you've got a new admirer. I hope I won't have to fight him to get the first dance."

"No. The first dance b-be-belongs to you," said Krista. "But if it happens, just think of your poor toes. I need to practice on someone."

"I'll keep that in mind," whispered Brennan.

"How's the proposal coming, Brennan? Should I bring anything up with Mr. Gautier?" Mr. Dexter asked.

"We're moving right along." Brennan slipped onto the stool to the right of their boss. "Krista, you want to jump in here?"

Shaking her head, she picked up her glass and sipped from it. She got tongue-tied around Mr. Dexter. She wanted to finish her glass of wine, listen to the music, and enjoy her evening. Let Brennan play big businessman and dazzle Mr. Dexter and the Gautier people.

Brennan cleared his throat. "We're putting together some things that I'll present to you in the next two weeks."

"Better be great," said Mr. Dexter.

"It will be," Brennan promised, ordering a scotch over ice.

Nodding, Mr. Dexter shifted his gaze past them. "Good. I see John Kee has arrived with our guests. Excuse me. I need to speak with him." He moved away and then stopped. "Come say hello once you're done here."

"Will do," Brennan promised, glancing over his shoulder before occupying the stool next to Krista. "Your first hit of the night."

She grinned, watching Mr. Dexter purposefully stroll to the people at the door. "Once you finish your wine, we'll start the mingling game," said Brennan.

Minutes later, Brennan stood and offered Krista his arm. She spun around and put her right foot on the floor, but her left foot got tangled between the two stools. A small gasp escaped her as she pitched forward. He stepped in front of her and wrapped an arm around her waist, breaking her fall. "I've got you," Brennan muttered against her hair and then caressed her forehead with his lips. "I've got you."

"Thank you," she mumbled, pulling the heel of her shoe free from between the stools.

"No thanks needed," he assured her, with a smile.

Flynn Parr slapped Brennan on the back. "Hello, my man." His gaze slid over Krista and his eyes widened and his mouth dropped open. "Krista? Look at you! Wow!"

She smiled politely, sidestepping Flynn's attempt to wrap an arm around her. "Thanks. I think."

Offering Krista a cheesy, unconvincing grin, Flynn said, "You're more than welcome." He turned his attention to Brennan. "Well, my man. We're coming down to the wire on this campaign. Are you ready?"

"We're there. What about you?"

"My team has been working steadily." Flynn folded his arms across his chest and rocked back on the heels of his shoes. "We're prepared."

"Good luck to you," Brennan stated, cupping Krista's elbow and steering her away from the bar. "Excuse us." As they moved away, he said, "Gautier's people are here. It's time to make our introductions."

Fear almost paralyzed Krista. She'd already stumbled and nearly fallen on her face. And that had happened within the first thirty minutes. What form of foolishness would occur before the French automaker?

Again, Brennan's solid, calming presence soothed her. His hand made a soothing path up and down her bare arm as he whispered in her ear, "You'll do fine. Come on. Let's do our thing so that we can enjoy the party."

They crossed the floor and waited in the reception line. When their turn came, Mr. Dexter waved a hand at Brennan. "Reynolds, this is Brennan Thomas and Krista Hamilton. They are part of one of the two teams working on your campaign."

Brennan stretched out his hand and gripped the Frenchman's in a firm handshake. "Mr. Gautier, I'm not going to bore you with shoptalk. We've got plenty of time for that later. But I am pleased to finally put a face to the information we've gathered."

Mr. Gautier was a handsome, older man with a full head of graying hair. He stood slightly under six feet and had a compact build.

"My name is Reynolds. Please use it," Mr. Gauthier said, with a slight French accent. "I'm looking forward to seeing your work."

Brennan turned to Krista. "This is Krista Hamilton. She's been working with me on your ad. She's a wonderfully talented IT specialist. And, let's not forget, a beautiful woman."

Heat rose from the pit of Krista's belly and burned her neck and finally settled into her cheeks. Krista found it uncomfortable to be pushed into the limelight this way. She smiled softly, silently wishing the conversation would shift to something different or someone else.

Reynolds Gautier gave Krista his full attention. His eyes sparkled as he shook her hand. "It's a pleasure to meet you. Let me introduce you to my wife, Michelle. Cherie, this is Krista Hamilton."

Krista turned her attention to the Frenchwoman at Mr. Gauthier's side. She was definitely a trophy wife. Blond, curvy, and expensively dressed, Michelle Gauthier stood at Mr. Gautier's side, with a possessive hand on his shoulder, listening to the conversation.

She gave Krista a quick nod of acknowledgement before focusing on Brennan. Her gaze did a leisurely stroll over him before returning to his face. If her expression revealed her thoughts, Michelle Gauthier liked what she saw, a lot.

Krista didn't like the predatory gleam in Mrs. Gauthier's eyes. A stab of jealousy coursed through her. Brennan was hers.

At that moment Flynn stepped forward. "Hello, Reynolds. It's good to finally meet you in person. I'm Flynn Parr."

"Ah. Flynn. Finally, we meet," said Mr. Gauthier. "We've talked so much. I feel as if I know you. How are the fish biting in Canada?" The men shook hands and then stepped out of the reception line to continue their conversation in low, almost secretive tones.

Mouths open, Krista and Brennan exchanged shocked glances. Phone calls? No one had told them they could contact Reynolds Gautier before the presentations. They thought all of the personal stuff had been handled through Connor Dexter or John Kee.

Shrugging, Brennan nudged Krista out of the reception line, and they explored the first floor, stopping at tables to greet other Dexter Kee employees and guests. Several members of Brennan's team made room at their table for the couple to join them. Although Krista didn't contribute much to the conversation, she enjoyed the gentle banter and sparring between her coworkers.

Krista relaxed a bit until she saw Erin Saunders enter the restaurant. Erin glided through Sweet Georgia Brown's door like a plane making a perfect landing at Detroit Metro Airport. She posed dramatically, tossing her sheer silver wrap over one bare shoulder. Her strapless scarlet dress hugged all the right spots. A silver chain graced her neck, and long silver earrings dangled from her lobes.

Erin scanned the restaurant until she located what she sought and then strutted across the room to their table. "Brennan," she greeted, placing a hand on his shoulder after dismissing everyone else at the table.

Krista tensed at Brennan's side, stirring uneasily in her chair. A warning voice whispered for Krista to be careful, to keep an eye on Erin.

"Hello, Erin," Brennan responded, getting to his feet.

"Mind if I sit here?" Erin asked no one in particular.

Brennan waved a hand at the table. "Help yourself."

One of the salesmen snagged a chair from a nearby table. He patted the cushioned chair before returning to his friends. Erin squeezed in next to Brennan, forcing him to move closer to Krista. He placed his arm around the back of Krista's chair and leaned in.

Erin snarled at Krista and monopolized Brennan's time. Krista didn't care. She was happy to remain silent while listening to the conversations floating around her. Every once in a while someone at the table would direct a question her way, and she'd respond.

Soft, nonintrusive music swirled around the restaurant as the evening wore on. Waitstaff dressed in white double-breasted jackets strolled the area, with trays of champagne and hors d'oeuvres.

The beat of the music changed. Brennan untangled himself from Erin's hold and rose. "You promised me the first dance," he said to Krista.

Krista stood and took his hand. They moved to the dance floor, and Brennan took her in his arms. She rested a hand on his shoulder as his arms wrapped her in his embrace, pulling her against his hard, warm body. They swayed to the music, leaning into each other's bodies.

Brennan looked down at her and whispered, "You look beautiful."

For the first time in her life, she believed those words. She felt beautiful. Being with Brennan made her feel special. Her feelings overwhelmed her, and she finally admitted what her heart had known for weeks. She truly loved this man. Those emotions frightened and thrilled her.

Krista stiffened. Brennan quickly glanced at her, with a question in his eyes. *Act normal,* she cautioned silently. *Don't think of him. That's in the past. Brennan's nothing like Paul.*

What did she plan to do about those feelings? Was she going to take whatever she and Brennan were doing to the next level? Or did she intend to return to her old ways and hide from all that life had to offer her?

Right now, she didn't have a clue. Until the evening was over, she planned to enjoy everything Brennan offered her.

Chapter 17

Krista felt like Cinderella. She attended the ball and danced with the prince. In this story, Cinderella didn't race from the castle at the stroke of midnight, the chariot didn't turn into a pumpkin, and Cinderella did not leave behind a glass slipper for the prince to find. Krista's prince escorted her from the restaurant.

Minutes after midnight, Krista left the restaurant hand in hand with Brennan. The evening had been magical, wonderful, and truly special. She had hated to see it end. The best part had been the discovery about herself. She loved Brennan, but admitting it was something she never intended to do. Krista had no idea where her emotions would lead.

They crossed the street to the parking lot. Brennan hit the remote, disarming the Saab. He opened the door and helped Krista into the passenger seat, handling her as if she were the finest of crystal, before climbing behind the steering wheel and starting the engine.

The car cruised along the deserted downtown section of Jefferson Avenue. Brennan took his eyes off the road for a moment. "You sure you don't want me to drop you at home?" he asked.

"No. Don't worry about it."

"Hear me out." Brennan squeezed her hand. "I don't like the idea of you driving home this late by yourself."

"It'll be fine," she assured him, pleased by his concern.

"If you're worried about your car, it'll be fine at my place until tomorrow."

"No. I'm not," she answered. "I would rather take myself home in my car. Less h-ha-hassles. Besides, if you took me home, I'd still have to find a way to get my car tomorrow."

"That's not a problem. Liz and I will come by with your car." He concentrated on the road for a few minutes. "There's no way I'm going to let you drive home this late alone. If you won't let me drive you, I'm going to follow you."

"Brennan!"

"Krista!" he mimicked, taking his eyes off the road long enough to grin at her. "I can't help it. I want you to be safe."

She giggled. The thought of Brennan being concerned about her safety gave her the warm fuzzies. She liked the idea of someone caring enough about her to want to watch over her.

"I'll tell you what," she said.

Smiling at her, Brennan said, "What?"

"I'll call you when I get home. That way you'll know that I made it okay. How's that?"

Lips pressed together, Brennan shook his head. "No. Not good enough. How about I follow you home, and then I'll be certain you made it safely?" He grinned at her. "Besides, what if something does happen along the way? I wouldn't know for hours. How's that?"

Laughing, Krista threw her hands into the air. "You win."

"Thank you, madam."

They were silent for a few minutes. The Saab ate up the short distance from the restaurant to his town house. Krista didn't know what to say next, so she sat quietly, watching the buildings sweep by.

"Krista?"

There was an urgent note to his tone, which spooked her. She gazed at him and found his face set in a stern mask. She touched his arm. "Is everything okay?"

"Yeah. I want you to know how much I enjoyed tonight. Being with you felt great. In fact, it was perfect." Fascinated, Krista watched the shifting emotions on his face. "Thank you for the first dance. It was fabulous. You were fantastic."

"Do you have a-an-any toes?"

He laughed out loud and then said teasingly, "One or two are pretty bruised. But I think I'll survive." He paused. "Seriously, the evening was great."

Nodding, she agreed, "Yes, it was."

"Once this campaign is over, we'll have to do it again."

Her heart leapt in her chest. Was he asking her out on a date? This was more than she'd ever hoped for. Maybe Brennan had feelings for her. "I'd like that."

He turned into the Harbortown complex and zipped through the parking lot to his garage, hitting the remote clipped to the car visor. The garage door rumbled, rising slowly. The car shot into the empty space next to Liz's Ford Five Hundred.

Brennan switched off the engine and turned to Krista. "Are you coming in?"

"Yes. Just for a minute. My stuff is in Liz's room."

Nodding, Brennan got out of the car and ran around the hood. He opened her door and took her hand. Krista stepped out of the car. Brennan tugged on her hand and drew her against the hard planes of his body. Using a finger, he tilted her face up so she could look into his eyes. Her breath caught in her throat. The heat from his lean frame warmed her body, making it ache for more. Krista felt a fluttering in the pit of her belly as his mouth covered hers, awakening her senses.

His head bent to her neck, dropping a trail of kisses on her bare skin. She closed her eyes, arching her neck to give him better access. Brennan nibbled his way along her jawline and covered her mouth with his, exploring the recesses of her mouth. His tongue scraped across hers, stirring a gentle fire within her. Krista responded, lifting her arms and wrapping them around his neck.

The pressure of his mouth eased and then vanished completely. Brennan released Krista, watching her through tiny slits.

She ran her tongue across her lips, enjoying the taste of champagne and the unique flavor of Brennan. "We need to go in now."

"You're right." He reclaimed her lips.

Eager for more, Krista felt a warm tingle surge through her, stirring the flame of desire into a gentle fire. She wanted more. But it was way too soon to do anything about it. She needed time to think. Krista stepped away and started for the door. Brennan grabbed her by the arm and swung her into the circle of his arms. His lips settled on hers, warm and sweet, drinking deeply. After a moment, he lifted his head and grinned down at her. "Now I'm ready to go in," he whispered.

He wrapped an arm around her shoulder and led her to the door. They entered the kitchen. Brennan dropped his keys on the wall rack near the door, went to the refrigerator, and removed a bottle of water. "Want one?"

She shook her head. "We should be quiet. Liz is probably asleep."

"No, she's not."

Krista folded her arms across her chest. "How do you know?"

"She's my sister. Liz is the nosiest woman I know. I'd bet money, she's probably waiting up to hear about our evening."

Shaking her head, Krista giggled.

He took her hand and led her toward the front of the house. "Let's find our personal busybody and give her all the gory details."

Eyebrows arched into a curve, she asked, "All?"

"The Cliff Notes version," he amended.

Krista expected to see Liz in the living room, stretched out on the sofa or sitting in a chair, watching television. But the room was empty, although images flickered on the TV screen.

Surprised, Brennan raised his eyebrows.

She shrugged.

"Liz did a lot today. Maybe she's in bed," said Brennan. Forehead wrinkled, he headed for the staircase.

"And I don't want to disturb her." Krista put her foot on the first step. "I'm going to tiptoe into the room and get my stuff, and then I'm gone."

He nodded, returning to the living room.

She bounced up the stair to the landing and turned down the hall. "Brennan!"

Seconds later, he crested the second floor and turned down the hall. At the doorway to the bathroom, he halted. Liz sat slumped against the bathroom door. Her generally happy features were pale and drawn.

"This is how I found her," said Krista.

When he reached the pair, Krista stood and moved away, making room for him.

"Liz?" said Brennan. Kneeling down next to his sister, he touched her cheek.

Liz opened her eyes and groaned, "Pain!"

"Where?" said Brennan.

"Baby," whispered Liz.

Gently lifting Liz into his arms, Brennan turned to Krista. "Krista, in the kitchen, next to the phone, is a number for Liz's doctor. Call him and tell him we're on our way to the hospital."

Heart pounding, Krista raced down the steps ahead of the siblings and through the house, to the kitchen. Once she finished making the call, she met Liz and Brennan in the hallway as he stepped off the bottom stair.

"I need you to go to Liz's room and get her bag," said Brennan.

Krista was halfway up the stairs when Liz spoke.

"No. No bag," Liz moaned.

"What?" Brennan demanded.

"Not packed. Ohhh!" Liz groaned, going stiff in her brother's arms. She rode out the pain, breathing hard. "Can't wait. Go! Worry about it later."

"Okay." Brennan started for the kitchen. "Krista, grab my keys."

At the door, Krista said, "Brennan, it's going to be a problem to get her in your car."

With the back door open, he glanced at the Saab and then turned his attention to the Ford. "You're right. Get the keys to Liz's car. They're next to mine." He rushed into the garage and stood Liz on her feet next to the Five Hundred.

Krista handed the keys to him and then concentrated on her friend. "It's going to be okay. Just hold on."

Liz grabbed Krista's hand and squeezed, biting her lower lip. Krista held on to Liz's hand throughout the contraction. When it was over, Liz's head bobbed forward before flopping against the car. Brennan opened the back car door and helped his sister onto the rear seat.

He climbed into the front seat and looked back at Krista. "Come on. We don't have time to waste."

Fear knotted Krista's insides. Her eyes grew large as she took a step away from the car. She expected them to head to the hospital, and she would lock up and go home. "I, you. You want me to come with you?"

"Please," Liz pleaded. "Come."

"We need you," Brennan confirmed.

Krista climbed in next to Liz and brushed the hair away from her eyes. "I'm here. I'll be with you as long as you want."

Liz and Krista held hands all the way to the hospital. Brennan stopped the car at the revolving doors to the hospital emergency entrance. He hopped out and ran into the building. Seconds later, he came out with a wheelchair, followed closely by a hospital attendant and a nurse.

Things moved quickly after that. They rushed Liz away, with her brother on the heels of the hospital staff. Krista followed at a slower pace. She felt like an intruder. This was a private moment.

Suddenly, Brennan stopped and retraced his steps. He took Krista's hand and pulled her along beside him. "Come on. You're family. We have to support Liz."

For a moment Krista debated whether she had heard him correctly, and then her heart sang with delight. Brennan and Liz wanted her with them. She felt a warm glow flow through her. For the first time in her life, someone needed and wanted her to be part of their family. Tightly gripping his hand, she hurried down the hall at Brennan's side. *I won't let you down,* she promised silently before glancing in Brennan's direction. *Neither of you.*

The birth room was brightly lit and colorful. Liz sat up in a bed, connected to a machine at her side. Krista took a moment to glance at Brennan. Perspiration peppered his forehead, and he shifted from one foot to the other.

"Are you going to be okay?" Krista asked, stroking his cheek with the back of her hand.

Brennan squared his shoulders and drew in a deep breath, letting it out slowly. "I promised Liz I'd help, and I'm going to. Let's do this." Determination shined from his eyes as he took his sister's hand. "Hey, Lizzie girl. It looks like my nephew is coming. You ready?"

Moaning softly, Liz nodded, shutting her eyes against another contraction. Krista noticed how Liz's grip tightened on Brennan's hand. The knuckles of his hand were white. When the pain subsided, he wiped Liz's forehead with a white facecloth. "I'm here. I'm here," he said.

"Where's Krista?" Liz asked.

"On your left," Krista teased, moving within Liz's line of vision. She squeezed Liz's shoulder. "We're both here for you."

Liz shut her eyes against a new contraction.

Five hours and thirty-eight minutes later, Joshua Brennan Gillis made his entry into the world, weighing eight pounds, thirteen ounces. Liz held her son, cuddling him close before exhaustion overtook her. Brennan swept the infant from Liz's arms as she drifted off to sleep. "Steve," Liz whispered.

Looking away, Krista fought back tears as sorrow gripped her. Liz's last waking thought involved her husband.

Krista observed Brennan, feeling her love for him rise to the surface. Like the proud uncle he was, he held Joshua in his arms, admiring him. "He's perfect," cried Brennan.

Laughing at the big, strong man drooling over the baby, Krista agreed. "Yes. He is."

"This was amazing. I didn't think I could get through it. But I did." He glanced over at his sleeping sister. "I wanted to do this for her." His voice wavered. Brennan stopped and cleared his throat before continuing. "I know how much she misses Steve."

Sadness invaded Krista's body. She felt so bad for Liz. "You're right."

"I wish I could have taken that pain from her," he muttered, pacing the floor with his nephew. "Being here during his birth was amazing."

Brennan moved across the room and stood in front of Krista. Legs spread apart, he rocked from side to side with Joshua in his arms. "Do you want to hold him?"

"Me?" she squealed, jumping to her feet. Her heart hammered in her chest. Shaking her head, she admitted, "I-I-I. I don't know. I haven't held a baby in a long time."

"Sit," Brennan commanded, pointing at the chair Krista had just vacated. "Maybe it's time you did. Here." He placed the small, blanketed bundle in her arms. "There you are."

In awe, Krista looked into the face of Liz's newborn and

felt her heart uncoil and open to this brand-new life, filling her with love. Red and round-faced, with a thatch of straight dark brown hair, Joshua was a beautiful baby. She touched his cheek, running a finger along the soft skin. He moved his head, seeking comfort.

Her thoughts turned to her own future and the changes in her life. Would she ever have a family of her own? Children? A husband? If so, would she ever give birth to a child of her own? Who would it resemble?

Reverently, she drew Joshua against her breasts and rocked him contentedly. He was so precious.

"Krista?" Brennan called.

Shaken from her private moment with the baby, she glanced his way. "Yes?"

"The nurse is here for Joshua."

Embarrassed, Krista handed the baby to the nurse and then brushed a lock of hair from her eyes. "Sorry."

"You okay?" he asked, helping her to her feet.

"Yeah."

He examined her silently. "It looks as if the baby got to you."

"Little bit," she admitted sadly.

Smiling down at her, he wrapped an arm around her shoulders and steered her toward the door. "Liz is asleep. Let's get out of here and give her a chance to recover."

Chapter 18

Brennan pulled the Ford into the townhouse garage around four thirty in the morning. He switched off the engine, leaned back against the headrest, and shut his eyes. "Man, it's been one long night."

"Yes, it has," Krista agreed, mimicking his gestures.

He pocketed the car keys and hit the door locks. "Come on in for a minute."

Krista considered his offer and then shook her head. "No. It's so late. I should get home."

"I know it's late. But there's something I'd like to talk to you about. It'll only take a few minutes."

The tone of his voice touched a nerve. A variety of emotions flashed across Brennan's face. Although he was trying to appear calm and casual, Krista sensed something more. "What's this about?"

"Just a thing or two I want to clear up," he hedged.

Pursing her lips, Krista checked the digital clock on the dashboard. It was really late, but maybe it was a good time to reveal a few secrets of her own.

"Besides," he continued persuasively, "I don't want you to rush off without my knowing you're fully awake. It's been one hell of an evening." He patted her hand. "Don't worry, I'm still going to trail you home. First, let's mainline some caffeine, and then we'll get on the road."

She touched his arm. The flesh leapt under her fingertips at her simple caress. "You just said it yourself. It's been a hell of a night, and you're worn-out. I can make it home without an escort."

"That's not going to happen."

Krista laughed out loud, feeling very precious. "I think we've had this conversation already."

Chuckling softly, he agreed. "Yes, we have. But that was before everything went crazy."

"At least everything had a happy ending." Krista sighed as the tug of a long-repressed maternal instinct made its presence known. "You've got your NBA player. Joshua is a beautiful baby."

Brennan grinned. "Yeah. He is. Come inside. Let me make you a cup of tea." He got out of the car and ran around the back to open her door and helped her from the Ford. He dropped an arm around Krista's shoulders and led her to the back door. "Do you need to call your aunt? I know it's kinda late. Does she know where you are?"

"Mm-hmm. I slipped out of Liz's hospital room for a minute and called her. I didn't want her to worry."

"Did you tell her when you'd be home?"

Krista shook her head. "Nah. I told her I was staying until after the baby came. She knows babies arrive when they get ready and not before."

"True."

When they entered the house, Brennan reached for the light switch. The room was immediately illuminated with light. He hooked his keys on the wall rack near the door and waved a hand at the kitchen table. "Have a seat."

Exhausted, Krista sank into a chair and waited. Brennan puttered around the room, preparing tea and setting the table with silverware, napkins, cream, honey, and lemon. Minutes later, he sat a steaming cup of green tea in front of her before taking the chair opposite hers. She stirred honey into her cup before cautiously sipping the hot liquid. The brew surged through her veins, energizing her.

Silently, they sat sipping their drinks. Once Krista finished, she rose from the table, went to the sink to rinse her cup, and placed it in the dishwasher.

Brennan followed, caging her between the edge of the sink and his body. Stepping closer, he turned her so that she faced him and enfolded her in his arms. "I need a little pick-me-up."

Turning in his arms, Krista felt the heat radiating from his body where their flesh met. The smoldering flame in his gaze made her pulse gallop, and an edge of alarm coursed through her. "Oh?"

"Mm-hmm." Brennan nibbled on her earlobe. Krista tilted her head, offering him greater access. His tongue outlined the shell of her ear as a ripple of excitement mixed with a touch of fear filled her.

His lips trailed along her jawline and settled on her lips. Her knees went weak. Brennan's tongue explored her lips and moved inside, tasting her as his tongue tangled with hers.

Krista gave in to the need to be close to Brennan, resting her hands on his shoulders and leaning into his body. He felt warm and inviting, causing butterflies to flutter in the pit of her belly.

Brennan gathered her closer and brushed his lips across hers. The sweet, intoxicating taste of him overwhelmed her.

Krista felt as if she were drowning in a sea of sensations, and she couldn't get enough of him. Their kisses grew in intensity. One kiss ended and another began. She stroked his back and arms, loving the way he responded to her touch. His hands were everywhere, caressing and kneading her flesh. She wanted to show him how much he meant to her. But the nagging voice in the back of her mind refused to shut up.

Tell him, the voice whispered as a knot of anxiety diminished

Krista's haze of desire. *He needs to know,* the voice in her head kept reminding her. It crept into her thoughts and tainted the love and affection she felt for Brennan.

Panting softly, Krista drew away and shook her head. She gazed into his earnest face and knew she had to tell him. If she wanted something special with Brennan, she had to bare her soul and let him know everything about her. He deserved the truth. Trapped between the sink and Brennan, Krista lowered her head and studied the patterns on the ceramic tile floor.

Frowning down at her, he asked, "What's the matter?"

"I can't do this."

He cupped her face between his large hands and gently kissed her lips. "Honey, we don't have to do anything."

Her voice trembled as misery knotted her insides. "No. You don't understand."

Smiling at her, he leaned forward and tasted her lips a second time. "Make me. What's going on in your head?"

She drew in a deep breath and let it out slowly. "I've made some bad mistakes."

Frowning, Brennan studied her expression. "Everybody has. You're no different."

The words trembled on the edge of her lips. "They're pretty bad."

"What kind of mistakes?" he asked softly.

"My junior year in high school, I-I-I . . ." She paused, wringing her hands together. "This boy in my class started acting like he liked me. It was the first time anyone had ever treated me like that."

Brennan teased, "Oh. Young love."

"Let me finish." Krista patted his warm chest.

"All right."

Chilled, she rubbed her hands up and down her arms. "No one had ever been that nice to me before, and I ate it up. The kids at school pretty much treated me like they do at work.

When Paul paid me a little attention, I loved it. I started skipping class to be with him and meeting him after school."

His expression slowly shifted from playful and fun to somber as understanding dawned. "Krista, you don't have to tell me this. You're an adult. What you did in the past isn't my business."

Sadness and regret waged a conflicting war within her. He was so sweet. Unfortunately, when he heard what she had to say, he'd probably run screaming from the room with disgust.

As she spoke, one hot tear rolled down her cheek. Maybe this was why she had never allowed herself to open her heart to anyone. She'd found it easier to dress like a frump and let everyone think she was okay with that. "I thought he loved me."

"Sssh!" he muttered, wiping away her tears with the pads of his fingers. "Don't do this to yourself."

Krista knew she didn't have to. But it was the fair thing to do if they planned to have a relationship, a lasting relationship built on more than physical attraction. "I was starved for affection, and naturally, we got closer. Paul kept insisting that if I loved him, I'd want to make love with him. Well, I let him, and days later I learned he was bragging to his friends about bagging the geek. And how boring and stiff I was. Paul told his friends that not only was I ugly, but I was a boring screw."

"Stop!" Brennan demanded. "None of that is true. You're a beautiful, talented woman. Don't let anyone take that from you."

Krista smiled sadly at him. "That's not the end of the story. Something else happened."

His forehead crinkled into a frown. "What?"

Wanting to cry, Krista bit her lip. She had to finish telling him. He had to know everything. "I got pregnant."

"Oh my God!" Brennan's hands dropped to his sides.

"It took me a while before I realized what was wrong with me."

"Oh, sweetheart!" he moaned, wrapping his arms around her and rocking her back and forth. "What happened?"

"Miscarriage."

He kissed her forehead and offered soothing words. "I'm sorry. I'm so sorry you had to go through that."

Her voice broke miserably. "It wasn't your fault. You weren't there. It was my fault for being so naive."

"You weren't stupid. You were being you, loving and trusting. That ass took advantage of all the things that made you special."

His expression stilled and grew somber. He took a step away from her. She noted a flash of guilt. She wondered about it but quickly dismissed the notion.

"I was so stupid. I should have known better." She laid her head against his chest. The reassuring beat of his heart gave her the strength to continue. "I thought Paul liked me and saw beyond the clothes and hair to who I was. The real me."

"I don't ever want to hear you say anything like that again." Brennan took her by the shoulders and gave her a quick shake. "You are beautiful, funny, and good-hearted. There aren't a lot of people with those qualities." He brushed his lips across hers. "Don't let some idiot destroy the person you are."

Maybe it was because she'd never told anyone her story, or the fact that Brennan hadn't rejected her, but Krista began to cry. She wept aloud as hot tears burned their way down her cheeks. She tried to stem the stream of tears, but all she did was cry harder. During all of this, Brennan held her, offering soothing words as he rocked her back and forth. Finally, after what seemed like hours, Krista got herself under control. She felt physically drained. "What did you want to tell me?" she said.

Brennan's expression changed. She felt as if someone had pulled the cord that shut the blinds.

"Just that I l-l-love you," Brennan stammered.

Her heart swelled with happiness. Although she believed him, there was a part of her that felt this wasn't the confession he had planned to make earlier. After everything she'd told him, Brennan still loved her. She gazed into his eyes and said, "I love you, too."

Brennan tugged on her hand, leading her through the house. "Come on. It's been a long day, and we're both tired."

She followed without resistance.

He led her up the stairs to the second floor and escorted her down the hall to a door. Brennan pushed the door open. She could see his bedroom.

Krista focused on the large bed in the center of the room. Swallowing hard, she faced Brennan. "I-I-I'm . . ." She paused and then started again. "I'm not ready for this."

Obviously, there was something in her expression, because Brennan began to explain. "This isn't about sex or making love. I'm not letting you drive after what you just told me. You'll stay here until later in the morning, and then I'll take you home."

"Oh. I don't know."

He raised his hands and assured her. "No funny business. All I want to do is hold you, be close to you, and give you comfort."

Krista remained silent for a moment longer.

"We've shared so much tonight," Brennan added. "The birth of Liz's baby and the stuff you've been holding inside you. I think we need to be together."

She nodded and took his hand, following him into the room. The queen-size bed dominated the room. A tall armoire stood near one wall, while a dresser with a mirror covered another. Brennan strolled across the room, opened a dresser drawer, and removed a white T-shirt. He returned to the spot where Krista stood and handed the garment to her. "You can sleep in this."

Krista took it. "Thank you."

Taking her hand, he led her across the room to another door. "Here's the bathroom. Under the sink is a new toothbrush. Everything else you need should be within reach." Brennan gave her a tiny push toward the door and left.

She went into the room and changed out of her dress and slipped on the T-shirt. After washing her face and brushing her teeth, she returned to the bedroom to find Brennan already in bed. With a bit of trepidation, she crossed the carpeted floor. Brennan opened his arms, and she ran into them.

"Hey, sweetheart," he muttered, tossing the light blanket over them and then brushing the hair away from her face and kissing her lightly on the forehead. "Get some sleep. I'm right here. I've got you."

Chapter 19

Thrashing around in the bed, Krista yelled, "No! No! Stop! Please, Uncle Nick, help me."

A firm hand shook her. She heard someone calling her name, "Krista. Krista. Wake up, honey. You're dreaming."

Krista fought her way out of the fog of sleep, reaching toward wakefulness. She opened her eyes and focused on the man leaning over her, with a worried frown on his handsome face. "Brennan?"

"At your service. You scared the hell out of me." He leaned over her, caressing her cheek. "Okay now?"

Weary, she settled against the headboard and sighed deeply, using her hand to wipe away the fine sheen of perspiration forming on her forehead. "I'm sorry I woke you."

"No problem. You were having quite a dream there."

"Nightmare."

Brennan scooted into the spot next to Krista, drawing her into his arms, and gently stroked her back as he spoke. "What about?"

Krista sat quietly, pleating the soft silk sheet. "Nothing."

"It might help to talk about it." He smiled encouragingly. "I promise anything you tell me will not go beyond this room."

"I'm not worried about that," she answered.

Brennan placed a finger under her chin and lifted her head, gazing intently into her eyes. "Then what?"

She shrugged and admitted, "I don't know."

"Look at me."

Relenting, Krista held Brennan's gaze with her own.

"You can tell me anything. Whatever it is, I'll listen," he whispered softly, tucking a lock of hair behind her ear.

Tears filled her eyes. *I'm not going to cry,* she vowed, taking in large gulps of air to control her oversensitive emotions.

He held her against his bare chest, rocking her back and forth. Krista laid her hand on his chest and sighed. It felt so good to be here with him. His skin felt warm and inviting under her hand. Unconsciously, she caressed his chest as she spoke. "I had a dream about the baby."

"Mm-hmm."

She brushed hair from her eyes. "Talking to you must have brought those memories to the surface."

"Could be." He caressed her back in slow, circular movements. "Tell me about the dream or what happened. Or we can stay quiet. It's your choice."

Did she want to tell him all the gory details? She'd been alone with this burden for so long, it didn't seem right to expect someone else to understand or even sympathize. *Will I feel better if I tell him? You've already told him part of it. Maybe he can be trusted with the rest.*

"I didn't know what I was going to do," Krista admitted, laying her cheek against his chest. The steady beat of his heart and the darkness of the room boosted her courage. "One thing I did know. My aunt was going to kill me."

"Had you told anyone?"

"When I realized I was pregnant, I went to Paul. I hoped he would understand and stand by me. I waited in the hallway for the school's basketball practice to end, and when he came out of the locker room, I caught up with him." Shivering, she scooted closer, seeking Brennan's warmth.

"Go on. What happened next?"

"I told him. He called me a liar and said it wasn't his. We argued back and forth for a few minutes, and then he told me he'd get the whole team to swear to it that they had had sex with me."

Brennan's arms held her tighter as she continued to tell him this sorry story.

"I said everybody knew that I didn't mess around and that my aunt wouldn't believe him. He got mad and punched me in the stomach. I fell against a row of student lockers and hit my head. Paul laughed at me and walked away, calling me a loser."

"Is that when you lost the baby?"

She shook her head. "No. That happened later. That night I woke up with terrible cramps. I could barely make it to the bathroom. Actually, I didn't make it."

"What do you mean?"

"I must have passed out on my way to the bathroom. I was unconscious in a pool of blood when my uncle found me on the bedroom floor. He called EMS and got me up, and they took me to the hospital. When I woke up, the doctor told me that I had lost the baby."

Brennan rested his chin on her hair. "What about your aunt? Did she give you a hard time?"

Shaking her head, Krista chuckled humorlessly. "It was fate. My aunt had left that morning for a weeklong church retreat. And for once she didn't demand that I go with her. Amazingly, I was home and back to school before she saw me. That was one little hospital trip I kept to myself."

"The hospital didn't keep you long or insist on talking to your family members?"

"No. Besides, Uncle Nick went to the hospital with me, and he kept my secret. The hospital kept me two days. I had a D & C, and they checked my hemoglobin before sending me on my way," Krista explained. "They gave me a prescription for pain and told me to go to my doctor for follow-up care. The nurse suggested I eat leafy green vegetables and take iron to build up my blood."

"You were what? Fifteen? Sixteen?"

"Sixteen."

Silently, for several minutes, Brennan continued to hold her, stroking her arm. "That was a big dose of responsibility for someone so young. How do you feel about all of this?"

"Bad. I felt like a fool for believing Paul. I never had a chance to really consider the baby, and then it was gone. In my head, I know it was probably for the best. But my heart can't help feeling as if I should have known better. Acted differently. I don't know."

"Don't think like that. Losing the baby was not your fault." Brennan planted a tender kiss on her forehead. "Paul knew what he was doing. I'm pretty sure he hit you with the hope that it would cause you to lose the baby."

She considered his words. Could he be right? Was she beating herself up for something she had had no control over? "Maybe. I don't know."

"What about this Paul joker? What happened to him? Did he help you?"

"No."

"What do you feel for him?"

"Paul hurt me in a way that I still don't believe has completely healed." Words trembled on her lips. "H-h-he took my innocence, trampled over my trust and the little confidence I had. Paul made a fool out of me and then made sure everyone in our class knew what he had done to me."

Brennan looked away and shifted on the mattress.

"I felt betrayed," Krista admitted, turning away so that he didn't see the tears shimmering in her eyes. The next words came out just above a whisper. "I thought he loved me. I was little more than a game to him. A joke he could brag about."

Brennan's eyes clouded over. But he didn't make any comments. He continued to stroke her arm.

Used to his comforting presence, she wondered about this shift in mood, about what was going on in his head. Krista rose up on one elbow and glanced down at the man next to her. Maybe she'd revealed too much, expected too much from him. "Are you okay?"

"Mm-hmm. Thinking about that ass Paul and how I'd like to get my hands on him."

"He's not worth it."

She had the oddest sensation. Was Brennan worried or upset about something? He refused to look at her. Did he feel differently about her now that she'd revealed the details of her past? She wasn't the sweet, innocent virgin he had probably assumed she was.

"Have I shocked you with my not-so-perfect history?"

"No. Not at all. Besides you weren't responsible for that dog. Your feelings were pure. You cared for him. I understand that."

Her eyebrows curved inquiringly. "Are you sure? Because I don't feel you're with me here. Did I say something that b-bo-bothers you? Maybe it's all too sordid for you to deal with?" She moved away from him and tossed her legs over the side of the mattress, preparing to leave the bed. "It's all right if you don't like what you've heard. Believe me, I'm not proud of it."

"God! No! You've got it wrong. I love you." He held her close. "Yes, it bothers me that you went through all of that. More than that, I hate that you were hurt by some stupid fool who didn't think about or care about your feelings. This jerk caused you pain and then went on about his life. Given a chance, I'd put my fist through his face."

Krista reached up and touched his cheek. "This is the first

time anyone has defended me. I've never had anyone in my life like you. Thank you."

"Don't thank me. I want you to be happy."

Brennan's head dipped, and his lips sought her mouth, softly touching her lips. Her pulse accelerated with excitement. His lips pressed against hers, and then his tongue slipped inside, exploring and teasing as he urged her closer to his warmth with a gentle hand at the small of her back.

His hands seemed to be everywhere at once. Warm and sweet, tantalizing, yet tender, he coaxed a response from her lips.

Slowly releasing her lips, Brennan rewarded her with a wonderful smile. Joy bubbled up inside her, threatening to explode. Unable to resist him, she smiled back.

When he leaned in to take her lips, she eagerly returned his kiss, with a hunger that belied her earlier shyness. She kissed him again, savoring every second.

Brennan's fingers caressed the soft swell of her breast through the cotton fabric. Her eyes flew open. *Oh boy!* she thought. *I'm not quite ready for this. How do I slow things down?*

"Wait! Wait!" Krista said, pushing against his chest as she scooted away. "I'm not sure I'm ready to take things any further."

Eyes shut and breathing hard, Brennan reluctantly drew away, lightly banging his head against the bed's headboard.

"Brennan," she said, touching his cheek. "I'm sorry."

"I didn't mean to frighten you." His eyes were smoldering with suppressed fire. "What do you want from me?"

"Everything."

He asked, "Are you sure?"

"No." Krista's voice wobbled as she squeezed his hand. "I'm scared." Embarrassed, she turned away, avoiding his gaze as she looked everywhere in the room, but not at him. Whispering, she confessed, "I keep thinking about the things Paul said and did to me. It's hard to forget the way he treated me."

Brennan listened to all she had to say without comment, stroking her cheek. "My poor baby. That man was an idiot. You're beautiful and desirable. And if you let me, I'll prove it to you."

Perched on the edge of the bed, she was frozen in place by fear. Afraid to believe Brennan, Krista mentally sifted through a laundry list of reasons why she shouldn't do this.

Brennan studied Krista from his position on the bed. A wicked little smile replaced his thoughtful expression as he moved closer to where she sat. "You know I'm a salesman."

"Yeah?" she asked in a breathless whisper, responding to the delicious sensations his hand stirred as it glided along the slope of her neck. His fingers swept across the swell of her breasts and tugged a lock of hair behind her ear.

"And"—Brennan's tongue followed the path of his hand—"I persuade people to buy or do things that they don't plan to do."

"I get that."

"Let's pack Paul and all the bad memories attached to him away for good. We're going to build some new ones. Are you interested?"

Was she interested? Didn't he hear her panting each time he touched her? Krista nodded, cautiously wondering what she was letting herself in for.

"Good. The first thing you need to do is relax. We'll use a couple of sales approaches to achieve our goals," Brennan explained in his best professional voice. She noted a spark of humor behind the words, mixed with naked passion. "Here are the rules. If I do anything that makes you nervous or uncomfortable, just tell me and I'll stop immediately. After all, I aim to please. Understand?"

"Understood," she answered, a bit unsure about what she'd just agreed to.

"Relax," Brennan said softly, stripping the T-shirt from her body. He settled comfortably against the headboard and drew Krista between his legs. He massaged her shoulders, working the tense muscles, gently kneading her flesh until she swayed in the direction of each stroke of his hand.

Krista settled against his chest, enjoying the feel of his hands stroking the soft flesh of her arms. His lips nibbled at her bottom lip as his fingers worked their magic, stirring her senses and building a gentle fire between her legs.

Lifting his head, Brennan asked in a whisper, "You like?"

Eyes shut, she breathed, enjoying every caress of his tongue and hands. "Oh yes. Yes." Her skin tingled every place he touched, while heat continued to pool at her core.

"What about this?" he asked, taking a nipple between his lips and sucking on it. His fingers stroked the other breast, turning Krista into a quivering mass of jelly. "You like?"

"I'm not sure," she muttered, stroking his head while he kept his mouth on her breast. "Do it again. I need to think about it for a minute."

"Whatever mademoiselle wants. I'm here to please."

Krista's soft moans of pleasure were the only sounds in the bedroom for several minutes.

"I like," Krista confirmed urgently. "I like a lot."

"Good. That's my girl." He sounded pleased. "Let's try something different." His hands molded to Krista's soft curves as they stroked their way down her body.

Brennan took her hands and placed them on his bare chest. "Touch me." Encouraged by him, she ran her tongue across his taut nipple, feeling a sense of power as he moaned.

Krista grinned. "You like?"

"Most definitely," he answered.

His finger drew circular designs as it traveled a path from her breast down over her belly, dipping into the indentation of her navel and finding the curls protecting her nub. Exploring her, his fingers moved back and forth across the tight nub.

Arching against his hand, Krista swayed with the movement of his fingers.

Each sweep of his hand drew her further away from the rational woman she knew she was and closer to a world filled with sensations.

"Come on," Brennan encouraged in a sensual whisper while he continued to finger her. "That's it. Let go. Come on."

The tension built higher and higher. Krista couldn't control it, feeling the walls quiver and shake as she reached for her first orgasm. Slowly recovering from the wonderful feelings, she watched as Brennan turned away and opened the drawer and removed a foil-wrapped packet. He tore it open and removed the latex item, rolling it over his engorged flesh.

Brennan positioned himself between her legs and slowly, inch by inch, pushed into her hot wetness. Hovering on the edge, he shut his eyes, absorbing the sweet sensations, before he began to move, kicking them into a gentle, but steady rock. Instinctively, her body responded, arching to meet him as wave after wave of sensual pleasure bombarded her.

Each stroke came harder, faster, and stronger than the last, until for the second time, Krista crossed over the edge, allowing Brennan to carry her to a new level of sensations. She cried out at the exquisite, pulsating feeling leading her from one exquisite peak to the next until she plunged headlong over the cliff of passion to her release.

Seconds later his harsh cry signaled his climax.

Brennan rolled away from her, quickly removing the condom and dropping it into a wastebasket next to the bed. He returned to her, pulling her against his side.

"I think this campaign was a major success," Brennan murmured, kissing her lips. "You surpassed my expectations. Forget Paul. He was a young fool."

"Who?" she asked.

Chuckling, he rolled onto his side and cradled Krista in his arms. "So, tell me. Did you like?"

Panting, she answered, "Yes. I liked a lot."

Safe in the haven of Brennan's embrace, Krista rested her cheek against his chest, listening to the steady beat of his heart. After a while, her fingers trailed across his chest, along his flat belly, and her hand curled possessively around his shaft. His flesh responded to her touch, stretching and growing under Krista's curious handling.

Krista rose up on one elbow. She outlined the curve of his ear with her tongue, whispering softly, "You like?"

"Oh yeah! Don't stop!"

Chapter 20

Krista stepped out of the shower, whipped off the shower cap, and shook her head, freeing her hair. She ran her fingers through her locks. The plastic bonnet went into a basket on the counter. She wiped the steam away from the mirror with her towel and studied her reflection.

It didn't show. She didn't look any different. Yet in the space of an evening, a million things had changed inside her. She wasn't the same woman who had allowed people to treat her any way they chose. Loving Brennan gave her focus and balance.

Returning to the task at hand, Krista dried her breasts, flushing red hot, remembering how Brennan had made her feel when he suckled one of her nipples, causing heat to pool between her legs. Brennan had taken care of that ache while erasing the unpleasant memories of Paul's selfish possession of her body.

Turning away from the mirror, Krista concentrated on drying herself before slipping into a fresh T-shirt, Liz's rose-colored robe, and flip-flops.

She hurried down the steps to the first floor, following the faint male voice and the aroma of freshly brewed coffee. Brennan paced the length of the kitchen, with the cordless telephone attached to his ear. He wore a pair of tan, loose-fitting cargo shorts as he moved freely around the kitchen.

Brennan caught sight of her in the doorway and beckoned her with an outstretched arm. Eager for his embrace, Krista rushed across the room and into his arms. She gazed into his eyes, feeling her love for him swelling to impossible heights.

How had she gotten so lucky? This wonderful man wanted to be with her. No more Paul, with his lies and schemes. This had been the best morning of her life.

His arm stretched across her shoulders, holding her against the long, lean length of his body, while he spoke into the receiver. "Good morning, Lizzie girl."

Brennan listened for a moment and then added, "Sorry. It's after eleven. I figured you'd be up. I'm coming to visit my nephew this afternoon."

Krista heard a loud squeal and a few choice words from the other end of the telephone.

A huge smile spread across his face, and his shoulders shook with silent laughter. Brennan looked down at her and winked. "Remember, you still have to come back here," he said.

Krista strummed a disapproving finger at Brennan. He shrugged but continued to laugh.

"Is there anything you need for me to bring? What about your stuff? Do you need it?" he asked Liz.

Krista smiled. He knew exactly what to say to put Liz back on track. She could hear Liz barking out instructions.

"Okay," Brennan agreed, gently kissing Krista as his attention drifted from his sister to the woman in his arms. The kiss was a gentle teasing of the lips, making her feel alive, safe, and at home in a place where she belonged.

"I'll bring Krista with me. And we'll see you around four or five. Love, you too," said Brennan. He disconnected the call and placed the phone on the counter. "Morning," he muttered, wrapping both arms loosely around her and drawing her closer for a second kiss.

Snuggling closer, Krista wrapped her arms around his neck. Starving for the sweetness of Brennan's lips, she rose on her toes.

"Morning," she responded, running her hands over his broad shoulders. "How's Liz?"

"Crabby. Ready to come home."

"Is her doctor releasing her today?" Krista asked.

"No. Probably tomorrow."

Krista nodded. "Good. She gets a day of rest before the real fun begins."

He snorted. "For both of us. Lizzie girl had a laundry list of things she wants me to do before I get to the hospital."

"That's to be expected. You're the older brother. It's time to help your sister. What about the baby? How's he doing?" she asked, returning to her tiptoes to kiss him a second time.

"Joshua's fine. I could hear him in the background, demanding his breakfast. The boy's got a pair of lungs on him."

Giggling, Krista untangled herself from him and moved to the coffeemaker. She grabbed a mug from the deep green mug rack and poured a cup. Turning to Brennan, she asked, "You want a cup?"

He pointed to the counter where the telephone sat, and she noticed an empty mug. "Had mine."

Nodding, she sipped the coffee, enjoying the way the brew surged through her veins, awakening her senses. "Poor thing. Her job has just begun. Did she say anything about Steve?"

"Yeah. Liz got in touch with his unit. Steve'll get the message."

"That's good."

Brennan strolled to where Krista stood and studied her for several quiet moments. "Are you okay?"

She smiled at him. "Better than I've been in a long time. Thank you for asking."

"You are more than welcome." His expression sobered. "I love you. You believe that, don't you?"

"Yes." Krista glanced past him at the clock and sighed. Anxiety twisted her heart. "I better get dressed. My aunt is going to have a fit."

"I didn't think about it until now. Didn't you get in touch with her last night? Can't your aunt get in touch with you?" He hunched his shoulders. "You know, by cell phone? I just assumed you had a phone because everyone does."

"I have one for emergencies. But I didn't bring it with me. I figured I'd be with you, so I didn't need it. Aunt Helen knows I'm with your family. She won't worry too much. At least I hope she won't," Krista amended, swallowing the last drops of coffee. She placed the mug on the counter and started for the door.

Brennan caught her arm as she passed him, halting her. "Good." His tone turned seductive. "So you can stay a little longer."

She felt her pulse leap. "Maybe. What have you got in mind?"

"Oh." He smiled seductively. "A little morning delight."

Her brows rose. The idea sent her spirits soaring. "Interesting." Krista took his hand and started for the door, marveling at how bold she felt this morning. Brennan held back.

Confused, she stared back at him. "What?"

"Not there."

Curious, Krista her tilted head. "Where?"

His lips pursed, he tilted his head in the direction of the table. "There."

Krista smiled, feeling naughty and excited at the same time. "Oh my."

Brennan grinned broadly and led her to the table. He lifted her and sat her on the edge.

Eyes wide, she stared at Brennan. Anticipation and surprise swelled within her.

"Here. Let me help you with that," Brennan offered, smiling engagingly at her as he untied the belt at her waist and pushed the garment off her shoulders. It pooled around her on the tabletop. Next came the T-shirt. He whipped it over her head and tossed it on the floor.

Brennan's gaze dropped from her eyes to her shoulders to her breasts. "Exquisite," he praised reverently.

A tingling sensation started in the pit of her belly and radiated throughout her. Hungry for his touch, Krista reached for him, pulling his head down for her kiss. She freely gave in to the passion of his kiss. His tongue sent shivers of desire racing through her.

Brennan released her lips and planed tiny kisses down her neck, creating a damp path to her breast. He took a nipple between his lips and rolled the nub, sucking strongly on it as his fingers sought the tight bud between her thighs.

Sensations assaulted her. Heat pooled between her legs as she held his head against her breast. Lifting his head, Brennan blazed a wet path across her chest to the other breast and gave it the same treatment.

His tongue left her breasts and moved over her stomach, taking a moment to worship her navel before continuing on its designated path and stopping inches from the curls shielding her essence.

Krista's eyes flew open. She pushed at his shoulders. "Don't!"

"You don't like?" Brennan asked, referring to his query from the previous evening.

"I-I-I don't know," she admitted. "No one's ever done anything like this before."

Exploring her thighs, his hands covered her breasts, using the pads of his thumbs to flick back and forth across the tight nipples. "Let me do this for you," he said. His hand moved from her breast to cup her bottom and bring her closer.

"I love the way you smell. So beautiful. So unique," he

said. He ran his tongue along her seam, lingering as he drew in a deep breath.

With the first sweep of his tongue, her body jerked instinctively. She'd never felt anything like this before. She never imagined any man would be this intimate with her.

Her leg quivered involuntarily. She couldn't make herself calm down. Brennan laid a hand on her belly, holding her in place as he made a second pass, diving between her slit to touch her nub.

This was too much. She felt too much. The feelings were far too intense.

How would she ever be able to look him in the face after this? His mouth latched onto her and sucked. It felt so good. One thought stayed in her head. *Just don't stop.*

The hot, wet torture of his tongue continued, building in intensity. Her legs shook uncontrollably around his head. Brennan held her so she couldn't pull away as he loved her with his mouth and tongue. Whimpering, she clung to him, riding out the sensations as she climaxed.

Krista stiffened, letting out a primal cry of release as she reached fulfillment. Chest heaving, breast quivering, and heart pounding wildly, she fought to catch her breath and control the tiny tremors racking her body. Releasing her, Brennan crept up her body, covering her petite frame with his own, taking her lips in a mind-shattering kiss.

Brennan stepped away from her, shoved his hand inside the pocket of his shorts, and removed a foil wrapper. Barely able to move, Krista stared at him.

Grinning sheepishly, he shrugged, unzipping his shorts and allowing the garment to drop to the floor. He stepped away from the garment, kicking it away from the table. "I grew up a Boy Scout. I'm always prepared. Or in this case, I was hoping."

He scooped her into his arms and laid her gently on the ceramic tile floor. The floor felt cool and hard against her back.

Bolder than she'd ever been in her life, she beckoned for Brennan to lie down next to her. She plucked the condom wrapper from his hand and tore it open. She took a moment to caress his hard shaft, lovingly running her fingers up and down his length and across the head, rubbing the moisture into his smooth skin as she learned the texture and feel of his shaft.

Brennan groaned, pulling her closer to him, seeking her lips. She returned his kiss, tasting her essence on his lips. It was unique, erotic, and exciting, another first for her to savor when she was alone. She wondered how he would taste.

Right now Krista needed him, so she filed those thoughts away for another day and concentrated on rolling the latex over his heavily aroused flesh. She ran her hand from the base to the head of his organ, checking to make sure it fit perfectly. But, truly, she wanted to feel him, touch him, and admire the man who fulfilled her fantasies.

"Here. Let's try something a little different," said Brennan as he guided her on top of him. Inch by inch, she descended onto his shaft, taking him into her body. He rested his hands on her hips, urging her to move.

Embarrassed, she looked away from him. As he moved inside her, her embarrassment was easily replaced by more pressing sensations. Instinctively, his body arched upward. His hands roamed intimately over her breasts as he repeatedly lunged into her. Krista caught the rhythm of his body and met his upward thrust with a downward stroke. Feeling herself stepping closer to the edge, she panted, loving the feel of his thick shaft sliding in and out of her wetness.

Soaring higher and higher, their bodies were in exquisite harmony as they moved together. The first tremor started deep within her, radiating out. The second and third tremors pulled harder, and she groaned. Suddenly, it was all too much, and she exploded, crying out her release.

With a harsh cry, Brennan made one final lunge. She felt his hot, wet release.

He took her face between his large hands and drew her down for a kiss. "Babe, for a newbie, you sure pick up things really fast."

Krista rolled to Brennan's side and grinned at her lover. "I always liked being at the top of my class."

Chapter 21

Sunday afternoon the sun was high in the sky when Krista stepped from the Chevrolet Caprice. With a heavy sigh, she started up the driveway to the side door. If her luck held out, Auntie had used the church bus to attend services. If that had happened, Krista had a little more time before she had to face her aunt.

She pursed her lips when the doorknob turned in her hand. No church today. Auntie was home.

The aroma of bacon and coffee greeted her. From the second floor, Krista heard the shower running. The old girl had cooked and eaten breakfast before returning to her bedroom to get dressed.

Krista dropped her garment and make-up bags on the bench near the door and made for the kitchen. A fresh pot of coffee sat on the warmer. Krista poured a cup, added sugar and cream, and then sat on a stool at the island, sipping her coffee. She might as well get comfortable. Her aunt would be down soon enough.

Thirty minutes later Aunt Helen stepped off the last stair and turned toward the back of the house. Leaning heavily on her cane, she entered the kitchen and moved across the tile floor to the cupboard. She removed a mug and then poured herself a cup of coffee. Unlike her niece, she took her coffee black, no sugar.

"Well, you're home. Good morning to you. Oh, excuse me. Good afternoon," Aunt Helen taunted as she headed for the den. She placed her mug on the end table before flopping down on the sofa and reaching for the remote. Bryant Gumbel's voice floated through the air, reaching the kitchen. "Did that gal have her baby?"

"Yeah. Big, fat boy. Liz named him Joshua Brennan."

From Krista's angle at the island, she watched Aunt Helen channel surf. Krista shifted on the stool, finishing the coffee. The old girl was drawing out the tension, waiting for the right moment to strike.

Krista hopped off the stool and took her cup to the sink. She rinsed it and loaded it into the dishwasher. She stood in the doorway, saying, "I'll come back down later. I'm going to shower and then take a nap."

"Don't think you're foolin' me," Auntie called to Krista's back.

Krista halted. "What?"

"Haircut, clothes, and parties at the job. You ain't foolin' nobody."

"I don't understand."

"This is all about that man."

"What man?" Krista asked, well aware of who her aunt was referring to. She was going to play dumb for just a little longer.

"That gal's brother. The one you work for."

"Auntie, I'm only going to be working with Brennan until the end of September. After that I go back to my old department."

"So what. You're all starry-eyed over him. Don't let that man break your heart."

A gentle smile formed on Krista's lips as she remembered how she'd spent the past hours with Brennan. Auntie was wrong. Brennan loved her the way she loved him. He'd never hurt her.

"That man's gonna get you in a whole lot of trouble," Auntie prophesied. "You're cruisin' on dangerous ground."

"What?" Krista turned in the doorway to glance at her aunt.

Folding her arms across her chest, Auntie answered, "You heard me. If you keep goin' at things the way you are, you'll end up hurt."

"I'm not doing anything."

Auntie shook her head. "Baby, you sound just like your momma."

"We've had this conversation before. I'm nothing like her. How could I be? I don't remember the woman."

"Think about your mother and how she was blind to so many things. She ended up in a world of trouble that we couldn't get her out of."

"I'm not like my mother," Krista said, feeling anger rise inside her. Why did her aunt always bring up her mother?

"You've got some of her ways in you."

"Aunt Helen, I'm not going to end up like her. My life is different."

"How do you know?" Auntie challenged.

Krista's mellow mood quickly veered to anger. "Because I'm not a party girl. I don't go out and leave my baby with anybody that'll keep her. I have a job and a sense of responsibility. And I don't"—Krista paused, swallowing loudly before continuing—"have a baby."

"Mmm."

Krista stepped into the den and stood over the older woman. "You've raised me. Don't you expect anything better from me?"

"I want better for you, just like I did for your mother. But she couldn't stop chasing behind any man that told her she was pretty. And look what it got her."

Close to tears, Krista hung her head. She'd heard this story so many times. "Have a little faith."

"Jewel ended up dead because she wouldn't listen to me."

"I know, Auntie. I know."

"I don't want that for you. You're all the family I have left. I raised you from the time you were a baby, and I don't want things to go bad for you."

"Auntie, look at me. Think about the girl you raised. I've never gone to parties and stayed out all night." *Except for last night,* she amended silently. "I don't go to after-hours joints. That's what my mother did. Not me."

"Yeah, but she died. Jewel had you when she was fifteen. Fifteen! She should have been having fun with her friends. Instead, she was rocking a baby." Aunt Helen threw her hand in the air. "Hell, she didn't rock it. Everybody else did. And she never stopped running the streets until she ended up dead."

"Auntie, my mother was in the wrong place at the wrong time. She didn't want her life to end like that. How was she supposed to know that those idiots would pull out guns and shoot up the place? Face it, Auntie. Bullets don't have names on them."

"Yeah. Jewel would be here today if she'd kept her butt at home."

"We can't change what happened. My mother is gone."

Auntie turned a worried gaze on her. Krista squirmed like a worm on a fishing pole. "And you're here. I don't want no man to hurt you. Baby, be careful. I know you think you know what you're doin'. But do you really? Are you sure?"

The strength of Brennan's love filled her, and she smiled at her aunt. "I think I do."

"It looks like you've made up your mind. So all I'm going to say is, I'm here for you when the time comes. Remember that."

"I do. And I will."

"Good. Go on and get your nap. After the night you had, I bet you need it."

Brennan slipped his keys on the wall rack and strolled quietly through the house to the living room. Liz sat on the sofa, with Joshua in her arms, softly humming the words to Anita Baker's "The Men in My Life". Silently, he sat in the chair across from the sofa and watched his sister.

His chest swelled with love for this miracle placed before him. It felt good to see Lizzie so happy and content, and the bonus footage was that he got to be part of his nephew's life.

After a moment, Liz rose and gently placed the baby in the bassinet in the living room. She covered him with a blue blanket before returning to her spot on the sofa. "Hey."

"Hey to you."

Stretching out on the sofa, she asked, "Krista get home okay?"

Brennan couldn't help smiling when he thought of Krista and how great it was to have her in his life. "Yeah, she's fine."

Lying on her side, Liz eyed him for several silent moments. "When did you plan to tell me what happened between you two?"

He laughed out loud and rose from the chair. Strolling around the coffee table to the sofa, he lifted Lizzie's legs and sat down on the sofa beside her. "You don't get the details."

"Don't want them." She rolled her eyes toward the ceiling. "I'm not a voyeur. Remember, I did tell you that you had feelings for Krista. I always know. You were too stubborn to admit it."

Krista's image floated through his head as he remembered the sound of her gentle voice and the feel of her tentative touch. "Yes, you did. Are you happy?"

Liz shrugged. "Little bit."

"I'm scared, Lizzie."

She frowned, tilting her head to the side as she stared back at him. "Why? Things looked pretty good between you guys when you brought us home from the hospital."

"I could lose her."

"True. That could happen. What is this really about?"

"The bet."

"Ahh," she muttered softly. "That is a problem."

He sighed, shaking his head. "Yeah, it is. I'm not sure how to handle it."

"Yes, you do know," she prompted.

"You're not going to cut me any slack, are you?"

"No. My big bro has found the woman for him, and I'm going to make sure you do right by her."

"I tried to tell her the other night. But she told me some things that stopped me dead."

"Like what?"

"Bad sexual experience in high school. Some other stuff that I don't want to repeat."

"You knew it wouldn't be easy when you decided to get involved with Krista. It's time for you to sit down with her and tell it all. Brennan, she deserves the truth."

"I know. And I plan to tell her all of it. But I don't want to lose her."

Liz eyed him somberly. "What do you need to do?"

"Clear up this crap ASAP."

"Good. Now you're talking." She gave him a thumbs-up sign. "That's a great first step."

"I've already set things in motion."

"Oh?"

Brennan rubbed his fingers back and forth across his forehead as if it hurt. "When I went to work this morning, I planned to talk with Flynn Parr and get him to call off the bet. That idea got shot to hell. He didn't come into the office today. He was in the field with a new recruit. So I have to wait."

"Do you think he'll do it?"

"I hope so." Worried, he thought about the confession Krista had made Saturday night. If she found out about his stupidity, it could destroy them before they had a chance to really get to know one another.

Lizzie dropped her feet onto the floor, sat up, and faced him. "To be honest, I don't want her to find out about my part in this. She's come so far. The confidence I see in her makes me feel that we've done the right thing. And there's another part of me that doesn't want Krista to stop trusting me. I don't want to lose that."

Brennan chuckled humorlessly. "That little woman has gotten under both our skins."

"I like her. I told you that before we started this business. And I still do. She's been a good friend to me. I won't forget that."

"Krista was at your side when you went into labor."

"Do you think Parr will be in tomorrow?" Liz asked.

He hunched his shoulders.

"This is how I see it. The sooner you put an end to the bet, the better," said Liz.

"I hear you. Trust me, that's what I want to do. Resolving this stuff is at the top of my to-do list."

"Good. Keep it as your priority until it's done." Lizzie reached for the remote and hit the ON button. The room was illuminated with the colors from the high-definition television. She surfed through a series of channels before stopping to watch *Deal or No Deal*. They sat quietly together until the commercial break.

He turned to her, asking, "What about you? How's Steve?"

The biggest grin spread across her face. Brennan hadn't seen Lizzie this happy since she gave birth to Joshua.

"He's coming home in ten days."

Brennan jumped to his feet, dragging her along with him and hugging her close. "Yes!"

"Sssh!" Liz poked a finger at Brennan's chest. "If you wake up that little boy, you'll be the one walking the floor with him."

He glanced toward the bassinet. When all remained quiet, he studied his sister. "When were you planning to tell me?"

"Tonight."

"I guess I can't complain. When you got pregnant, you were ready for maternity clothes before you told me anything."

She giggled. "True." Somberly, she added, "Steve'll only be here for ten days."

"That's okay. I can live with this," he said.

"I'd rather have him here for a short period than not at all. Unfortunately, things will be incredibly busy while he's home," Liz explained.

"Why?"

"We're going to try and get the baby christened while Steve's home."

"That's a tall order. I can ask my assistant to help you."

She shook her head. "No. I'm going to ask Krista. I think she'd enjoy helping and being with the baby. What do you think?"

"I think you're right."

"Brennan?"

The change in her tone drew him away from the program on the television. "What?"

"Steve would have done this himself if he were here. But he's not. So he asked me to."

Frowning, he waited. This must be something important.

"We would be honored to have you as Joshua's godfather."

Shocked, he sat there staring at his sister. Godfather. Hell! He hadn't seen that coming.

Liz balled her hand and knocked on his head. "Hello! Are you in there?"

"I'm here."

"What do you say?"

He drew her close and hugged her. "Thank you. I'd love to do it."

"This is not in name only. I expect you to do your job as godfather. Watch over my son, and help him out while his father is away."

Brennan pretended to consider her comments. "I can do that. Besides, this is my basketball star. Someone has to show Joshua the ropes and have his back when you start PMSing."

Liz groaned dramatically. "My child is doomed."

"Who are you planning to ask to be the godmother? I hope you're not going to ask that nutty friend of yours, Jasmine." Brennan shuddered at the thought. "She'll make your baby crazy."

"Don't say that. No, she won't."

"It's the truth. Make your choice wisely," he warned.

Liz relaxed into the sofa's soft leather. "I already have. I want someone I can depend on. I'm going to ask Krista."

Grinning, Brennan nodded approvingly. "Now you're thinking logically. Wise choice. That's my girl. I think you'll be happy with Krista, and she'll be honored."

Chapter 22

Two weeks after Joshua arrived, Krista sat in the front seat of the Saab as Brennan drove them to his town house. Liz had called and invited Krista to dinner to meet her husband, Steve.

With a nervous giggle, the new mother had assured Krista that her craving for seafood had finally ended, and she wouldn't subject them to another meal of fried catfish. Liz also admitted this meal was sort of a welcome home celebration for Steve.

"Has your house finally settled down now that the baby has been with you for a while?" Krista asked as Brennan took the I-75 exit eastbound to Jefferson Avenue.

"Yes," he answered, with a grin. "I was just getting used to having the baby wake me up at two in the morning, and now I have a grown man wandering through the house at all hours."

"Poor baby. You do have your hands full." Krista reached toward the steering wheel and stroked Brennan's hand. She smiled, amazed at how different things were between them. Two months ago she would never have taken the initiative and touched him. Yet now she felt comfortable in expressing her feelings for and to him.

"Don't get me wrong," he said. "I'm happy for Lizzie. I

know it was really hard on her to have Joshua without Steve. But they seem so happy that I feel like an intruder in my own home. Most evenings, I rush through dinner and head to my room so that I don't bother them."

"W-w-when did Steve get in?"

Brennan hit the turn signal and merged into the right lane, preparing to enter his townhouse complex. "Tuesday." He pressed the button on the remote and pulled into the garage, cutting the engine. "I'm warning you before you go in there. This place is like a madhouse right now. So go with the flow."

"I can do that."

He leaned across the transmission gear and held her chin with his hand, kissing her lips softly. Unable to resist, she deepened the kiss, allowing her tongue to sweep across Brennan's. Slowly ending the kiss, he played with a lock of her hair. "I've missed you."

"I've missed you, too."

Brennan grinned. "I needed to hear that. With everything going on in my house, I'm afraid I haven't had a chance to be with you the way I'd like to or spend time with you."

"We're busy. And you have a sister and nephew that need you. I understand that."

"I don't want you to think that I've forgotten you. You're important to me, too."

Before Krista could respond, the door opened and Liz stood there, peering into the car. "Hey, you two. Come on in."

Brennan smirked at Krista. "It's like having kids that interrupt at every opportunity."

Laughing at his joke, Krista climbed out of the car and approached her friend. Immediately, she was swept into a big bear hug and rocked from side to side. "I'm so glad you came. Come in," said Liz.

Krista hugged her back, happy to be in a place that she felt safe and comfortable in. "It's good to see you. Where's the baby?"

"With his daddy. Steve and his son are inseparable." Liz reentered the house, with Krista on her heels. The aroma of broccoli, garlic, and lamb filled Krista's nostrils. Steam rose from a variety of pots on the stove. She had expected to find the kitchen table set for dinner. Other than an empty glass, the table was bare.

Brennan shut the door and strolled past the pair. "I'll let you spend a little time together. I'm going to check my voice mail and e-mail."

Liz waved him away. "Go. We don't need you standing over us while we talk. See you in a few."

He asked, "Krista, you okay?"

"I'm fine."

He waved and strolled out of the room.

"Everything's under control," said Liz. "We have a few minutes before I'll put the food on the table. So let's head into the living room and chat." Liz slipped her arm in the crook of Krista's arm and led her through the house. In the dining room, candles illuminated the walls.

"Want a glass of wine?" Liz asked.

Krista nodded.

Liz reached for the dark green bottle chilling in a clay carafe. She removed a wineglass from the sideboard and filled it. After handing the glass to Krista, she picked up a can of 7UP, and they strolled to the living room. Liz took a seat on the sofa and patted the spot next to her. Krista slipped onto the cushion next to Liz and sipped her wine.

A sly smile spread across Liz's face.

Krista shifted uncomfortably on the leather sofa. "What?"

"I don't know how to say this delicately, so I'm just going to put it out there. I'm happy about you and my brother."

Quickly, Krista looked away. Instantly, she felt heat filling her cheeks. She wasn't used to this, and her relationship with Brennan was still too new for her to feel comfortable talking about it.

Liz took her hand and squeezed it. "Don't be embarrassed. I'm not prying. I want you to know that I think you're good for him."

All of Krista's shyness came back with a vengeance. She felt tongue-tied. Being in a relationship was new to her.

"You don't have to say anything," Liz cooed. "I just wanted you to know that I'm happy for you and my brother."

"Sweetheart," called a new voice, which must have belonged to Steve. He entered the room, with Joshua in his arms. It seemed strange to see the tiny infant in the arms of this brawny man. What intrigued Krista the most was the gentle way Steve held his son. "I think he needs to be changed."

Giggling, Liz shook her head and rose from the sofa. "And you couldn't do it yourself?"

Steve grinned down at his wife. "I think Joshua needs you for this part. I'm just a new dad."

"And I'm a new mom," replied Liz. Arms outstretched, Liz winked at Krista. "My husband, a military man and pilot, is diaper challenged. Hand him over."

Steve kissed the baby on his forehead and gently placed him in Liz's arms.

"I love how you delegate responsibilities for our son. Must be all those years in the military," said Liz.

Krista couldn't help laughing at the couple. They were so comfortable with each other.

Steve finally noticed Krista sitting quietly on the sofa. "Hi. I'm Steve."

"Krista," she responded softly, quickly focusing on the rug. She still had trouble meeting new people. It took her a while to warm up to them.

Standing with her feet spread apart, Liz rocked the baby to and fro. "Oh, I'm sorry. Steve, this is Krista Hamilton. She and Brennan got me to the hospital and stayed until after Joshua arrived."

Although Krista had seen pictures of Liz's husband, she

wasn't prepared for the sheer breadth of the man. He wasn't exceptionally tall, maybe around five feet ten. But he commanded attention and respect. His skin was the color of rich brewed coffee, and his brown eyes sparkled with a hint of mischief. A thick mustache covered his upper lip, while the dark brown hair on his head was cut close to his scalp.

Steve approached Krista with an outstretched hand. She rose from the sofa and extended hers. They shook hands, and Steve looked down at her with appreciation in his eyes. "Thank you for being here with Liz. I worry about her, and it's good to know that she has a friend that she can count on. I appreciate everything you did for my family."

"You're welcome," replied Krista as she pushed a lock of hair behind her ear. "I didn't do much. We had fun."

Liz bumped up against her husband with her hip. "You should thank her. She's the one that went to Frankenmuth with me so that I could get your fudge. She tolerated me very well that day."

"I'm glad Lizzie didn't have to travel that far alone," said Steve. His sun-roughened face broke into a grin. "Thank you. Thank you. Not just for the fudge. But for being there with my wife."

Krista shifted around on the sofa. This much praise didn't sit well on her shoulders. She wished Steve would stop. "No problem."

"Hey, where's that brother-in-law of mine?" Steve asked, glancing around the room.

"Checking e-mail," Liz responded. "Krista, I'll be right back. I'm going to change him and put him down. Then we'll be ready for dinner."

Steve sank into the chair across the room and picked up the remote. He turned on the television and channel surfed until he found *Real Sports with Bryant Gumbel* on HBO.

As Liz started down the hallway to the first-floor bathroom, Brennan entered the living room. He slipped into the space Liz had vacated and stretched an arm along the back of the sofa. "Hey, man."

"Hi, Brennan," said Steve. "I haven't seen much of you. We're not running you out of your house, are we?"

"Nah. Everything's fine," replied Brennan. He moved closer to Krista, putting an arm around her shoulders and drawing her against his side. "Although those first two days after Joshua came home, I thought I would have to put your wife and baby out."

Laughing, Steve said, "Don't do that. I really wouldn't get any rest."

"Don't worry. Things are great now," Brennan explained. "I wasn't used to having a newborn demanding to eat every couple of hours. That little boy is too greedy for me."

Grinning, Steve added, "What can I say? He takes after his dad." Turning to Krista, Steve said, "I understand you and Brennan work together."

She nodded. "Temporarily. Normally, I work at the help desk in IT."

Brennan took over. "Krista was reassigned to my area to help with a new project. She's a whiz with computers and software. I, on the other hand, am an idiot."

Laughing softly, she touched his hand. "No, you're not."

Liz appeared in the doorway. "Dinner's on the table. Let's eat."

Brennan rose and helped Krista to her feet. He led her down the hallway to the dining room.

The lights were turned off, and the candles that graced the dining room table added an intimate mood to the room. Brennan sat at the head of the table, with Krista at his right. Steve took the chair opposite Krista, and Liz rounded out the group at the far end from Brennan.

Rack of lamb, rice pilaf, and a vegetable medley made up of broccoli, cauliflower, and carrots filled the table. A garden salad and rolls and butter completed their meal. Brennan stood, went to the sideboard, and returned with the bottle of wine. He filled everyone's glass.

"Lizzie girl, everything looks wonderful," said Brennan.

Steve added, "Sure does, honey."

Krista added her praised to the group. "You did a good job."

Grinning mischievously, Brennan added, "And to think, the world contains food other than fish."

Stabbing a fork in her brother's direction, Liz warned, "Watch it. Or I'll cut you off. No more dinner for you."

"I'm not worried about your threats," said Brennan. " The only thing I wish is for your son to let us eat in peace. Then I'll be happy."

"Joshua's not that bad," Liz defended, passing serving trays. "He's used to being in a warm, confined place. It takes a little while to get used to this new environment."

Once their plates were full, the group got down to eating and enjoying the wonderful meal that Liz had prepared. After a few minutes, Liz glanced at Steve, and he nodded. He cleared his throat. "Folks, Liz and I have a request for you guys."

Brennan and Krista turned to Steve, waiting for the rest of the story.

"Before my return to active duty, we'd like to have Joshua christened."

"That's a good idea," Krista responded.

"Liz and I have already scheduled it for this Sunday. Brennan, we'd like you to be Joshua's godfather."

Brennan grinned. "Thank you. I'd be honored."

"And, Krista," Liz said, "we'd like you to be our son's godmother."

Overwhelmed with emotions, Krista raised her hand to her mouth. *Oh my!* She felt so honored to be asked. All of her insecurities hit her at once. *But why would Liz ask me?* Krista wondered. *Liz has friends. Good friends. Why me?*

"Are you sure?" Krista asked, breaking her roll into tiny

pieces. "I mean, I'm sure you have friends that you'd like to do this for you."

"No. You've been good to me and Joshua," said Liz. "If something were to happen to me, I want someone that I can trust to make the right decisions for my son. We have similar ideas about life, and you are one of the most caring people I've met. And I know you would take care of my baby. I choose you." She paused, brushing away a tear. "Plus, with my brother as Joshua's godfather, I'm sure he'll have everything he needs and wants."

Liz's words made Krista feel useful, wanted. She never thought of herself as being someone who could raise a child. But if it became necessary, she'd do her very best.

"Thank you. I promise that I'll be the best godmother," replied Krista.

"I know you will," said Liz.

"So, now that's settled. It's going to be a small affair with just us, my mother and father, and my brothers and sisters and their families," said Steve.

"Wow!" Krista muttered. "You guys move fast."

Liz cleared her throat and said, "Steve's only here for ten days. He'll be leaving before the end of next week. We wanted to get this in before he has to return to his unit."

Krista felt so bad for Liz. She just had a baby and her husband had just made it home and now he had to go back to Iraq.

Putting on a brave smile, Liz said, "We're not going to worry about Steve leaving right now. We decided to live in the moment. Everybody dig in and enjoy your food."

Chapter 23

Sunday morning dawned bright and warm. The birds outside Krista's window kept up a steady stream of chatter as they sat on her window sill.

Normally, she'd shoo them away so that she could sleep a little longer. Today was different. This Sunday was special. Baby Joshua would be christened, and she would become his godmother.

They would be connected for the rest of their lives. She felt honored that Liz and Steve trusted her with their baby's life.

Filled with excitement and pushed by a touch of fear, she made a silent promise to be the best godmother any child could ask for. However, she really wasn't sure what was expected of her. She rolled over in her bed, rubbed her eyes, and tossed back the light blanket. Time to get ready.

Krista dressed carefully for the day, choosing a floral dress cut from an airy, soft fabric that was pink and cream, with splashes of blue. The dress hugged her hips and caressed her thighs, ending just above her knees. Cream hosiery and leather sandals completed her outfit.

After preparing breakfast and lunch for Aunt Helen and making sure the old girl had everything she needed, Krista hurried out the side door and headed downtown, to Brennan's town house. She arrived on his doorstep and rang the bell, taking a quick peek at her watch while waiting for him to answer the door.

It was much earlier than Krista had expected. She hoped it wouldn't be a problem. Brennan greeted her with a warm hello and a sweet kiss on her lips.

"Hey," he whispered, taking her lips in a second kiss as he ran his fingers down her bare arm. Her skin tingled under his hand.

"Good morning to you, too," Krista answered, wrapping her arms around his neck and kissing him back. She felt safe with Brennan. Nothing could do harm to her when she was with him. Krista glanced over his shoulder. "Where's everybody?"

"Liz, Steve, and Joshua are upstairs getting ready," he explained.

A bolt of uneasiness struck her. She took a step back toward the door. "Am I too early? I can go over to IHOP on Jefferson Avenue and have a cup of tea and then come back later."

"Relax, honey." He took her hand and squeezed it reassuringly. "You're fine. Family can be early."

Family? Brennan considered her family?

Krista hadn't realized it, but she'd been holding her breath. She smiled, releasing the air from her lungs slowly. "Good. I want to help if I can."

Brennan pointed out the window. A white van with DREAMS COME TRUE written on the sides pulled up to his back door. A man and woman dressed in identical white shirts and black trousers got out of the van and approached the back door. "There's the caterers. They'll be setting up while we're at the church." He grinned down at Krista as his finger gently stroked her cheek. "There's nothing for you to do but enjoy yourself and stay close to me."

She smiled back at him. "I can do that."

"That's my girl." He rested an arm around her shoulders and steered her down the hall toward the living room. "Come on. We can relax until Steve's family arrives."

"Does Steve come from a big family?"

"It's four brothers and two sisters."

"Wow!" she said, getting comfortable on the sofa when the doorbell rang.

"Speak of the devil. I'll be right back." Brennan strolled out of the room and down the hallway to the front entrance. Greetings and welcomes filtered to the living room. Minutes later he returned with a middle-aged couple, six younger couples, and a horde of children on his heels.

Krista jumped to her feet. Her heart leapt in her chest. There were so many of them. Conversations with strangers still made her feel incredibly nervous. Could she pull it off? Mentally, she had braced herself to meet Steve's parents, but not this entourage. She hoped she didn't make a fool out of herself.

Steve rushed down the stairs and raced into the room, yelling, "Momma, Dad!" He reached for his mother, smothering her in a large bear hug. Seconds later, his father swallowed him in his embrace.

"Glad to have you home, son," said Mr. Gillis as he placed a hand on Steve's shoulder.

"Thanks, Dad. I wish I was here to stay," said Steve.

"Me, too, son. Me, too," replied Mr. Gillis.

Krista noticed tears in the older man's eyes before he quickly wiped them away with the back of his hand. Mrs. Gillis allowed her tears to flow freely and mopped them up with a tissue from her purse.

"Come on, Mommy, Dad. I want to see him, too," said a man who looked very much like Steve. He nudged Mr. Gillis senior out of the way. Smiling, he studied Steve before offering his hand. Laughing heartily, Steve took the man's hand and then pulled him into an embrace. "Good to see you,

Gerald." Other members of the Gillis family followed suit, hugging Steve and exchanging information about their lives.

"What's all the commotion about?" asked Liz as she entered the room, with the baby in her arms.

"Liz!" Mrs. Gillis exclaimed, rushing to the doorway. "Let me get a look at my grandbaby."

Everyone turned to the doorway, and the Gillis family immediately converged on Liz and Joshua to get their first glimpse of the baby.

"He looks like you did when you were a baby," Mrs. Gillis said to Steve while holding the baby's tiny hand.

"Nah. Joshua's better looking," Gerald teased.

Throughout this exchange, Krista stood on the sidelines with Brennan, watching the Gillis clan. She enjoyed the banter, closeness, and joy at being together. Being on the edge of so much love made Krista wish she had grown up in a larger family. Maybe having siblings to bounce things off of would have made her a different person. Hugging and kissing didn't happen often when she was growing up. But she knew that her aunt and uncle loved her and wanted the best future for her.

"We need to get to the church. The ceremony starts at eleven," Brennan pointed out, taking charge of the arrangements. "Krista and I will be in my car. You guys can follow me to the church. It's west on Jefferson, near downtown. If you pass the Renaissance Center, you know you've gone too far."

Steve took the baby from Liz. "Ma, Dad. Why don't you ride with Liz and me?"

"That makes sense," Mr. Gillis said.

Steve pointed toward the kitchen. "We're parked in the garage. Let's head that way."

"We'll wait for them in the car. This way, folks," Brennan instructed, ushering the Gillis folks out the front door.

* * *

The well-wishers gathered in front of the building for the ceremony. They made their way into the small church to lend their support to the couple and their infant.

As they stood at the front of the church, the sun shone through the stained-glass windows. Brennan and Krista stood beside Steve, Liz, and baby Joshua, with the minister. Steve's parents, Mr. and Mrs. Gillis, and his siblings were the only guests.

The christening ceremony was simple, moving, and beautiful. Brennan and Krista pledged to be godparents.

An hour later they returned to the town house, to a light buffet-style meal. Baby Joshua's toothless grin and happy disposition won over his grandparents as he was passed from arm to arm. As expected, his grandparents fawned over him, marveling at how perfect an infant their new grandson was.

Brennan's town house was in an uproar. The house wasn't meant to hold this many people at one time. The Gillis family was everywhere, parked in every available seat. The group had returned from the christening and had dived into the buffet spread, organized for Liz's convenience by her brother.

Music from the compact disc player streamed through the house. The kids were laughing and teasing each other as they munched on wing dings and sandwiches.

Steve's parents had found a spot to eat on the sofa. Steve's siblings and their children were everywhere, dishing up plates of food from the buffet and searching the house for a place to sit.

Liz and Steve were upstairs, enjoying a greatly deserved and needed moment of peace and quiet. Krista had volunteered to care for the baby while Brennan entertained their guests. Humming softly, she sat on the sofa, feeding Joshua.

There's something special about holding a baby, Krista thought. The infant's eyes fluttered shut as he sucked on the bottle, concentrating on his meal.

A moment of sadness held Krista in its grip as she thought

of all that she had lost. She'd never gotten the opportunity to hold her baby. Nor had she had the time to learn to love the baby the way he or she deserved. She'd never had a chance to be a mother. That was okay. Joshua would get all of that love and pampering.

From across the room, Brennan watched Krista, with a slight smile on his face. The gleam in his eyes made her heart flip. She glanced at him and then mouthed the word "What?"

Chuckling, Brennan crossed the floor, with a napkin in his hand. He handed it to Krista and scooted into the place next to her. He leaned close to her ear and whispered, "You're a natural."

Looking down at the baby, Krista shook her head. "Hardly."

He reached out and stroked her cheek. "Don't believe that. You're great. Joshua's loving your attention."

They watched the baby in silence, enjoying the sense of peace and togetherness. "He's so sweet," whispered Brennan.

"Yeah. He is."

Brennan's fingers stroked her arm, sending her pulse into a gallop. "You are so beautiful."

"That's Liz's doing."

"No. That's who you are."

The intensity of his expression was too much for her to handle. She focused on the sleeping baby in her arms.

"Krista, look at me," he commanded.

She raised her head and gazed into Brennan's eyes. "You are beautiful. I'm talking about the woman you are. Who you are inside. I love that as much as I love the way you look."

Did Brennan mean it? Or was he trying to make her feel better because he knew about her baby and felt sorry for her?

She tried to read beyond the mask he generally wore. Love and respect were the only emotions she read in his eyes.

Brennan cleared his throat before admitting, "I'm getting really attached to the little one myself." A spark of sadness flitted across his face and was quickly hidden. "I don't know what I'm going to do when Liz and Steve move out. I don't think I'll see my basketball star on a regular basis."

"Sure, you will. That's a long way off, isn't it?"

He dabbed at the milk escaping Joshua's eager lips. "Probably not. This is Steve's final tour of duty. Hopefully, he'll be home permanently within six months to a year."

"Do they plan to stay in Michigan?"

"Yes. Liz wants to buy a town house in this complex. I hope she does. I'd like for her to stay close."

"I can understand that. I hope it all works out."

"Me, too," he replied.

Krista handed the bottle to Brennan. He placed it on the coffee table. She settled the baby on her shoulder, rubbing his back in a slow, circular motion. After several moments, a loud burp escaped the baby. Giggling softly, she said, "Well, I think you're done."

Brennan laughed out loud. "He's a pig, too."

"Don't say that. He's just a baby." She scooted to the edge of the sofa and rose. "I'm going to take him upstairs and put him down."

"Want me to go with you?"

"No. I'm fine. Besides, I don't want to disturb your sister. She and Steve need this time together." She gave the room a quick, sweeping gaze and said, "You entertain your guests."

He nodded. "Thanks."

"You're welcome. I'll be back in a minute." She zigzagged her way through the people in chairs and on the floor.

With the sleeping baby in her arms, Krista reached the top of the stairs and turned down the hall toward Liz and Steve's bedroom. The door was slightly ajar, and Krista felt confident she could knock without causing an embarrassing moment.

As she drew closer, Krista stopped outside the door, debating whether to interrupt the couple. *I'll listen for a moment. If they are busy, I'll take Joshua back downstairs and come back later,* she decided.

"Come on, Liz," Steve pleaded. "Don't do this."

A teary Liz replied, "I can't help it."

Tears! Not Liz. She'd kept such an upbeat attitude about life during the time Steve had been away. Crying seemed so out of place for Krista's happy friend.

"Why now?" Steve asked. "We've got less than a year to go."

"I don't know," Liz replied through her tears. "I just have this bad feeling that won't go away."

"Well, tell it to go away or ignore it. This is almost over. Six months to a year from now, I'll be done, and we can get on with our lives."

"I'm sorry. I don't mean to bring you down."

"I know you don't. You've been great through everything. Don't let anything get you down now. You're the one that held me together. I need your strength."

Liz's tears broke Krista's heart. Liz always seemed so confident and in control. This was not the way Krista envisioned her friend. She seemed vulnerable and in need of her husband's comfort and reassurance.

"Maybe because this is the last time you have to go over there. I'm more worried then before," Liz admitted.

"It's going to be fine. Say that whenever you feel blue. When I get back, we'll buy that house we want and settle down for good."

"Steve, I'm scared. When you left the last time, I could see you coming back. The three of us were together, and that was before Joshua was born. I knew everything would work out."

"And now?" he asked cautiously.

"I don't see or feel it. I'm lost." Liz's tears followed.

"Babe, don't cry. I hate it when you cry."

Sniffling, Liz admitted, "I'm sorry. I can't help it."

"What can I do to make you feel better? Just tell me."

"Come back safe and in one piece," she said.

"Done. I promise."

"Can you?" Krista heard the desperation in Liz's voice. "Don't make promises you can't keep."

"Oh, I plan to keep this one. You find us a house, and I'll make sure we move into it."

"Steve, I love you."

"Me, too. I love you. Nothing will keep me from coming home to you and Joshua."

Silence followed. Krista suspected they were kissing. *Time to make my escape,* she thought.

Feeling like a voyeur, she shifted the sleeping baby from her right arm to her left, eased away from the door, and started for the stairs. *I'll come back later,* she thought. Krista hadn't meant to listen so long but had hoped for a moment where she could break into their conversation and put the baby in his crib.

Her thoughts went back to what she'd heard. No one expected Liz to be happy about Steve's trip to Iraq, but Krista had never heard this level of desperation in Liz's voice. It worried Krista. Until Steve returned, she planned to stay close to her friend and provide comfort and support over the rough spots.

Chapter 24

Brennan leaned back in his chair, watching the flickering images on his laptop. Connor Dexter had finally scheduled the Gautier presentations for the week following Labor Day, and his team was working on the bullet points for the written speech.

Pleased by the end results of Krista's hard work, Brennan nodded approvingly. The short skit worked effectively with the larger-scale promotion he intended to launch. She'd done a bang-up job of crunching numbers to determine what demographic market to target with their online campaign. It had taken a boatload of time and effort to convert the film version of their commercial to a computer format.

Smiling, he thought of how Krista had changed his life. Her quiet presence offered encouragement, strength, and direction when he felt low. Although he would never admit it, his sister had been right. Krista was an intricate part of his life.

Although his team was prepared, there were a few things that still bugged Brennan about Gautier. After attending several lunch meetings with the French automaker, he felt out of the loop with the company execs. Mr. Gautier's aloofness made it difficult to pin him down on any topic related to what he expected and wanted in a campaign from Dexter Kee, making Brennan feel as if he were the odd man out in this particular game.

Flynn Parr sat in at every meeting with the Gautier brass, gauging what information Brennan chose to reveal and how much he actually learned. His salesman instincts told him Flynn had established a far better rapport with Mr. Gautier. That offered Flynn an edge, which Brennan had been unable to penetrate.

A sharp rap on the door drew his attention away from the presentation. Brennan looked up in time to see the door open.

Flynn Parr stuck his head inside the room. "I heard you were looking for me, Thomas."

"Come on in." Brennan stood, shutting his laptop. He didn't want Flynn to know any details of their campaign. Flynn had enough of an edge as it was. Brennan waited as the other man shut the door and strolled across the office to where Brennan stood behind his desk. "I came by your office yesterday."

"Oh yeah?" Flynn slipped into one the empty chairs across the desk and laced his fingers together, placing his hands in his lap. "What can I do for you?"

Brennan cleared his throat as the first beads of perspiration formed on the back of his neck. He hoped this worked. Krista and his future rode on how well he handled these negotiations. "Actually, I have a favor to ask."

"From me?" Flynn snorted. "No."

"I haven't asked my question yet."

"I'm not going to drop out of the Gautier campaign."

Running a finger along the bridge of his nose, Brennan faked a laugh, hating the joke and disliking the pretense. "You're so funny. But I think you're a bit ahead of yourself. The game isn't over yet."

"It will be up in two weeks." Flynn offered his best "I got you" smile. "Admit it, Thomas. I'm ahead in this game."

"Maybe in your own mind. But it's far from over." Brennan lifted a hand in the air. This was not the direction he wanted to go with Flynn. "That's enough about the automaker. I need to talk to you about something that has nothing to do with Gautier."

"Then you must need advice about women." Flynn chuckled at his own joke.

You're closer than you think, Brennan thought wearily, but answered, "Something like that."

Flynn's blue eyes narrowed as he rolled that idea around in his head. "What's going on?"

"I need you to call off the bet."

"No."

Simple, concise, final. Brennan had expected that, but he had still hoped for something different. Now came the hard part, finding an angle to change Flynn's mind. He wasn't the top salesman for nothing. His skills of persuasion were his best tool to work with Flynn. The biggest problem was, Flynn had the same arsenal of weapons, and he recognized every one.

Brennan tapped his finger on the top of the desk, examining the other man for weaknesses. There had to be a way to convince him. "Why not?"

"Because I don't want to."

"Look, I know we agreed to this, but I've thought things through and have had a change of heart. You and I are not the only ones this bet may affect. If we continue down this road, Krista could end up emotionally crushed."

Chuckling, Flynn drew one leather-clad foot over the opposite knee, smoothing a hand over the fabric covering his leg. "Too bad. You agreed to the terms. We set the rules. Live with it."

Bastard, Brennan thought. *This isn't working. I need to try something different.* He stroked the velvety curve of his eyebrow while searching for another approach.

"You're right. It is good no one else knows about the bet." *That's right. Agree with him. Make Parr believe he has a connection with you. Find common ground.* "One of my concerns is that this is a bad time for us to stick our naked asses in the air. We're both in highly sensitive positions. If the details of the bet got out, it could end our careers."

Grinning broadly, Flynn shrugged. "Then we should keep the details between us."

"Doesn't it bother you at all?"

"No. Why are you bothered?"

"I'm not," Brennan denied quickly, laying his palms on the desk. "But we both have got a lot on the line right now."

"Suck it up, Thomas. I'm not letting you out of it."

"What will make you reconsider?"

"Nothing. We agreed to go until Gautier makes its decision. I'm not going to let you slither out of the bet."

"That's not what I'm doing."

"Right." With an expression of contempt on his face, Flynn added, "We're going to see this through to the end. You don't deserve special consideration. Besides, I think you've done more than your share of underhanded crap."

Confused, Brennan asked, "What the hell are you talking about?"

"Oh, come on. Don't act so innocent. You go behind my back and get Krista switched to your department and under your direction."

"There wasn't a rule against that."

"Right. You got that little gem. That's your quota. Our meetings are scheduled for two weeks from now. Once they're over, we'll settle up."

A feeling of desperation filled Brennan. He couldn't have this bet over his head. Not now. Not with so much at stake.

If Krista found out about the bet, she'd be devastated. The way that idiot Paul had treated her, the loss of the baby, and the baggage she'd carried about that miscarriage almost put her over the edge. He couldn't bear to do that kind of damage to her fragile confidence a second time.

"Look, I'm willing to pay out the money. Give you the amount we agreed on. I just want this stuff over," said Brennan.

"Nope."

"What do you mean nope?"

Flynn grinned and put his foot on the floor. "My momma's old phrase comes to mind. You made the bed. Now you've got to lay in it."

"The way things stand right now, you're the one on the losing end. Krista's shining, coming out of her shell, and performing in a professional manner. This could be your way to keep that money in your pocket."

"Don't worry about my pocket." Flynn rose from the chair. "It's not your concern."

I'm not going to get anywhere with him, Brennan thought. *I'm going to have to find another way.*

Flynn scratched the side of his face with a long finger, eyeing Brennan suspiciously. "You're the one wanting out of the bet. I have to think there's something more going on. I've got time. There are still plenty of hours in the day for Krista to embarrass the hell out of you and herself. I want to be there to see it."

"Krista won't. She's come too far."

"Yeah, but it ain't over till it's over. I've got hopes. I think something more is going on. Maybe Krista's beginning to revert to her old ways. Clumsy, can't talk. I don't know. Trust me. I'll find out."

"That won't happen," Brennan answered quickly.

A knowing smile spread across Flynn's smug face. "The game isn't over yet. I'm going to wait and see how things work out." He stood, balled his hand into a fist, and playfully punched Brennan on the arm. "It'll all come out soon enough."

Brennan rubbed a hand over his face. This hadn't gone well at all. What if Flynn figured out Brennan's true motivation?

Krista had suffered so many indignities at the hands of cruel and unthinking people. He wanted to protect her, fight anyone who dared to come between them or cause her any harm. He couldn't or wouldn't let anyone else take advantage of her gentle nature.

Most of all, Brennan didn't want to lose her. He didn't want to see her expression of admiration turn to hate. Initially, his motives had been for her own good. It was his fault that they were in this position, and it was up to him to resolve it.

Suddenly, he had the overwhelming need to see Krista, to talk with her and hold her in his arms. Brennan needed to re-assure himself that they would be all right regardless of the problems facing them.

He rose from the chair and skirted the edge of his desk, heading toward the door. As he put his hand on the doorknob, there was a knock. Surprised, he took a step away as Erin Saunders pushed the door open and filled the entrance.

"Hi, Brennan," she cooed, running a hand over her hips to draw his attention to her short skirt.

Finding Erin standing in his doorway didn't sit well with Brennan. He'd already dealt with one unpleasant visitor this morning. He wasn't in the mood to deal with a second. Besides, he'd seen the way Erin treated Krista. She insulted and made fun of Krista at every opportunity. He also suspected Erin passed on much of her work to Krista, and his sweet baby was too tenderhearted to complain. He planned to change all of that. But not yet. His hands were tied until he got that monkey of a bet off his back.

"What can I do for you?" Brennan asked.

Erin stepped into his office and shut the door behind her. Brennan was taken aback. Why was she here? he wondered. They shared very little work, if any.

Slowly strolling back to the desk, he moved around its edge, took his chair, and pulled it up to the desk. What did she want?

"Does Rachel need something from me?" he asked.

Erin shrugged, taking a minute to sit and cross her legs. "No."

Her skirt was so short, Brennan could see the tops of her thigh-highs. She noticed the direction of his gaze, and a knowing, satisfied expression settled on her face.

This didn't feel right. Whatever her agenda, he wanted nothing to do with it. "If Rachel didn't send you, what do you need?"

"I thought I'd drop in and see if there's anything I can do for you."

Brennan tossed his hands wide, pretending to be surprised by her comment. "Thanks, but I'm good."

"I bet you are."

He shifted in his chair. This woman made him feel uncomfortable in his own office. He'd had enough of that. "Is there something in particular you need?"

She offered him a sly, seductive smile. "Mm-hmm."

"And that is?"

"You."

Nervous, he stood. "Will you excuse me? I need to talk with Krista about a few things."

"What?" The pleasant façade cracked, revealing an angry, very upset woman.

Smiling, Brennan helped Erin to her feet and guided her to the door. "We've got the Gautier campaign, and I just remembered something that she needs to look into for me."

Brennan escorted Erin from the office and stood outside, in the bull pen. "Thanks for dropping by." Relieved to be rid of Erin, he turned away, blew out a hot puff of air, and headed to Krista's office.

He knocked on her door but received no response. Opening the door, he peeked inside. The lights were on, but the office was empty. Surprised, he looked for signs that she'd arrived at the office today. Her briefcase sat in one of the chairs, and Microsoft Vista ran on the laptop she normally used.

Leaving the office, Brennan shut the door, giving the area a quick scan. He pursed his lips as he considered where she could be.

Chapter 25

Intent on completing her expense report, Krista stepped off the elevator and crossed the bull pen to the supply closet. Softly humming Najee's "Joy" she turned on the light before moving farther into the room, then searched the shelves for blank copies of the triplicate form.

Preoccupied with locating the supplies she needed, Krista barely registered the sound of approaching footsteps. Seconds later, she heard the sharp click of a door shutting. Unconsciously shifting toward the copy machine, she glanced toward the door.

Brennan was leaning against it.

"Hi," she said casually, maintaining an outward appearance of calm. At the same time, her heart pounded in her chest, and her skin tingled.

"Hey." He pushed away from the door, strolled across the room, and captured her hand in his.

A fleeting expression of despair skated across his face and quickly disappeared. That look, coupled with his one-word greeting, touched a cord deep within Krista's heart.

Concerned, Krista cupped his cheek and examined him carefully. "Brennan? Are you all right? Is something wrong?"

"Nothing." He shook his head and then glanced into her

eyes, smiling in that special way that made her heart flutter in her chest and her pulse quicken. "I needed to see you for a moment. That's all."

Still unconvinced, she studied his face a beat longer, trying to see into his head and heart. What was bothering him? Before she had time to form another thought, Brennan swept her into his arms, holding her in the warm circle of his embrace. Her soft curves molded to the contours of his lean frame.

Brennan's breath fanned her face as he whispered, "Krista, I love you." He released her, took her face between his hands, and softly kissed her lips. The brief caress tantalized and teased her senses while offering a too-short glimpse of heaven. Not satisfied with that fleeting touching of lips, he deepened the kiss, exploring the interior of her mouth with his tongue.

Krista moved closer, savoring the sweet taste of coffee mixed with cream and the unique essence of Brennan. She wound her arms around his back, holding him close.

Blood pounded through her veins. Fire roared within them.

Reluctantly, they parted, putting a few inches between themselves as they fought for control. Brennan's hands left her shoulders, kneading them before drifting lower. Reverently, he stroked her breasts through the soft fabric of her blouse while planting tiny kisses along the slope of her neck. Her nipples puckered under his personal and special ministry.

Krista's hand wandered down his chest, paying homage to his taut male nipples. Her fingers circled the aureole, rolling the flesh through his dress shirt. She ran her hand across his belly, admiring the flat surface, and then paused at his waist before moving lower.

Krista stroked Brennan's trouser zipper, pulled the tab down, and reached inside, feeling a sense of power when he moaned against her lips. His erect shaft pulsated through the cotton fabric of his briefs.

Sanity returned for a moment. Krista removed her hand. A

frustrated growl left his lips as he gazed at her with passion-filled eyes. She asked, "What are we doing?"

"Don't know. But it feels good." His mouth covered hers hungrily. He took her hand and returned it to the opening of his trousers.

Yes, it did. He felt perfect, wonderful.

It amazed her that after a few weeks of being with Brennan, she felt so little embarrassment about the things they were doing inside the walls of their place of business. As that thought struck her, Brennan's hand moved lower. His fingers lifted the hem of her skirt, slipped under it, and touched her thigh, heating the places where they rested on her warm flesh.

Her breath caught in her throat as his hand moved higher and fingered the lace of her thigh-high nylons. *Thank you, Liz,* she thought, remembering the day the other woman had insisted she purchase the thigh-high hosiery. His fingers moved higher and slipped under the elastic band on her panties and touched her intimately as his tongue continued to ravage the sweet interior of her mouth.

"Mm!" she groaned. Her hand outlined his hard shaft.

Brennan moaned low in his throat. "Babe, don't stop."

With boldness she didn't know she possessed, Krista slipped her hand inside the slit in his briefs and freed him. Her hand ran up one side of his hard flesh and down the other. She rubbed her thumb across the head as he pushed himself farther into her hand.

Following her lead, Brennan invaded the confines of her panties and found her moist and ready. He rubbed the tight, swollen nub as her juices started to flow. Using his thumb to continue rubbing her nub, he stuck a finger an inch inside her, moving in and out. Unconsciously, her hips began to rotate, receiving pleasure from the naughty caress.

Oh my, I like this, she thought. Krista's eyes widened as the sensation intensified, surging through her. This was wonderfully wicked and exciting. She couldn't get enough of him. Finding a miniscule amount of control, she took his shaft in her hand and imitated his movements. She closed her hand around him and began to pump up and down his length. Involuntarily, his hips swayed against the direction of her hand, adding friction to her movements.

Brennan's moans of excitement encouraged her. She rubbed her hand over the tiny slit, smearing the liquid over the smooth head.

"Brennan!" Krista dug her nails into his shoulders. Her legs trembled uncontrollably as she drew closer to her climax. She felt as if all of her strength had been drained from her. With one final push inside her, he added a second finger and rotated it, sending Krista over the edge as wave after wave of sensation gripped her. She rode out the pleasure as she climaxed.

As the first wave of passion crested, she heard his muffled cry, and the wet release from his flesh filled her hand.

Krista's legs gave out, and she started to sink to the floor. Brennan's arm encircled her waist, and he lifted her against his chest, whispering, "I've got you."

He reached beyond her and picked up a discarded piece of paper from the copy machine. Propping Krista against the machine, he took her hand and wiped away the small amount of liquid in her palm. Balling the paper into a wad, he shoved it inside his trouser pocket. "I'll get rid of this," he promised.

Completely sated, she nodded slowly.

Brennan leaned close and kissed her lips before righting his clothes. "Thank you."

Dazed, Krista tossed the paper towel in the trash basket and stared at her reflection in the mirror. She smoothed her hair into place and then ran a hand over the soft silk fabric of her skirt. The new hairdo and clothes were only a small part of the changes in her life.

That was all well and good, but what about who she was on the inside? Had she changed that much in the last few weeks? Or was it her feelings for Brennan that had made the biggest and most significant change to who she was?

Krista drew in a deep breath and let it out slowly before leaving the ladies' room. She strolled purposefully to her office, opened the door, and moved across the room to her chair. She sank into her chair and swiveled it toward the window, gazing absently at Cobo Hall.

"Brennan," she muttered softly, seeing him in her mind's eye. Her heart raced when she thought of what they'd done in the supply closet. She couldn't believe how hot he'd got her using his fingers while she caressed his hard flesh.

Krista shook her head, trying to wipe the images, sounds, and smells from her mind. Giggling nervously, she couldn't believe she'd done those things with him and within close proximity to the people they worked with. She ran her hands up and down her arms, still feeling her skin tingle from Brennan's touch, and smelled the heat of their passion as they exploded together. Her hand covered her cheek. Oh my! How would she be able to face him again?

The door opened. Erin Saunders stepped inside the office and shut it after her.

Instantly, Krista's good mood dissolved. The scowl on Erin's face told a story of its own. She was here to cause trouble.

Get yourself together, Krista warned silently. *You know Erin is not here to offer goodwill and cheer.* "Is there something I can help you with?" asked Krista. She paused. "Does Rachel need something from me?"

"No." Erin slithered across the room to the desk. Her eyes narrowed to piercing slits, although her voice remained soft and enticing. "Actually, it's what I can do for you."

"Oh?" *How did I get so lucky? Since when has Erin cared about anything to do with me? She hates the sight of me.*

"Mm-hmm."

Krista waited. Erin had something special in mind.

"I don't want you to make a terrible mistake."

Surprised, Krista blinked several times. "How so?"

"I saw you and Brennan leave the supply closet a little while ago."

Instantly, Krista flushed to her hairline. Her hand fluttered around the neck of her top. *Stay calm,* she warned.

Satisfaction gleamed from Erin's eyes.

"And that means what?" Krista swiveled the chair to face the other woman.

"Anyone with eyes can tell that you like him a lot. You probably think you're in love with him."

"And if I am?"

"I know you remember Paul and how that turned out. I don't want to see that happen to you again."

Krista's hackles rose the instant Erin mentioned Paul's name. Ready to send Erin packing, Krista paused, mentally calming herself and studying the situation from an analytical angle. She'd suffered so much at Paul's hands, and Erin had been around to see everything, including how broken up Krista had been once Paul revealed how he'd used her. Why would Erin want to help her?

Brennan and Paul were two very different men. No, that wasn't right. Paul had been a boy, pretending to be a man. Brennan was a man who loved and wanted the best for her.

"Aren't you sweet," Krista muttered sarcastically.

Erin ignored the biting remark and took the chair facing Krista. "There's something you need to know before you make a complete fool of yourself."

"No thank you. Whatever it is, I don't want to know."

"It involves Brennan," Erin taunted softly.

Panic rose in Krista. Had she taken a peek inside the supply closet while they were too busy to notice? Did she know what they had been doing? Or was the other woman guessing? Erin was fishing for answers by insinuating she knew something that she didn't. Maybe she should hear Erin out, learn what she knew, and then talk to Brennan about it.

"Oh?"

"To be more accurate, this includes Flynn Parr and Brennan."

Flynn Parr? Krista leaned back in her chair, offering the other woman a relaxed pose. At the same time, her insides practically cried out for Erin to say what she wanted to say and then get the heck out of her office.

If Flynn Parr was involved, this could involve the Gautier account. Anything to do with that account interested Krista. She leaned back farther in her chair, striking an indulgent pose. "You've got my attention. What's this all about?"

"Remember the picnic?"

Embarrassed, Krista blinked as her hand fluttered over the keyboard. She wished she could forget it. As usual, she'd made a fool of herself. Nodding slowly, she waited to hear more.

"After you left, Brennan and Flynn had a nice little talk about you."

Why would they talk about her, and together at that? They barely spoke to each other when they were in the same room. Yet, she'd seen Flynn leave Brennan's office this morning when she got off the elevator. "Why would they talk in front of you?"

"They didn't. I was close enough to hear everything they said."

"In other words, you were eavesdropping."

Erin shrugged. She didn't deny the accusation or appear ashamed. Instead, she bulldozed her way to what she wanted to say. "You were the topic of discussion. They were laughing at all the stupid things you do. Flynn kept talking about the crazy ponytails at the back of your head. Brennan commented on your clothes. And then he asked why anyone would wear a skirt to a picnic. I think it was Flynn that said someone needed to help you. They talked about ways. Flynn said you were a hopeless loser who would always be out of step with everybody else."

Shocked, Krista sat still in her chair. This wasn't happening to her.

Warming to her topic, Erin got more comfortable in her chair and added, "Brennan said maybe we should get you on one of those guerilla makeover shows and see if they could do something with you. Fix you. Work with you. That sparked the bet, and Flynn bet Brennan a lot of money to see if he could redo you."

Pain shot through Krista. No! She refused to believe it. Not again. Not after Paul.

Tears burned Krista's eyes. But she refused to let them fall in front of Erin. She wouldn't allow this malicious bitch to humiliate her. There was still one question that needed to be answered. "Why are you being so good to me?"

"I remember Paul. You were so lost after everything fell apart. We can't afford to lose the Gautier account, and you are a big part of that."

This little tattletale session has nothing to do with me and everything to do with showing me that she has the edge, that she knows what is going on around Dexter Kee. She just wants to cause trouble while looking good. Krista drew in a deep breath and stood, moving around the desk to where Erin sat. She led Erin to the door and shut it after her.

Completely dazed for a different reason, Krista returned to her desk and fell into her chair. Face in her hands, she sat, trying to determine the truth of what Erin had just revealed.

Had she been betrayed a second time? The thought of it sent chills down her spine. If so, Brennan had the ability to strip her bare emotionally.

This hurt so much more than when Paul lied to her. Although she had thought she loved Paul, those childish feelings were nothing compared to how she felt for Brennan. And for the second time in her life, a man had used her feelings against her.

It couldn't be true. It just couldn't be. She was older and understood people better. Besides, Brennan had told her that he loved her. Would he go to those extremes to win a bet?

One thing she knew for sure. She needed to talk with him, learn the truth, and then go to Erin and set her straight. Put the troublemaker out of her life before she did any more damage.

Chapter 26

Krista made it her business to avoid Brennan the rest of the day. Confused, she needed time to think, evaluate the situation, and come to a decision on what course of action to take.

Vehemently praying that Erin had been wrong and that Erin's motivation was the desire to hurt her, Krista refused to think that Brennan would treat her so shabbily.

They had built their relationship on love, respect, and trust. Brennan would never do anything to jeopardize what they shared. He wasn't anything like Paul.

But, if he'd agreed to take part in the bet, his sister was involved. Liz hadn't just fallen into Krista's life by accident. They must have planned it.

Her stomach clenched into knots. She felt as if she might throw up at any moment. Fighting back tears, she wondered, *Why do these things keep happening to me?* For the second time in her life, supposed friends had stuck a knife in her heart. She believed she had outgrown the childish games and backstabbing. Apparently, she had been wrong.

Krista fought back tears. Her head throbbed.

When the day ended, she hurried from the office and out of the building to her car. With a sigh of relief, she started the engine and left the parking lot. She'd gotten away without dealing with Brennan. Maybe by tomorrow, she'd have everything sorted out and could confront him with Erin's lies.

As she exited the Lodge Freeway, she turned left onto Clairmont Street and drove several blocks before reaching Woodrow Wilson. She turned right, feeling a sense of peace as the frustration and pain from the day oozed from her body.

Krista zipped into the parking space in front of the house and frowned. Why was a brown and yellow realtor's sign mounted in the center of the lawn?

This must be a mistake, she thought, examining the houses in the immediate area. Maybe the realtor had placed the sign on the wrong lawn.

Before leaving the house this morning, she'd spoken with her auntie. The old girl hadn't said anything about wanting to leave her place. How did she plan to sell without making the house look presentable? Heck, Aunt Helen couldn't bear to go into Uncle Nick's apartment. Besides, her aunt would never put the house on the market without talking the decision over with Krista.

Well, the only way I'm going to find out is to go in the house and talk with my auntie. She got out of the car, rushed up the drive to the side door, turned the knob, and pushed. This time the door didn't budge. Surprised, Krista gave the door a second nudge but received the same results.

Krista's eyebrows rose to her hairline. "Wow!" She removed her keys from her purse, then unlocked and opened the door. When she stepped onto the landing, she heard Whitney Houston's strong gospel voice coming upstairs from the basement apartment.

For a minute, she panicked. Who in the world would be in the basement? As she turned to leave, she heard, "Krista?"

"Aunt Helen?"

The old girl appeared at the bottom of the stairs, with Uncle Nick's robe tossed over her arm. "Who else would it be?"

Curious, Krista moved down the stairs to see what Auntie was doing. Open cardboard boxes covered the floor of Uncle Nick's apartment. Aunt Helen dodged them as she made her way out of the living room. Minutes later, she strolled out of the bedroom, with an armload of Uncle Nick's clothing. She dumped the shirts, trousers, and ties on the sofa and then started to fold the items, placing them in separately marked boxes.

Stunned, Krista silently watched her aunt before asking, "What are you doing?"

The old girl gazed up while continuing her work. "What does it look like I'm doing?"

Krista picked up one of the shirts. "These are Uncle Nick's clothes."

"I know."

"What are you doing with them?" Krista asked, tossing the garments over the back of the sofa, clearing a place for her to sit down.

"It's time to start getting this place in order."

Krista's heart began to race. This couldn't be what she thought. Aunt Helen had finally decided to clear out the basement apartment. Why? And, more importantly, why now?

"For what?"

The older woman dropped the shirt in her hands in her lap and gazed around the dimly lit room before turning to her niece. Krista saw tears swimming in her auntie's eyes. "Nick and your mother are gone."

Krista reached across the pile of clothes and squeezed her aunt's hand reassuringly. "I know."

"Denying it don't make it different. It's time for me to make my peace with the past and move to the next point in my life."

"How are you planning to do that?"

"First thing I'm going to do is clean out this apartment."

Krista cleared her throat and fidgeted with a lock of hair before asking, "Is that why there's a For Sale sign on the lawn?"

"Partly."

"Tell me about the rest."

"You're grown. I can't hold you back anymore. If Nick and me did our job right, you'll be fine. We put everything in you that you need to make it in this world." Aunt Helen muttered a second time. "Do just fine."

"So you're selling your home because I'll be just fine?"

"No. That's not the only reason. This house is too big for one person, and before you say anything else, I know you live here, too," she hastened to add, reaching across the sofa to gently stroke Krista's cheek. "But not for long if everything you said to me is true. Soon enough you'll be heading on to your life and not playing on the edges of mine."

Krista rubbed her hand across her forehead. She wished that were true. And that her life included Brennan and his family. A big question mark hung over her head regarding that issue. There were several issues that needed to be cleared up before she could say her life was headed in a new and exciting direction. But she didn't plan to tell her aunt. "You don't have to move because of me."

"Yes, I do. But not just because of you. This house is too much for me. I'm going to one of those senior places."

"Auntie, you'll hate that."

"Not if it's part of the church," Auntie reasoned.

True. Their church had recently built a senior facility.

"Don't you have to go on a waiting list for that kind of place?"

"Normally, yes." Auntie gave Krista a secret smile. "But I've got clout. There's a place in Redford Township coming up real soon, and I plan to make that move as soon as it's ready."

"And the house?"

"The realtor said a lot of young folks are moving back into this area. She thinks I can sell really quick. I hope she's right."

Krista couldn't quite wrap her mind around her aunt's quick decision to move. The life she'd always known was changing faster than she was able to keep up with.

"What's going on with you?" Auntie asked.

"How do you know something's wrong?"

The old girl laughed. Her shoulders shook. "I raised you. I know a lot of stuff. Baby, you've never been able to keep things from me. So, come on. Tell me what's going on."

Krista bit her lip, debating how much she should tell her aunt. "I heard something today that could change everything."

"Like what?" Auntie asked, leaning into the sofa.

"One of the women at work told me something about Brennan that could end our relationship."

"Hmm."

Krista hated it when Auntie did that. No answer, just a grunt.

"Did you ask him?"

"No," Krista answered.

"Hmm."

"What do you think?"

Auntie reached for a gray cardigan sweater and folded it. "I think you've condemned the man without a trial."

"How can you say that?"

"Easy." She ticked off items on her fingers. "First, you don't know if this woman is telling the truth. You need to ask this man and hear it from his lips. All you doin' is worrying yourself. Who is this woman, anyway?"

Krista rubbed her forehead. How much did she want to tell her auntie? Would she understand all the stress and pain she went through at work? "Someone I work with."

"And how does she know things?"

"How come you're not asking what Erin said?" Krista asked.

"It's not my business. Besides, you're grown. You got to make your own decisions."

Krista folded her arms across her chest and said, "Right. But you always want to add your two cents."

"It's not for me to tell you what to do. You know what's right and what you truly want to do. But here's my take on things. If somebody told me something about a person I care about, I'd question the source. Go to the man and talk with him. Tell him what the girl said and ask him up front what he knows."

"What if it's true? How do I handle that?"

Auntie shrugged. "I don't know. That's for you to make up your mind. But you can't get anywhere until you know the truth, whether it's good or bad." She pointed a finger at Krista. "You've got to know."

Chapter 27

After a sleepless night, Krista rose from the bed when the alarm clock went off. She went through her morning routine of making her bed, showering, and getting dressed. Once those tasks were completed, she made her way to the kitchen.

She stood in front of the sink, gazing out the window. The thought of food twisted her gut into knots. Krista opted for the soothing effects of a cup of green tea before saying good-bye to her auntie and heading out the door to work. With little enthusiasm for the day, she climbed into the Caprice and headed for downtown Detroit.

This was a critical day in her relationship with Brennan. His answers to her questions would either cement their relationship or end it for all times.

After parking the car at Cobo Hall, she strolled across the street to the Roney & Company building and slowly approached the elevators. Her anxiety increased with each step.

I have to talk to Brennan, she sang over and over in her head the entire way to work.

Heart pounding, Krista checked out the people in the elevator, certain they could hear it. *I'm scared,* she admitted silently, automatically stepping off the elevator and into the salesmen's bull pen when the doors opened.

Erin's words echoed in her head. "Flynn and Brennan bet Brennan could change you from a geek to a lady." Erin's laughter was tinged with malice. "I must say he did a pretty good job."

Why was this happening to her? For the first time in her life, she had all the things she'd every dreamed of and never expected to have: a loving man, good friends, and a chance at happiness.

It looked as if her happiness was built on a deck of cards that might come tumbling down if a strong wind whipped up. But that wasn't all. Unfortunately, Krista's professional and personal life were intertwined with Brennan's. Her best friend, Liz, and her job had all come about because of her relationship with Brennan.

Everything rode on this conversation. Lord knows, she didn't have a great track record when it came to men and relationships. If she screwed it up, she could lose not only Brennan, but Liz and Joshua, too.

But they couldn't maintain a relationship built on lies. She needed to know the truth.

Taking in a deep, shaky breath, she let it out slowly. *I can do this,* she chanted too low for anyone to hear while navigating her way through the maze of cubicles to her office.

What if Brennan did agree to the bet? How did she intend to handle that?

As she passed his office, she saw Brennan behind his desk, working his way through a pile of reports. Krista wished he'd open his arms and she could run into his embrace. She wished he would hold her and tell her he loved her and that he'd never allow anything or anyone to hurt her. None of that happened. Brennan failed to see her as he made notes on a white pad.

With a heavy heart, Krista continued to her office, unlocked the door, and stepped inside. All morning she'd fought the urge to cry. She leaned against the wood frame of the door, fighting for control. After a minute of self-pity, she regrouped and crossed the floor, dropping her briefcase in a chair and placing her purse in the desk drawer. Smoothing her hair into place, Krista straightened her skirt before leaving her office. Seconds later, she tapped on Brennan's door.

"Come in," he called.

She opened the door and stepped inside.

Brennan looked up. A warm smile of welcome spread across his face. She responded by returning his smile.

Standing, he crossed the room and took her hand. "Hey," he muttered in a husky tone that touched every nerve ending inside her.

She shook off those sensations and slipped into the guest chair.

Puzzled, he returned to his desk. "I called you a couple of times last night. I put a few fillets of salmon on the grill, and Liz and I wanted to invite you to dinner. All I got was your voice mail."

"I was helping my aunt."

"Oh?"

Krista fidgeted with the hem of her blouse. "She's decided to put her house on the market."

Surprised, he raised his brows, and he leaned toward her. "Really? What does that mean for you?"

"I'm going to have to find myself a place to live." She placed a hand on the desk, nervously rubbing the smooth, cool surface.

"There may be other options," he declared.

Krista shrugged. "Maybe."

Brennan leaned back in his chair and stroked his chin. For a beat, he studied her before asking, "Is everything all right?"

Krista's gut cramped. This was it. "Actually. No."

"What is it?" Concerned, Brennan leaned closer and reached for her hand.

Quickly, she placed her hand in her lap. Her gesture didn't

go unnoticed. When she looked into his eyes, there was a question.

"What's going on? Is there something I can help you with?" said Brennan.

Krista's chest felt as if it would burst. Her resolve weakened when she saw the familiar face of the man she'd learned to love.

Forehead crinkled into a frown, he asked, "How can I help?"

Krista fingered a lock of hair, thinking, *You can't hide. It's time for the truth.* "Yesterday, Erin Saunders came by my office."

"And?" he asked softly.

"She was being Erin, talking a lot of crap. But she did say one thing that bothered me, and I wanted to ask you about it."

Nodding, he responded, "Okay."

"Did you make a bet with Flynn Parr about me?" There. It was out. She'd asked the question that hadn't allowed her to sleep last night. *Please let him tell me no.* That Erin was talking trash, trying to cause trouble. She needed to hear him deny Erin's claim.

Silence filled the room. Brennan rubbed a finger up and down his nose. Krista could tell that he was thinking hard and working out an answer, maybe a lie.

"I want the truth," she demanded, fighting the edge of hysteria.

"Yes."

Ice spread through Krista's belly, numbing her. It amazed her how one little word could change your whole life. With a slow nod of her head, Krista rose from the chair and headed for the door.

"Wait!" Brennan leapt from his chair and hurried across the floor, sprinting in front of her to block the entrance.

Stopping in front of him, she gazed into his eyes. Guilt blared back at her. "For what?"

"Let me explain."

"There's nothing to talk about. We've said it all."

He took her arm and tried to lead her back to the desk. For a moment, Krista resisted, before allowing him to push her back into the chair she'd just vacated. "I know this looks bad. But hear me out, please."

"Was Liz in on this, too?"

A red stain crept up his neck and filled his cheeks. She shut her eyes, praying that she could get out of this office without making a complete fool out of herself.

"Yes," he admitted softly.

During the long predawn hours, Krista had considered every angle, including Brennan's possible lies and Liz's involvement in the bet. Although she knew it was a possibility that they had conspired against her, she had held out hope that it was all part of Erin's lie.

"Don't blame Liz. She didn't want to do it," he said.

Anger flared, and Krista shot back, "Then why did she? What did she get out of this?"

Again, that awkward silence filled the room. With deliberate movements, Brennan made his way around the side of the desk and took his seat.

"Well?" she prompted.

Hands flat on the desk top, he remained as silent as night, while the red stain in his cheeks grew even brighter.

Krista laid her hand on the desk and started to rise.

Instantly, Brennan halted her by putting his hand on top of her. "Don't. Let me explain."

Krista returned to her chair. Brennan could explain and talk all he wanted. When she left this office, everything was over between them. "Go ahead. I'm listening."

With a sigh of relief, he returned to his chair. "It all started at the picnic. Once you left, I read those guys the riot act, told them they couldn't keep treating you so badly."

He paused, gathering his thoughts. Krista felt certain he was searching for the best approach to convince her.

"And?"

Brennan waved his hand in the air. "I didn't get anywhere with those jokers. So I told them that I better not catch them mistreating you, and then I started for my car."

"Mm-hmm."

"Flynn Parr caught me before I left the park, and he started talking a lot of crap."

"Such as?" She believed that. Flynn always seemed to be stirring up a mess wherever he went.

"I-I-I." Brennan paused and then continued. "He goaded me into a bet, with a promise to have his people leave you alone."

Krista stared at him. Some of what he'd said made sense. Flynn's salespeople had been outstandingly easy to work with since the company picnic. But she wasn't stupid enough to believe Brennan's motives were all for her benefit.

After a moment, he added, "Plus, he talked about getting the VP job over me, and he flashed a check. I caved. I admit it. And I'm sorry that you had to hear this stuff from Erin. I should have told you."

"Then why didn't you?"

"Because I was afraid you wouldn't be able to see past the bet. We'd lose everything. Truthfully, I was scared that we couldn't get beyond this."

She rose from her chair and started for the door. "Your fears have been realized. We're through."

"No!" Brennan raced across the room to the door. "Stop and think about what you're doing."

Staring at the floor, she stated, "Get out of my way."

He took her hands in his and drew her into his embrace. Normally, her skin tingled and came alive every place he touched her. Not today. She felt alone, cold, and betrayed.

"Krista, think. I know this is far from the perfect situation.

But, if I hadn't agreed to the bet, we wouldn't be together. We'd never have fallen in love. Something good and true came from that awful bet. In a weird way, Parr made us truly look at each other in a different light. Can you see what I'm saying?"

"Yes. I do. Now hear me. We're done."

"Stop being silly." He grinned persuasively, brushing a finger along her jawline. "We love each other."

"Doesn't matter. Truthfully, I've never felt this way about anyone else in my life. But I won't be involved with a man that I can't trust." Krista's voice dropped an octave. "Let go of me."

"Of course, you can trust me. I've never done anything like this before, and I promise it'll never happen again."

"Too little. Too late." Her hand sliced through the air, dismissing his remark. "From now on, this is the way it's going to play out. Until the Gautier account is settled, I'll do the work and finish the presentation. Once they've made their decision, I'm back to IT."

"You don't want to stay in my department? I planned to create a job here for you. Think about it. You won't have to deal with Rachel and her lazy crew."

"Brennan, you're not hearing me. I'll work on the campaign, but there is no us. Unless it involves work, I don't want to hear it."

She put her hand on the doorknob and glared at him. Shocked, he stepped aside and allowed her to wrench open the door and leave. Holding back tears with superhuman strength, Krista hurried to her office and sank heavily into her chair.

Krista felt so empty. She imagined this was the way people felt when they lost a loved one.

Head bowed, eyes closed, Krista fought the urge to scream, toss things around the room, and cry. She stayed that way for several minutes as she struggled to hold back tears.

Why couldn't life be easier, simpler? Like some cruel joke, each and every time she believed she'd found paradise, it was snatched from her.

Enough. She'd allowed herself to be used for the last time. Pulling herself together, Krista decided, no more. She was tired of being hurt by callous men and people who didn't give a damn about her. From now on, she'd concentrate on her career and leave love and relationships to someone who knew what they were doing.

Feeling stronger, she lifted her head and glanced out the door's windowpane. Erin Saunders stood at the administrative assistant's desk. Her gaze was glued on Krista. With a smirk, she waved and sashayed away from the desk.

Something unnatural and ugly rose in Krista. "Bitch!"

Chapter 28

Bone tired and mentally drained, Brennan climbed out of the car and headed for the back door to the town house. This had been a hell of a day, and he was glad to see the end to it. He turned the knob and entered the house.

He reached inside the kitchen and hit the switch. Light filled the room.

Tonight no meal waited for him. No pleasant aromas tickled his taste buds when he stepped into the kitchen. He placed his briefcase next to the door and plucked a glass from the cupboard, filling it from the water dispenser in the refrigerator door.

Brennan took a seat at the kitchen table and finished his water, glancing around the room. He noticed a large pot filled with clean baby bottles. His poor sister had been busy today. Baby bottles, laundry, and taking care of a baby consumed her day. Since Liz had brought Joshua home from the hospital, regular meals had been preempted by baby formula and feedings. It didn't matter. He felt too tired to even make a sandwich.

The faint voices from the television reached his ear, and he followed the male voice until he reached the living room. Liz sat on the sofa, with Joshua in her arms. She hummed softly as she rocked the baby back and forth.

When he entered the room, she glanced up, with a smile on her lips. The smile quickly faded, replaced with a frown. "Hey."

He flopped down next to her and rested his head against the back of the sofa. "Hi. How are you and my little man doing?"

"We've had a day. Mr. Man here has been fussing all day long. When I pick him up, he whines until I put him down. The minute I put him down, then he wants to be picked up. We're going to have to come to an understanding real soon."

Chuckling sadly, Brennan stretched out his legs in front of him. "I think Joshua is going to win. So you better get ready for it."

She looked down lovingly at the baby in her arms. "You're probably right."

Groaning softly, he undid his tie and shut his eyes.

"What's wrong?" Liz asked quietly.

Opening his eyes, Brennan studied his sister. "Krista found out about the bet."

Liz gasped. "Oh my god. No!" She scooted to the end of the sofa and rose, placing her son in the bassinet next to the chair. She returned to her spot next to Brennan. "I was afraid that might happen."

"You did warn me that we could get burned by this."

"Brennan, what happened?" she asked, running her fingers through her short brown hair.

"This woman in the office, Erin Saunders, told Krista about the bet between me and Flynn."

Shaking her head, Liz asked, "How could that be? I thought you and the other guy agreed to keep the bet between yourselves."

"We did."

Frowning, she captured her bottom lip between her teeth. "Do you think Flynn Parr told this Erin Saunders?"

Shutting his eyes, Brennan mentally went back to the day of the picnic and his encounter with Flynn Parr. "No. The day we made the bet, I remember seeing Erin near my car. Truthfully, I didn't pay her much attention and dismissed her at that time.

But she must have heard what we were talking about. The woman is slick. Erin kept the info to herself until she felt the need to use it."

"If she kept things to herself this long, what made her decide to do it now?"

Brennan snorted. "Yesterday she came into my office and hit on me."

"And you?"

"I put her in her place. I'm with Krista. I don't want or need anything Erin has to offer."

"Eww! Woman scorned."

He nodded, running a finger up and down his nose. "Pretty much."

"Now what?" Liz asked.

"I don't know." He shut his eyes against the pain. "I don't know if I can fix this. Krista is so hurt. She's so distant. When I talk to her, I feel like there's nobody there."

"There has to be a way. Do you think I should talk to her? Maybe I can help explain the situation and tell her how much we care about her."

"I don't think she'll listen."

"Krista's always been so sweet. Of course, she'll listen to you. Give her a day or two, and then try again."

"You don't understand. The person who walked into my office today and demanded answers wasn't the gentle woman we know. She's suffered too many times and refuses to listen. Krista was livid, and it was like she'd had enough and refused to allow anyone to hurt her again. I don't know if she'll ever trust me again."

"Big bro, you can fix this," Liz stated, with confidence. "I know you can. All you need to do is think things through and come up with a plan."

Brennan didn't have the heart to tell her that he didn't think there was a way to fix things. The one woman he truly loved was well beyond him at this point. He didn't know what to do next.

Chapter 29

This was it, Brennan thought, pacing back and forth outside the executive boardroom. The day had arrived. Gautier International Motors presentations would be held within the hour. The French executives were in the building and waiting to be dazzled by Dexter Kee ad teams and their presentations.

Breathing hard and fast, Brennan tried to calm his nerves. He ran a hand over his face and tried to focus on the work ahead.

Thirty minutes earlier, he'd seen the Gautier entourage head into Connor Dexter's office for a powwow session with the management team. Once that meeting ended, Brennan and Flynn's presentations would start.

Everything was ready. Brennan had worked his way through a checklist of items, including the computer, LCD projector, and the conference room seating arrangement, more than once. His presentation cards rested in the breast pocket of his suit jacket, while his words of welcome were permanently imprinted in his brain.

So much energy, hard work, and time had gone into this campaign. He wanted everything to go smoothly.

From the doorway to the boardroom, Brennan watched Krista stroll purposefully down the hall toward him. Dressed in a navy business suit that emphasized her petite form in all the right places, she looked beautiful. His gaze dropped lower. The skirt hit mid-thigh, revealing a wonderful length of shapely brown legs and thighs. His flesh leapt to life, straining against the zipper of his trousers.

No geek here. Regal, moving like the queen of Dexter Kee, and in control, Krista approached him.

Brennan swallowed loudly, balling his hands into fists at his sides. He wished he could touch her. Wrap his arms around her and hold her close. Feel the warmth of her skin against his and inhale the enticing fragrance she wore. An added bonus would be a taste of the sweet nectar from her lips.

Frustrated, he looked away. None of that was possible. Not anymore and not after the incident last week.

Since he'd admitted making the bet with Flynn Parr, Krista had withdrawn from him, constructed barriers that separated them. As promised, she had completed every request Brennan made as long as it involved Dexter Kee business and the Gautier account. The moment he shifted their conversation to anything personal, to Liz, or the bet, Krista went blank, shut down, and found an excuse to leave his office as quickly as possible.

He drew in a deep breath and let it out slowly. Liz's encouraging words filled his head. *Krista believed in us, and we destroyed that trust. You've got to find a way to talk to her. Make her listen.*

That was what hurt the most. Krista had always been so open to him. Whenever they'd been in the same room, she'd offered him that beguiling smile that took his breath away.

"Krista still loves you," Liz had insisted. "If she didn't feel anything for you, she could walk by you without a glance in your direction. Her feelings aren't gone. But you did break her heart, and the trust is gone. Now you have to work real hard to earn it back and give Krista a little space and time to recover."

Navy business suit, navy pumps, and laptop in the crook of

her arm, she moved with the grace of a queen. His heart swelled with pride as he watched her.

Krista halted outside the boardroom. She dipped her head in Brennan's direction and glanced past his right shoulder, refusing to make eye contact.

"You ready?" he asked.

"Mm-hmm. What about you?"

Automatically, his hand went to the knot of his tie and tugged. "Nervous. But I can handle it."

"That's all that counts." Krista peeked into the boardroom behind her and then checked the hallway. "Where are the Gautier people?"

"With Connor Dexter," Brennan answered.

Krista ran her tongue across her plum-colored lips, drawing his attention to her lush mouth.

The urge to capture that mouth with his lips made him ache with desire and filled him with loneliness. *Focus, my man, focus. Get your head out of your crotch, and focus on the presentation.*

Brennan cleared his throat and pointed at the computer in Krista's hands. "Do we need your laptop, too? The LCD is connected to the network."

A tiny smile flitted across her face and quickly disappeared. "Not really. But I believe in contingency plans. Besides, I have a few calculations and information that might come in handy."

Longing, deep and all-consuming, coursed through Brennan's veins. He missed her. Not just the physical contact of making love, but Krista, the essence of the woman standing next to him. When was the last time he'd received one of her gentle smiles or experienced a loving expression that made his insides crave more? Those gestures made it a pleasure to work with Krista.

"What kind of information do you have?" He wanted her to think he was all business just as she was.

"More statistical data in case the Gautier people want more details or decide to quiz us about the company." She patted the laptop. "I'll be able to pull up any info that we might need." She stepped into the room and stood inside the door, checking the layout.

"Krista?"

"Yes? I'm going to sit back here. If anything happens where you need me, I'll check it out on the Internet."

"That'll work." Brennan cleared his throat a second time and shoved his hands into his trouser pockets. "When we're done here, I'd like to take you to lunch."

She chose a spot and opened her laptop. "Not necessary."

"We have to talk."

"No, we don't," Krista answered softly, but firmly.

Brennan opened his mouth to add something and was immediately cut off when Connor Dexter stepped inside the boardroom with the Gautier president and senior vice presidents.

With difficulty, Brennan shifted into sales exec mode. With an outstretched hand, he marched across the room. "I'm glad you gentlemen were able to come. We've got an exciting campaign for you."

"We hope so. That's why we're here," Reynolds Gautier said, choosing a chair close to the front of the room.

The complete senior management team for Dexter Kee took seats in the boardroom. Flynn Parr followed.

Brennan waved a hand in Krista's direction. "Krista Hamilton and I worked exclusively on this project for the past several months."

She stood and nodded at the group of people before returning to her seat.

Everyone refocused on Brennan. "The Internet is a powerful tool that we would like to use in your campaign. It has the ability to reach more prospective buyers than television."

Brennan picked up the tiny remote and switched on the LCD projector. Using a laser pointer, he brought the group's attention to the screen. "What we are proposing is a simultaneous Internet and media presentation that will hit our target market in the two biggest mediums available."

He clicked the remote, and the images changed. A series of three-dimensional charts with legends appeared. "Ms. Hamilton did intensive research on who was most likely to buy Gautier cars. We learned that upwardly mobile professionals hit your Web site three times more often than any other group. So we decided to make that group our target market."

Mr. Gautier nodded.

"As you can see from this chart, we've collected extensive data and have studied your Web site and 2005–2006 sales. Ms. Hamilton, my team, and I have tracked the demographic information. From everything we've learned, this target group analyzes a great deal of information from your Web site. We decided to center the campaign on Gautier's three high-end concept vehicles."

Brennan continued the presentation with a description of their concept for the automaker. The idea of a simultaneous promotion that would include the Web site, all search engines, television, and movie theaters seemed to appeal to everyone.

The presentation moved smoothly until Flynn Parr raised his hand. "Excuse me."

Brennan faced his coworker. "Yes?"

"Everything you've said so far sounds wonderful on paper, but we need a few reality checks here."

"In what way?" replied Brennan.

Flynn stood, pushing his chair away from the table, then moved to the front of the room. "You've shown us statistics on a small portion of the market. Gautier makes fifteen other automotive products." Flynn pointed at the chart on the screen. "What about those vehicles?"

Instantly, Brennan knew what Flynn was doing. Before Brennan had a chance to counter Flynn's remarks, Mr. Gautier spoke up. "That's a good point. What about buyers who

can't afford the three products you're targeting? Is there anything for them?"

With a smirk on his face, Flynn returned to his seat. As he
passed Mr. Gautier, Flynn gave him a pat on the shoulder.
"Good point. In all that information you've gathered, do you
have any data on other income groups?"

Thinking fast, Brennan opened his mouth to rattle off some
statistical data that he hoped would satisfy the French automaker until he could plug up this hole in his presentation.
Not one word had left his lips when he noticed Krista. She
rose from her chair and made her way around the large conference table to the front of the room.

Smiling confidently at the people surrounding the table,
she said, "Mr. Gautier, I've also worked up several scenarios
for a variety of incomes." She removed the remote and laser
pointer from Brennan's hands and clicked back to the series
of charts. "Mr. Parr was absolutely correct when he said there
should be something for everyone. And, in that vein, we
didn't forget anyone."

Smoothly stepping into the spotlight, she continued. "If you
take a closer look at the items on levels two and three of this
chart, you'll notice we've completed a series of projections for
all of the Gautier line of cars. These groups were broken down
into income levels and the price of each car. The campaigns
would be similar. The only difference will be in how the information is disseminated. Also, the same information is available for you to look at in the packages in front of you."

Mr. Gautier leaned closer, squinting at the projection
screen.

Krista pointed a red beam at the figures, explaining what
each level represented. "As you suggested, Mr. Parr, we need
to match the proper cars with the incomes of your buyers. And,
if you look closer, you'll see that we have done exactly that."

Stunned, Flynn stared at Krista. It took everything in Brennan not to laugh. Another part of him was so proud of her.

She'd come through when he needed her and shown everyone in the room what a well-organized professional she was. Brennan's chest filled with love and pride at how well she'd presented the information.

"If there aren't any additional questions, I'll turn the presentation back over to Mr. Thomas and he can continue," said Krista.

Bowing her head a fraction, Krista handed the remote and pointer to Brennan. She returned to her position at the back of the room and quickly slipped into her chair.

Brennan cleared his throat. "Well, now that we've cleared up your questions, let me show you the video we've created. This is just a small example of what we can do for your campaign." He clicked the remote, and a jazzy flute began to play, and a chorus began to sing.

Everything went smooth as silk from that point on. Krista remained at the back of the room, monitoring the situation, adding needed info when required. At the end of the video, Mr. Gautier expressed praise for the thorough way Brennan's team had executed the presentation.

If Brennan didn't receive this contract, it wasn't because they hadn't tried. Everything had gone well, and Krista had made things run smoothly. Brennan would forever be in her debt for all of her hard work. As they filed out of the boardroom, he eased around the people milling around the door and caught Krista's hand. Curiously, she glanced up at Brennan. He squeezed her hand and whispered, "Thank you."

She gave him a tiny generic smile and answered as she walked away, "You're welcome."

"What about lunch later this week?" he asked hopefully.

The smile disappeared. "No th-th-thanks."

Chapter 30

At the conclusion of his presentation, Flynn returned the remote to the pocket next to the LCD projector and glanced around the room. After a moment, Flynn turned his attention exclusively on Mr. Gautier. "Thank you for listening. Are there any questions?"

The automaker rose from his chair and headed to the front of the boardroom, with an outstretched hand. Mr. Gautier pumped Flynn's hand enthusiastically. "Good job! Good job!"

Flashing each and every tooth in his head, Flynn grinned back at the Frenchman. "Thank you. I'm looking forward to working with you and your team on your transition to the U.S. market."

Flynn's gaze skipped over the older man's head, and along the conference table, to where Brennan and Krista sat side by side. Flynn winked and grinned broadly at them. Anger boiled inside Krista. He was still a jerk.

Parr thinks he's bagged the account and the position as vice president of marketing. It's not over until it's over, she thought, watching Reynolds Gautier gush over Flynn.

Mumbling among themselves, the Gautier entourage rose from their chairs and filed out of the room. They milled around in the hall outside the boardroom.

Connor Dexter cleared his throat, getting everyone's attention. "Those were wonderful presentations. I've made reservations at Coach Insignia, in the GM Renaissance Center." He waved a hand toward the end of the hall. "If you will take the elevator to the lobby and head out the Jefferson Avenue doors, you'll see several black limos parked at the curb."

Lunch! I'm not doing that! Panicking, Krista immediately rejected the idea of eating with the bigwigs. What if she knocked over her water glass or dropped food on her clothes. She couldn't sit for any length of time and converse with other people. No! Krista had created enough embarrassing moments to last several lifetimes. No more.

Still as night, Krista stepped back, trying to blend into the dark, wood-paneled walls. If she could wait until most of the people started for the elevator, she could slip away unnoticed. As their voices drifted off, Krista started down the hall in the opposite direction, intent on taking the stairs to her floor.

"Krista," Connor Dexter called, placing a gentle, but firm hand on her shoulder.

"Yes?" said Krista.

"You're included in this group," said Connor Dexter.

Trapped like a rat, she faced the agency president. "I'm going for my purse, and I'll meet everyone in the lobby."

"You don't need your purse. This meal is on me."

She smiled. "I'm a girl. I always need my purse. I'll be right down."

Mr. Dexter wagged a finger in the air, warning, "Don't let me have to come after you."

"I won't," Krista promised, hurrying toward the exit. She pushed open the door and rushed down the stairs to her office. After grabbing her purse, she caught an elevator to the first floor and went out the doors to the waiting limos.

At lunch, Krista found herself seated between Flynn Parr and Mr. Gautier. At first, Flynn dominated the conversation, speaking directly to the automaker while ignoring her. Cars, sales, and Detroit sites dominated the table discussion at first. When their entrees were served, Flynn excused himself.

After a few awkward moments, Krista and Mr. Gautier found common ground. "Do you have children, Ms. Hamilton?" asked Mr. Gauthier.

"N-n-no. And p-pl-please call me Krista."

He nodded. "That's a lovely name."

Definitely a charmer, she thought. "Thank you. Why do you ask about kids?"

He reached for his wallet and removed a photo, displaying Michelle Gautier and five children of different ages. "My wife and I are still debating where to live, and I wondered what community you think has the best schools."

Krista handed the photo to him, stammering, "Th-th-that's a h-ha-handsome group." She stopped and let out a hot puff of air, gathering her thoughts so that she didn't sound like the town idiot. *This is not the way you want to spend the rest of your life. So get it together.* She ran her tongue across her dry lips and tried again. "If you plan to stay in the tri-county area, there are several communities you should check out."

There. That was easier than she'd expected. *Take your time. You can do this.*

With a glass of wine in his hand, Mr. Gautier said, "Tell me more."

Mr. Gautier's request opened the door to a wonderful debate on the different communities and talk about school districts. For the balance of the lunch, they got to know each other by exchanging ideas about housing, raising children, and child-friendly locations.

At the end of their meal, Mr. Gautier excused himself. Krista swallowed the last of her water, took her napkin from her lap, and placed it on the table. That's when she noticed the white spot on her navy skirt. The blood pounded in her temples. She'd done it again, made a mess.

Calm down, she cautioned silently. *You don't want anyone to see this.* She studied the group for a beat, noting that everyone was engaged in conversation with others at the table. This gave her an opportunity to use her finger to determine what the small dot was. It was a drop of Swiss cheese from her French onion soup. Krista plucked the cheese off the fabric and placed it on the napkin. That still left a very ugly spot in the center of her skirt.

Think, Krista. Think. She rubbed a hand across her forehead. When this happened at Southern Fires, Liz had handed Krista a moist towelette under the table. Did she have one with her? Krista opened her purse and searched its contents. Her breath quickened as her cheeks became warm. *There it is,* she thought. Stuck under her comb and wallet was a white, square packet.

Beneath the table and in her lap, she tore open the packet and removed the damp sheet, dabbing the spot on her skirt. Several seconds later the spot disappeared. Although the towelette had created a wet spot, it wasn't large enough to draw a great deal of attention. For once she'd solved her own problem without making a bigger mess.

Satisfied, she folded the little towelette into a tiny square and returned it to the wrapper. Maybe she wasn't the most graceful woman, but she had learned how to clean up her own messes without making a fool out of herself.

By the time they reached the office, the spot was almost invisible. Brennan, Flynn, and Krista rode the elevator to their floors with Connor Dexter. He halted all three professionals before they stepped out of the elevator.

Holding the elevator open as he spoke, Mr. Dexter said, "You guys did bang-up jobs, and I'm really proud of you. Thank you for giving Gautier a great view of our agency."

Brennan and Krista picked up their messages at the administrative assistant's desk. Krista sifted through the pink scraps of paper and then turned toward her office.

Brennan touched her arm. Her skin tingled where his hand rested on her arm.

"I want to thank you for all your work. You saved the presentation when I lost it," he said, smiling gently.

"You're welcome," she answered.

Flynn slithered up to Krista as she opened the door to her office. "Congratulations. You really impressed the little Frenchman," he said.

"You mean Mr. Gautier?" asked Krista. She didn't like the way he described this pleasant person.

"Yeah. Whatever."

Nodding, she stepped into her office and started to close the door. Flynn slipped in behind her. As she moved past him, Flynn wrapped his hand around her arm. His voice dropped seductively. "What do you say you and I go out after work and get a drink to celebrate?"

"No, thank you." She pulled her arm, but he refused to let it go. "Excuse me. I've got work to do."

Flynn's gaze slid from her face and settled on her breasts. His expression grew heated and hungry.

Uncomfortable, Krista took a step away.

His beer breath fanned her face. "You know, you're looking really hot these days."

"Thank you," she said.

I keep saying that when what I really want Flynn to do is leave. Give me some peace so that I can relax and get back to work. When is he going to get the hint that I don't want him here?

"You should let me take you out," said Flynn.

"No." Krista shook off his hand and hurried across the room to her desk. "I don't date coworkers."

"Since when?"

Who did he think he was? "I beg your pardon?" she asked, with a hint of anger in her tone.

Flynn followed her across the floor and halted on the

opposite side of the desk. The scowl on his face made her nervous. "What do you call what you and Brennan Thomas are doing?"

"None of your business," Krista answered quickly. "If you'll excuse me. I have work to finish."

"With good old Brennan. Am I right? You know he was in on the bet. He agreed to it and then asked if he could have his sister work with him," Flynn taunted.

Logically, Krista knew Brennan would have needed help to transform her. But hearing Flynn admit to it with such glee twisted a knife into her heart. Pride kept her from showing any crack in her armor. Not this time. She was tired of people using her as their personal punching bag.

"I've tried to be nice. I don't think you deserve it. Number one, I wouldn't go out with you under any circumstances. You laughed and then made a bet against me. In my mind, that puts you on the low end of the food chain."

He raised his hands and spread them wide. "That was all a mistake. We weren't trying to hurt you."

Folding her arms across her chest, Krista stated, "Well, you did. I really don't care what you were trying to do. You made me look like a fool."

"Nah, honey. You've been doing that all on your own."

She stepped around the desk and got in his face. "Maybe in the past that was true, but not anymore. I don't play those games. Trust me." Her eyes skated over his lean frame, and her voice grew chilly. "I don't see anything special about you that would make me change my opinion enough to deal with you on anything that doesn't involve this job. I think we've said everything that needs to be said. Leave."

Flynn strolled to the door. With a hand on the doorknob, he turned to her. "Remember one thing. If I get this contract, I'm going to ask old man Dexter to assign you to my team. What are you going to do then?"

"When that time comes, I deal with it and you. Until that happens, stay out of my face."

"We'll see. Take care, Krista wolf," Flynn stated, shutting the door after him.

Krista gasped. How did he know about that? Erin. That was the only person that knew about the name the kids used to call her in high school.

Breathing hard, she dropped into her chair, covering her face with her hands. Would this torture never end? This situation was impossible. She didn't know how long she'd be able to keep this up. Brennan and now Flynn. They both knew too much about her and the way she'd changed since starting this job.

Chapter 31

Krista walked up to Brennan's door and raised her hand to knock. She halted. What was she doing? Did she really want to talk with him?

She pursed her lips as she considered her options. She rolled the vacation request form in her hand into a cylinder. She didn't want to bother Brennan. Nor did she want to have to spend time alone with him. Lately, every topic led them back to their relationship and problems.

Shaking her head, she turned away. *I'll call in sick. The only person I'll have to talk to is his assistant,* Krista decided, backing away from his door. Mere feet from her office, she stopped a second time. Calling in sick defeated the purpose of having vacation time. She'd accumulated a lot of leave, and if she didn't use some of it, she'd lose it. Besides, there were errands to run and things that needed her attention. A little time to apartment hunt and pick up her new car were high on her priority list. There weren't enough hours in the day to complete everything. She needed tomorrow morning off.

Stop wimping out. You have to deal with Brennan until Gautier makes a decision, and maybe even longer if they decide to go with Brennan's campaign approach. You're supposed to be a new woman, with more confidence and in control of your life. Get on with things. With her heart pumping erratically, she knocked on his door.

"Come in," Brennan called.

Krista entered the room. Brennan sat at his desk, with his back to the door, gazing out the window at the Detroit River. Taking a deep breath and letting it out slowly, she crossed the carpeted floor and stood on the opposite side of the desk.

With a heavy sigh, Brennan swiveled the chair in her direction and halted. Surprised, he opened his eyes wide before concealing his expression behind a façade of faint curiosity. But not before she saw the hot flame of desire leap to life.

Her body involuntarily reacted to that gleam in his eyes. The sound of his voice made her go weak at the knees, and Krista got a mental picture of them together. *Come on, girl. You're through with him. Brennan lied and used you. Let it go.*

Brennan stood, smoothing his tie into place. "Good morning," he muttered in the whiskey honey voice that surged through her like blood in her veins and touched every nerve ending in her body.

She responded softly, fidgeting with the form in her hands. "Good morning."

"What can I do for you?"

"Vacation. I need some time off."

Brennan held out his hand, and she gave him the form. He glanced at it before asking, "Doing anything special?"

"No."

Nodding, he opened his desk drawer and removed a pen. Going over the form, he signed the bottom and peeled off the top copy before handing her the rest.

Krista offered him a vacant smile. "Thank you."

"You're welcome."

Almost out of here without an incident, she thought as she turned the doorknob.

"Krista?"

She faced him. "Yes?"

Etched deep into his face was a different emotion, a combination of pain and tiredness that generally came from lack of sleep and worry. "Is this how things are going to be between us from now on?"

"I don't know what you mean," she answered. *Yeah, I know exactly what you mean, but I'm not going to acknowledge it.*

"Yes, you do."

"I'll be in around one tomorrow. Thanks for letting me have the time off."

"What if we get the contract? How are we going to work together then? You won't be able to ignore me."

"I'll deal with that when I have to. Have a good day."

"I didn't mean to hurt you," he continued, moving around the desk to catch her before she could escape.

For a moment, Brennan's physical presence overwhelmed her. His subtle scent wafted under her nose, bringing back memories of the times they had made love. Krista swayed unsteadily on her feet. Images of the tender way he'd held her and made her feel as if she was the most precious and loved woman in the world besieged her.

Krista pushed those thoughts out of her head and snapped her armor in place. "But it happened, anyway." She refused to look at him, focusing instead on the carpeting.

The sharp edge of pain and humiliation gripped her once more. Here stood the one person she had believed would never hurt her and who loved her. God, had she been a fool. Brennan had exploited her failings and laughed at her like everyone else. Krista was so tired of being the joke for everyone. She just wanted all of it to go away and to find a way to make the pain stop.

He took her hand between both of his. "Please listen. Let me explain. It's not the way you think."

Anger sprang to life inside her. "Then how was it? How did you e-en-end up making a b-be-bet about me?"

"It all started because of the park incident this summer. Remember, you fell in the lake that day?"

Krista grunted, jerking her hand away from him. How could she forget? That incident sat way up there on her embarrassment meter. The whole staff had been there, including the management team, and as usual, she had been the source of amusement, entertainment, and gossip for the employees of Dexter Kee.

"After you left, I read the riot act to the sales staff," said Brennan. "It didn't make any difference. They were just as stupid as ever."

She folded her arms across her chest and glared at him, without comment. It felt as if the weight of the world sat on her shoulders. *I'm so tired of going over the same territory.*

"When I walked away, Flynn Parr followed me and challenged me. He said if I cared so much about you, I should help you. But I didn't go along with the idea until Parr promised to have his staff back off you. For me, that made it worthwhile. So I agreed."

Disbelief fueled her next words. Her head shot up. Disgust and anger made her voice harsh. "Let me g-ge-get this s-st-straight. You did it to protect me? Am I right?"

"Yes. It's the truth. Think back. How did they treat you before the picnic, and what was different afterwards?"

Mentally, she did a quick evaluation of how Flynn's team had acted for the past two months. They had been less aggressive and easier to work with. But Krista refused to acknowledge his comment just yet.

Krista opened her mouth, but the words were cut off by a rap on the door. Instantly, Brennan took a step away.

Connor Dexter opened the door, filling the entrance. His eagle gaze rested on Brennan and then on Krista. He must have felt the tension in the room, because his eyebrows rose fractionally. "Good. You two are together. I have news."

Instantly, Brennan went stiff at Krista's side. He took in a deep breath and let it out slowly. "Come on in," he said.

The trio moved to the desk. Mr. Dexter and Krista took the guest chairs, while Brennan circled the desk and took his place. "So what's your news?" Brennan asked.

"Mr. Gautier has chosen a campaign," replied Mr. Dexter.

Krista's heart nearly skipped a beat. Mr. Gautier had made a decision.

Nodding, Brennan maintained a calm exterior, although under the cover of the desk, Krista noticed his hand tugging on the end of his tie.

Mr. Dexter scratched the side of his head. "They loved both campaigns. But yours touched them. Congratulations. Your team will head up the launch of Gautier International Motors in the United States."

Grinning, Brennan stood and grabbed Mr. Dexter's hand, shaking it enthusiastically. "That's great!"

Both men returned to their seats. Mr. Dexter propped an ankle over the knee of his other leg. "So. This means that we'll need you guys to shift into high gear. Krista, I understand you worked up more statistical data. I'd like to see that as soon as possible. Reynolds wants everything you suggested. Plus, the same computer and television programs for the moderate-priced vehicles."

Brennan nodded. "We can do that."

Tossing his hands wide, Mr. Dexter added, "Before you start any of that stuff, take a vacation. Give yourselves a few days and relax. I know you both have been working nonstop since Gautier approached us. I don't want to burn you out before we actually get started."

"That's a good idea. Thank you," Krista said.

"Connor?" said Brennan.

"Yes?" replied Mr. Dexter.

"Does that mean Krista will be permanently assigned to my team?"

Grinning, Mr. Dexter answered, "Absolutely!" He turned to the woman. "Krista, I think you've found your niche."

Mr. Dexter rose from the chair and headed for the door. He paused, with a hand on the doorknob. "I'm proud of you both. You put Dexter Kee on the map in the way I've always wanted. Thank you for that."

He stepped out of the office but returned seconds later. "Oh! By the way, this is your heads-up on the situation. Although this is far from a formal announcement, you'll be meeting with me and the rest of the management team to discuss your promotion to vice president of marketing, Brennan. Have a good day." Mr. Dexter shut the door and strolled off.

With a whoop of elation, Brennan gathered Krista in his arms and swung her in a wide circle. Without thinking, she wrapped her arms around him and hugged him back. He stopped, allowing her body to slide along his until her feet reached the floor. By the time her feet touched the floor, her body cried out to make love with him one more time.

He cupped her face between his hands and leaned close, nibbling on her lips. Unable to resist, Krista followed his lead, savoring the gentle touches. The tempo of his kiss changed, and he devoured her. After long minutes, he lifted his head and leaned his forehead against hers, whispering, "I love you."

Reality returned with a bang. She dragged her face away from him. "No! This isn't right."

He chuckled, planting sweet, tender kisses on her eyelids. "This is so right. We belong together."

"No. You and I are done. We can't go back." Krista stepped away from everything she craved and desperately wanted.

Brennan tried to take her into his arms. "We can get through this. Think about it. Do you want to spend the rest of your life alone?"

Her body stiffened. Heat burned her cheeks as she fought back tears. She was so tired of the complete sorry mess. She'd opened herself up to Brennan and allowed him to see her pain, believing he understood her plight. Brennan had betrayed her in the same way Paul had. There was a major difference: Brennan's betrayal hurt more because she truly loved him. Paul had been an infatuation who faded from her thoughts as quickly as snow melted in the summer.

"Give me a chance to make it up to you. I promise you won't regret it," said Brennan.

I need to get out of here, she thought. *I love him too much, and if I stay, I'll agree to just about anything.*

"No." Krista reached for the doorknob. "It's over. I can't trust you. It's time to move on. Let it go." She slipped out of the office before he could stop her.

Physically shaken and in need of privacy, Krista hurried to her office. She sat at her desk, staring blindly out the window. This situation could not continue. They had to find some common ground to work under. If they didn't, working together would be a thing of the past.

Chapter 32

Thrilled, Krista drew in a deep breath, holding that new car scent in her lungs for a moment before letting it out slowly. She giggled, feeling a sense of amazement and wonder as she found an empty space and parked her new Malibu in Cobo Hall's rooftop structure.

I love the feel of a new car, she thought, smoothing her hands over the leather burgundy steering wheel. After driving the Caprice for more years than she cared to remember, she'd finally gotten rid of the old Chevy and purchased her first brand-new car.

Her next move involved signing the lease on her first apartment. Finally, she was making a life for herself independent of her family.

Krista took the escalator to the first floor, exited Cobo Hall through a set of double doors, and jogged across Washington Boulevard. She entered the building housing her office and crossed the lobby to the bank of elevators. Minutes later, Krista stepped onto the sales floor of Dexter Kee and made her way through the bull pen, toward her office.

Krista passed Brennan's office on her way to pick up her messages. The lights were out. Surprised, she stopped and turned the knob and found the door locked. She pursed her lips. What was going on with him? she wondered and then shrugged off her concern. What Brennan did with his time had nothing to do with her. *That's a lie,* whispered a nagging little voice in her head. She did care deeply about what went on with Brennan. There was nothing she could do for or to him. They were done, finished. Krista tucked Brennan into the small recesses of her mind and continued on her way to the administrative assistant's workstation.

"Hi, Tanisha." Krista dropped her purse on the tall gray surface of the administrative assistant's cubicle and placed her briefcase on the floor, next to her leg.

"Hi, Ms. Hamilton," replied Tanisha.

"How are you?"

"I'm fine." The administrative assistant handed Krista several pink scraps of paper.

"Thanks." She sifted through her messages, discarding some and keeping those from people she planned to call back later. "Anyone looking for me?"

The dinging from the elevator caught Krista's attention, and she turned toward the sound, expecting to see Brennan step onto the floor. Instead, Erin Saunders strolled into the area, with a notepad under her arm. All of Krista's good cheer flew out the window, and the hair at the back of her neck rose. Why was Erin constantly on this floor? She didn't work here, nor had she been assigned any project involving the sales force.

Tanisha shook her head. "Nope. You're fine."

Refocusing on the assistant, Krista answered, "Good. That's the way I like it." She hated to ask, but she wanted to know. "Where's Brennan? Is he in a meeting? Or out of the building?"

"Neither. He called in," Tanisha answered over the soft hum of her printer. She pulled a fresh sheet from the machine and slipped it into a folder.

A twinge of apprehension flowed through Krista's veins, and she found herself studying Brennan's dark office for clues. That was odd. In the months she'd worked for the sales department, Brennan had never taken a day off or called in sick. If he needed to be out of the building, he always left word for her. "Really? Is he sick?"

"No. Mr. Thomas is home with his sister." Tanisha glanced around her and then answered quickly. "Apparently, they received word that Mrs. Gillis's husband has been reported missing."

"What?" Shock flew through her, and her mouth dropped open. Krista's heart pounded, while her hands shook. She stared at the assistant, waiting for more info.

The administrative assistant nodded solemnly. "Mr. Thomas told me that Mr. Gillis's plane went down somewhere behind enemy lines. They think he's being held as a hostage."

Poor Liz. She must be going mad waiting for information about her husband.

She felt drained and could hardly lift her voice above a whisper. "When did this happen?"

The phone rang. Tanisha lifted a finger and picked up the receiver. Once she finished the call, she replied, "I don't know. I think it happened sometime over the last few days."

Krista hadn't spoken with Liz since learning about the bet. Krista figured Brennan and his sister had teamed up to work the scam. To avoid all the apologies and recrimination about the incident, she'd avoided talking to Liz and refused to discuss anything other than work with Brennan.

But now things were different. Krista nibbled on her bottom lip. Liz needed all the support she could get.

Should she call? See if there was any way she could help? Or go to them? There was another dilemma. Would they welcome her presence in such a tense situation?

"Thanks. If you need me, I'll be in my office," said Krista. "Okay."

Krista started down the hall but halted as an idea hit her. "If Brennan checks in, I'd like to speak with him. Okay?"

"Sure. I'll transfer him to you," replied Tanisha.

Through her shock, Krista tried to smile. Her face felt stiff and unnatural. "Thanks." She made her way to her office, unlocked the door, stepped inside, and turned on the light.

"Oh, Liz," Krista moaned softly. She couldn't imagine what Brennan's sister must be going through. The conversation she'd heard between Liz and Steve came to mind. Liz had prophesied that Steve would be in danger, and she'd begged him to be careful. Steve, the ever confident pilot, had dismissed his wife's concerns with an understanding and reassuring pat on the shoulder.

Krista made her way across the floor to her desk and dropped heavily into her chair. Poor Liz. If Brennan was missing, Krista would be frantic with worry. Krista reached for the telephone, intent on calling and offering her support.

Stop, Krista. Don't go there. This is not your business. She understood Liz's plight. The love she felt for Brennan beat as steady as the rhythm of her heart. Although Brennan was here and she could touch him, she'd lost the love of her life when Erin snatched away her dream.

She returned the phone to its base and bowed her head. What could she do to help?

The door opened, and Krista glanced toward the entrance. Erin Saunders stood in the doorway. Without waiting for an invitation, the woman stepped inside and shut the door behind her.

Krista planted a calm, almost bored expression on her face. "Is there something I can help you with?"

"I just heard about Brennan." Erin slithered across the room. Her fangs dripped with blood. "Isn't it awful?"

Krista intertwined her fingers and responded calmly, "Yes, it is."

"You and Brennan are so close. I imagine you know all the details. Oops!" Erin covered her mouth with her hand and then giggled. "Sorry. That was before you broke up."

Krista's eyes narrowed into angry slits, and her nose flared with fury. Her voice dropped an octave. "Erin, what do you want?"

The other woman shrugged and answered, with a hint of malice, "Nothing that you can give me."

"Then leave." Krista rose and circled the desk.

Erin gasped softly, and her eyes widened. She quickly masked her surprise behind a snarl and a verbal attack. "My, my, my, Krista wolf. Aren't you feisty this afternoon."

"Don't call me that ever again. To you, my name is Krista or Ms. Hamilton."

This time it took a moment longer for Erin to recover from Krista's response. Erin's gaze swept over Krista and then dismissed her. "You really want to be called Mrs. Thomas. Too bad, so sad," Erin sang while her head swayed from side to side. "That'll never happen."

Krista moved closer, planted her hands on her hips. "Okay. I've had enough of you. You seem to have an inflated opinion of yourself. Let me put everything in perspective."

"Are you sure you can do it without tripping over your own feet?" Erin's smile faded a little.

A muscle quivered in her jaw, but Krista arranged her face into a calm mask. "Absolutely. You're right about one thing. It'll never happen"—she paused dramatically—"for you."

Erin's head snapped back as if she'd been slapped, but she mouthed off with the force of a punch to the gut. "You can give up on me calling you Ms. Hamilton. It'll be a gift if I call you Krista."

"I'm not in the mood. Nor is this the time for you and your cattiness. There are more important things going on." She pointed a hand toward the door. "Good-bye."

Erin's pretty features quickly twisted into a cruel mask of anger. "Krista wolf, you are not dismissing me."

Now it was Krista's turn to get angry. Since the day she'd started at Dexter Kee, Erin had haunted and taunted her. The woman had laughed at her and made ugly remarks about her hair, clothes, and personality. No more. Krista stalked up to the other woman. "No more!"

Erin sneered, "You think you're so important. Special. Let me clear things up for you. You're not!"

Krista didn't want to lose her cool. Erin would love that. It would be another tidbit to relay to all the staff and twist to her advantage. Not today. She planned to stay in charge and put Erin in her place.

"I don't care what you think. My name is Krista. Not Krista wolf or anything else you come up with. Understand?"

Erin snorted, dropping her hands to her hips. "And if I choose to ignore you and do what I want? What are you going to do?"

"I know you're an IT person. And you probably don't read much else. There are laws against harassment, and Dexter Kee must adhere to them." Grinning at the other woman, Krista shrugged. "People forget and think they can say or do anything. You can't. If I hear a whisper of those names come out of your mouth again, I'm going down to HR to file a grievance against you. It'll be easy. Think back. How many people have heard you use that phrase? You've been with Dexter Kee since you got out of college. How would you explain the gap on your resume if you omit the agency?" She perched on the edge of her desk, folded her arms, and grinned broadly at Erin. "Now that we've establish the rules, I suggest you go back to IT and do some work."

"We're not finished." Erin's face turned beet red.

"That's where you're wrong. Good-bye."

Erin stomped across the room, yanked open the door, and stormed out.

Krista laughed long and hearty, enjoying the feeling of liberation she felt at putting Erin in her place. That talk had been long overdue. No more. This was her life and she planned to live it and no one would hurt or use her again.

Chapter 33

After an afternoon of fielding questions about Brennan and Liz, Krista felt relieved to see the end of the day. Once she left the office, she sat in her car for several minutes, debating whether she should shoot down Jefferson and go to Brennan's house.

Finally, she decided it would be rude to drop in when there had been so many painful words between them. Instead, Krista steered the car toward the Lodge Freeway and headed home. Fifteen minutes later, she pulled the car into her spot in front of the house and turned off the engine.

On her way to the side door, Krista stopped and took a moment to glance around the neighborhood. Most of the well-maintained homes were owned by elderly couples. They'd watched her grow up and had offered advice when she needed it. A tear escaped and rolled down her cheek. This wouldn't be her home for much longer. The sensation of incredible loss filled her. This had been the only home she'd ever known, and she was about to lose it for good.

If Auntie had her way, the house would be sold, and they would be living elsewhere before Christmas. If the number of prospective buyers traipsing through the house indicated anything, it looked as if it might sell sooner rather than later.

She unlocked the door and stepped inside. The aroma of fresh-brewed coffee and fried fish filled the first floor. "Aunt Helen?" Krista called, heading for the staircase leading to the second floor.

"I'm in the den."

Krista changed direction and strolled through the kitchen to the back of the house. Katie Couric's perky voice filled the room as her image filled the television screen.

Aunt Helen sat on the sofa, watching the news. "Hi."

"Hey." She moved across the room, kicked off her shoes, tossed her purse on the coffee table, and curled up on the love seat, with her feet tucked under her. Silently, they watched the news together. Once it ended, Auntie used the remote to switch to *Wheel of Fortune.*

Krista smiled sadly. It had been a long time since they'd shared an intimate moment like this. She wanted to savor it and hold it close for the times when they weren't together.

"How's the car?" Auntie asked, taking her attention away from the contestants to question her niece.

Krista grinned. "Great!"

"Good. I want a ride Saturday if the weather's clear."

"Okay," Krista answered.

"You hungry?"

"Little bit," Krista admitted.

Nodding, the older woman pointed toward the kitchen. "Fried catfish, smothered potatoes with onions, and corn are on the stove if you want some."

"Thanks. I'll get it in a minute. How was your day?"

"Good. I had some folks in here looking at the house." Aunt Helen picked up her cup and saucer, sipping her coffee.

"How is it going?"

"Real good. Got an offer this morning."

Krista's belly twisted into knots. This was it. She was on the brink of the end of her childhood life and the beginning of her adult life.

Think positive, Krista. After all, this is what Auntie wanted. She swallowed her misgivings and said, "Wow! That's great! Are you going to take it?"

Aunt Helen looked around the room, and Krista saw tears swimming in her tired brown gaze. "I haven't decided. The people who were here today seemed real interested. I'll wait and see if they say anything."

"What makes them different?"

Auntie shifted around on the sofa, searching for a more comfortable spot, and placed her cup and saucer on the end table. "They were a young couple with two kids and one on the way. They need a place like this."

Nodding, Krista said, "I can see that."

Auntie cleared her throat and asked, "What was your day like? Anything interesting goin' on?"

"Crazy."

"Mmm?"

Krista stretched out on the love seat. "Liz's husband is missing."

Aunt Helen's brow crinkled into a frown. "Isn't that man in the army?"

"Air force."

Nodding, Auntie asked, "How's she taking it?"

"I don't know," Krista admitted.

"Isn't she your friend?"

"Sort of." She shifted uncomfortably under the older woman's steady gaze. "All that stuff with the bet is still between us. They made me feel like a fool."

"What's that got to do with anything? If you care about that girl, you'll get over there and see about her."

I don't believe she's saying this, Krista thought. "Even after everything that's happened between us, you think I should drop by and comfort Liz?"

"Stop and think. She just had a baby, and now her husband's God knows where. I'm sure her brother is doin' every-thang he can to help. But she needs a woman who knows them both and understands the situation." Auntie pointed a finger at Krista. "That's you. Don't turn your back on her."

"She probably does need help. But why does it have to be me?"

"That girl needs you. I'd bet good money, Liz feels too guilty to reach out to you. She knows you're hurtin' and she's responsible."

"I don't know. They hurt me, Auntie," Krista's voice quivered, and she fought unsuccessfully to bring it under control. "They hurt me so bad."

"No, they didn't. They shamed you. You can get over that. You look good. From what I've been hearing, you're holdin' you own against some other folks. They helped you."

No denying that. After years of abuse, she'd finally put Erin Saunders and Flynn Parr in their places. And it felt wonderful. She'd bought her first car and was looking for an apartment. The staff was treating her like a colleague instead of a geek. It was true, things had changed for the better.

"Think about how alone you've felt in the past. How people abandoned you when you really needed them. What that girl and her brother did wasn't right. But it's over. Remember what Reverend Jacobs says about forgiveness and understanding." Auntie placed her hands on her small bosom. "You can't move on unless you forgive. Be the bigger person. Go see them. Help that girl. Even if you don't patch up your differences with her brother, you'll feel better."

"I don't know."

"Yeah, you do. That's why you brought it to me." She chuckled. "You just didn't think I'd say this."

Krista started to laugh. "You are so right."

"I'm goin' to always tell you what's right. You may not like hearing it. But I'm gonna tell you." Auntie grabbed Krista's purse and tossed it at her and then tilted her head toward the door. "What you waitin' on? Go on over there and see about them. Don't rush back."

Krista dug in her purse and removed her key ring. Standing, she stepped around the coffee table and leaned down, giving her aunt a hug. "I know you don't like to hear it, but I'm going to say it, anyway. I love you."

"Go on, gurl," Auntie shooed her away with a wave of her hand.

For the second time that evening, Krista noticed tears in her aunt's eyes. Tentatively, Auntie's hand rose and gently caressed Krista's cheek. "I love you, too. You're the most important person in my life."

"Mine too, Auntie. We're family."

"Good or bad. We are." She dabbed at her eyes with the sleeve of her sweater. "Now git! Take care of your business."

Had she been selfish, ignoring Liz's needs? Should she be at Liz's side, helping her with Joshua, answering the door, and fielding calls? If their roles were reversed, Krista would want someone she cared about around to help.

Auntie might have been right, but Krista still had misgivings over how Brennan and Liz would receive her. That didn't stop her from pulling into a parking space near the town house. She locked up her car, walked up to the front door, and rang the doorbell.

Nervously waiting, Krista rubbed her sweaty palms against her skirt. *This is going to be all right. It's the right thing to do,* she chanted silently.

After a moment, the door swung open, and Brennan stood in the entrance. His eyes widened a fraction when he recognized the woman on his doorstep.

Dressed in a pair of denims and a loose-fitting sweatshirt, he looked wonderful. Krista's body quivered in response to seeing Brennan.

Repeatedly blinking at her, he muttered, "Krista?"

Nodding, she swallowed the lump lodged in her throat and gently patted her hand against her chest, trying to calm her rapidly beating heart. Clearing her throat, Krista asked in a soft, embarrassed tone, "Can I come in?"

"Sure." He stepped aside and waved a hand at the house's interior.

Once inside, she waited, awkwardly standing in the hallway, twisting the strap of her purse around her fingers. She grabbed a quick peek at Brennan before turning away.

Etched with heavy lines of fatigue and worry, his face was drawn into a tight, unhappy mask. Without another word, he marched past her to the living room. She followed at a slower pace, wondering why she'd let Aunt Helen talk her into this meeting.

"Liz is upstairs with the baby, I'll get her."

"Thanks." Jazzy, upbeat tunes from the DirecTV music channel greeted Krista when she entered the living room. She sat on the end of the leather sofa, picked up a copy of Bob Woodward's book *State of Denial*, and placed it on the coffee table after skimming the pages.

Hesitating, Brennan stood over her and asked, "You heard."

"Yes. How is she?"

"Holding up." He shook his head and then lowered his voice. "Hiding her true feelings."

Frowning, Krista glanced around the room. "Where's Steve's family? I thought they'd be here."

"They were. Liz sent them home. I think they were getting on her nerves. She promised she'd call when she got any news."

"I'm so sorry."

"Really?" His harsh tone caused Krista to flinch. "I would have thought you'd enjoy seeing us get what we probably deserve."

"I'm not here to gloat," she answered in a soft voice and

then looked into his eyes and saw pain. It twisted her heart. She wanted to wrap her arms around him and hold him close. It took everything in her to remain seated.

"Then why are you here?" Brennan shot back, hands on his hips.

"To help if I can," Krista answered, nervously fidgeting with her purse strap.

Brennan stood over her with his arms folded. His eyes flashed with contempt. "Right," he drawled. "For weeks you made it real clear that you don't want anything to do with me or my family. And yet today you're here wanting to play Florence Nightingale. Why?"

"For Liz."

His mouth spread into a thin-lipped smile. "If my memory serves me correctly, you were pissed at Liz because she knew about the bet."

"This isn't about you or me, Brennan. I'm still upset about the way you tricked me. It was cruel, and you hurt me. But that's not why I'm here. Liz needs all the support and comfort she can get, and I plan to be there for her, if she wants me. This has nothing to do with you."

"She's got me," he reminded.

"Yes, Liz does. And she's blessed to have you. You're lucky to have each other." Krista raised one finger and added, "I think in this case, she needs a woman to talk to, a person to help with Joshua, and time to be alone when she wants it."

There wasn't much he could say, and she knew it. He snorted and turned away.

"I know you can help with most of that," said Krista. "Although I'm pretty sure, you're not a woman. I think you've gotten really good with the baby, but a little added help wouldn't hurt."

Before Brennan could add another comment, Liz burst into the room. "Who was that at the door?" She halted, mouth wide open. "Krista?"

"It's me," Krista answered, feeling the unyielding coil of apprehension twist the knots in her belly.

With outstretched arms, Liz rushed across the room. Krista rose from the sofa and met Liz halfway, wrapping her friend in a huge bear hug. "You came," Liz cried into the other woman's hair. "Thank you."

Over Liz's shoulder, Krista glanced in Brennan's direction. One eyebrow rose with satisfaction. *I told you.* Silently, he backed out of the room and started down the hallway, leaving the women alone.

Chapter 34

With an angry twist of her wrist, Krista snapped off the radio. The escalating violence in Iraq tore a hole in her heart each time the news reported more details.

Fighting for control, she let out a shaky breath of air and gripped the underside of the countertop. If she were a superhero, the granite surface would have splintered into a zillion pieces.

Krista searched for something to focus on. Her gaze landed on the calendar hanging from a tack on the opposite wall. Steve had been officially declared missing in action for almost a month. Thirty long and wearisome days without an update, follow-up, or call from the military.

A lack of appetite, sleepless nights, and worry were taking their toll on Liz. The young woman was barely holding herself together. Something had to change soon because Liz's fragile façade was breaking down under the stress.

Krista did what she could. She dropped by every evening after work. For the past few weekends, she'd split her free time between Brennan's house, taking care of Joshua, and home, packing for the big move.

What a difference a month made. Aunt Helen had sold the house and had made provisions to move before Thanksgiving.

Krista had been so involved with Brennan and Liz, she hadn't found a place to live. If she didn't watch out, she'd find herself homeless.

A distressed cry blared from the baby monitor. Joshua was awake. Krista started for the staircase.

Brennan met her in the hallway and shooed her away. "I'll take care of Joshua," he offered, taking the stairs two at a time. Relieved from diaper changing duty, she returned to the kitchen, searching the cabinets for something delicious to serve to Liz.

Granted, Krista didn't produce Emeril-quality feasts, but she did have the skills to put together a reasonably healthy and tasty meal. She gathered the ingredients for spaghetti and meat sauce and then returned everything to the shelves. A tray laden with heavy food might turn Liz off. Maybe something light would restore the young mother's appetite.

Krista opened the refrigerator door, scanning the contents for something appealing. Finally, she settled on a sliced turkey breast sandwich on wheat with Swiss cheese, sweet iced tea, and pineapple slices. She removed the ingredients from the fridge, set the items on the counter, and went to work on making sandwiches.

Ten minutes later, Brennan entered the room, with Joshua in his arms. A few steps inside the kitchen, he pointed a finger in Krista's direction and said to the baby, "See, there's Krista. I told you she wouldn't leave without seeing you."

Krista grinned in approval. She loved the image of this large man with the infant in his arms. Her thoughts turned inward; at one point she had imagined Brennan with their baby. Unfortunately, her dreams of a happily ever after had quickly faded. Shaking off those disturbing thoughts, Krista concentrated on preparing lunch.

Brennan crossed the floor and stood next to her. Unable to resist the happy baby, she leaned close and kissed Joshua's cheek. Over the baby's head, she studied the man. Liz wasn't the only person affected by Steve's disappearance. Brennan was fighting his own demons. His voice was drawn, and dark circles created half-moons under his eyes. Although he was still fit, Krista could see his denims sagged from weight loss.

The desire to run her fingers across his forehead and smooth away his worry wrinkles nearly overwhelmed her. Turning away, she steadied her shaky hand by placing the sandwiches on a tray.

Brennan's unique scent wafted through the air and filled her nostrils, making her acutely aware of his virile presence and the sensual way he moved. Her belly twisted into knots. She couldn't deny what her heart and body kept telling her. The love she felt for Brennan hadn't died. It had grown stronger daily.

No matter what she believed or felt, their feelings couldn't be actualized, not anymore. The trust between them had been broken. Like Humpty Dumpty, it couldn't be put back together again.

A sort of truce had been established between them. The recent time they'd spent together had repaired part of the breach, but not all of it. They had rallied their forces in an effort to support and help Liz through this difficult time.

Watching him cuddle the baby, Krista realized how much she missed the closeness she once shared with Brennan. She found it almost impossible to remain focused and not react to his nearness when she visited the town house.

Brennan still made her heart sing. She wanted to touch him, kiss him, snuggle in his embrace, and forget all their problems. Sometimes when they transferred the baby from one to the other, she lingered a moment, enjoying the feel of his body intertwined with hers. Those feelings made her want to forget the past, throw herself into his arms, and tell him how much she still loved him.

Don't think about it, Krista warned, remembering how they'd made love in this room, enjoying their time together and savoring the moments. They weren't lovers anymore. But since Steve's disappearance, they had reclaimed their friendship.

"Hello, baby Joshua," Krista cooed, tickling him under his chin. He smelled of baby powder, lotion, soap, and that special scent known exclusively to babies. He giggled happily, squirming away while pushing her hand away.

Wouldn't life be simpler if she were as oblivious as Joshua? Tears sprung to her eyes, and she turned away, wiping them away with the back of her hand.

Moving closer, Brennan squeezed her shoulder and encouraged her softly. "It's going to be okay. Just hold on. Steve won't leave his family without a fight. Believe me, that man is stubborn and creative. He'll find a way to get back to his family."

"I know. Sometimes it's really h-ha-hard to stay positive, upbeat," she answered, dabbing at her tears with a paper towel.

"Tell me about it," Brennan muttered sorrowfully. He eyed the tray. "Is that for Lizzie?"

Krista nodded.

He sighed heavily and shifted the baby from one arm to the other. "I hope you can get her to eat. She's losing so much weight. I'm worried about her."

Biting her lip, she admitted, "Me, too."

"I don't think Liz has swallowed more than a couple of spoonfuls of soup all week." His eyes were dark with concern, while his voice turned husky with fear. "Lizzie can't keep going this way. She's going to make herself sick."

"I know." Now he needed her comfort. Krista patted his arm reassuringly and then reached down to link their hands. "I'll do what I c-ca-can to encourage her."

Brennan cleared his throat and said, "Thanks. I don't know what we'd do without you."

"Don't worry about that." She caressed the baby's cheek. "Does Joshua need anything?"

"No. I've got him." Brennan went to the refrigerator and removed a baby bottle filled with formula. He popped it in the microwave oven and programmed the machine for thirty seconds. "Joshua's been changed, and I'm going to feed him. You take care of Liz, and I'll take care of my future basketball star."

Smiling sadly, Krista picked up the tray and started for the hall. "Brennan, there are sandwiches in the refrigerator for you."

He saluted her with a wave of his hand before opening the microwave-oven door and removing the bottle. He sprinkled a few drops of formula on his wrist. "What about you? Do you want me to wait?"

"No. I think I'll s-st-stay with Liz until she's done."

"Thanks, Krista. I appreciate everything you've done for us."

I haven't done enough, Krista thought, wishing she knew of a way to persuade the young mother to eat and keep up her strength. "I'll be down in a bit. Will you guys be okay?"

He jostled the baby in the crook of his arm. "Certainly. Won't we, little bud? We have a lot to talk about."

Laughing gently, Krista strolled down the hall to the staircase. Balancing the tray of food, she climbed the stairs carefully, hit the second floor, and made her way to Liz's room. After tapping lightly on the door, she waited for a beat before entering the bedroom.

"Hi," said Krista.

Liz sat on the edge of the bed, with Steve's photo in her hands. "Hey."

The despair in Liz's eyes made Krista's gut cramp. Light-headed, she swayed unsteadily on her feet, mentally searching for a way to help her friend.

"I thought you m-mi-might want something to eat," Krista explained, crossing the carpeted floor.

"Mmm. I'm not really hungry," Liz responded.

Krista placed the tray on the dresser and returned to the bed. She sat down next to Liz and reached for the photo. "Let me have that."

Resisting for a moment, Liz held on to the framed print. Tears welled in her eyes, and she whined, "I miss him."

Pain squeezed Krista's heart. "I know." She gently pried Liz's hands from the silver picture frame. "But Steve wouldn't want you to fall a-ap-apart or get sick. Honey, you have a baby that needs you, too."

Nodding, Liz wiped away her tears.

Krista returned to the dresser and picked up the iced tea. "Come on. Drink this for me. I made it the way you like it."

Liz took the glass and cradled it between her hands without drinking.

Krista placed her hand under the bottom of the glass and lifted it toward Liz's lips. After a moment, Liz took a sip.

"It's good," said Liz.

Krista quickly went back to the dresser and returned with the tray. She placed it between them on the bed. "Maybe you should try one of the sandwiches."

Laughing softly, Liz asked, "When did you become so slick and persuasive?"

"It's in the genes."

Frowning, Liz gazed at Krista, with a question in her eyes.

"My aunt. That little woman knows how to make people do exactly what she wants."

Liz picked up half of one of the sandwiches and took a tiny bite. Nodding approvingly, she took a second bite and then a third. With a little encouragement, she finished off most of one sandwich and a pineapple ring. Liz brushed the crumbs from her T-shirt with a napkin and said, "Wow! I didn't realize I was so hungry. Thank you."

"You're welcome." Krista picked up the tray and started for the door.

"Krista?" Liz called.

Tray in hand, Krista turned toward the bed. "Yeah?"

"Don't go. Please."

The expression on Liz's face sent a chill down Krista's spine. The nervous edge of her voice and the way she kept pleating the comforter between her fingers made Krista wonder what her friend had on her mind.

"Sure. Let me get rid of the tray," said Krista. She placed the tray outside the door and returned to the bed, gingerly sitting on the edge of the mattress. "What's up?"

"Thank you," Liz uttered somberly.

"Anytime."

"No. You don't understand." She took Krista's hand and held it between both of hers. "Thank you for being my friend again. After everything that happened between you, me, and Brennan, I thought I'd lost that friendship forever. I didn't think we'd get beyond it."

Turning away, Krista shifted uncomfortably. This was not a conversation she wanted to have. Her feelings had been put aside to help Liz and Brennan, but she refused to dive into the most embarrassing and painful period in her life. "Let's not talk about that."

"We've got to," Liz pleaded. "Please hear me out. All morning I've been thinking about Steve and our life together. How we met. The good and bad times we shared." With a hysterical little giggle, Liz added, "Who could ever forget the arguments. We've had some shouting matches that would curl your hair. None of that matters now." The shadow of a smile flashed so quickly across Liz's face, Krista wasn't sure she'd seen it. "Having Joshua made it almost perfect. Getting Steve home safe is all I want." Liz burst into tears.

Unsure how to answer, Krista wrapped her arms around her friend and held her, letting her tears flow. Maybe it would help cleanse Liz's soul and give her the strength to keep going. After a few minutes, Liz drew away, wiping her eyes with the back of her hands.

Liz went on. "You've been so good to us, helping around here with me and the baby. I don't know anyone else that would do what you've done. My so-called good friends have deserted me. Yet you're here every day."

Uneasy, Krista tried to shift the conversation to a different topic. "Joshua is really growing. Your little man is really special."

"Don't change the subject. Let me apologize. Honestly, there's a part of me that feels that I've got what I deserved for hurting you." Her voice quivered uncontrollably. Liz paused and then started again. "For being arrogant and thinking that I had all the answers. And yet the logical side of my brain knows that it's all a coincidence. I know Brennan and I hurt you with the bet, and I'm truly sorry, Krista. So I want to make amends."

"There's no need. We're good." Intent on getting out of the room, Krista rose from the bed.

Liz caught her hand and held on. "No, we're not. I'm just telling you things you need to hear. Please listen."

Krista didn't know what to say. Maybe Liz needed to get all this old baggage off her chest so that she could breathe easier.

"This isn't just about me. It's about you and Brennan. Since you've been in my brother's life, he's been happier then I've ever seen him. He laughs more. Talks about you all the time and discusses his plans for the future."

"There is no Brennan and me."

"I'm sorry, honey. I disagree with you. Yes, there is. Whether you want to admit it or not, it's there. The chemistry, the feelings between you two are so clear, you can't deny them. It's like you two are connected, and when you're separated, you're not happy until you're together again. I know you're upset with him, and you have good reason to be. But I want you to consider two things. One. How would you feel if you never saw him again? Use my situation as an example. Could you live with yourself? Would you want to live without him?"

Liz's question jolted Krista. It made her consider how she would feel if Brennan disappeared from her life. Could she survive that? Would she want to?

"Two. I know love needs nurturing to survive. Do you really want yours to die?" Liz's voice cracked and broke over her words. "I'd give almost anything to have Steve home safe and sound. Are you willing to give up on Brennan so easily? Let the love die between you two and go on?"

That question was easily answered. No. She didn't want Brennan out of her life. But she didn't know how to trust him anymore.

Krista rose from the bed. Liz grabbed her arm before she took a step away.

"Listen to me. It's important," said Liz. "I love my husband, and I'd give just about anything to know he's safe and is coming home." Tears dotted Liz's cheeks. She ignored them, continuing to speak. "Anything could happen to him in Iraq and might already have."

Krista turned away, fighting her own feelings of pain and betrayal. She didn't want to go down this road.

Liz went on. "Brennan loves you. He won't bother you anymore or explain about the bet. But my brother is suffering as much as you are. He misses you. I see the pain and heartache in his eyes every day."

Krista looked away.

"You can ignore me all you want," said Liz. "I know the truth. You love Brennan as much as he loves you." Sighing, she dropped Krista's hand and brushed away her tears, wiping them on her denims. "Don't let your anger and pride keep you from love. You've come so far. Everything you've craved, respect from your peers and success on your job, is yours. Brennan told me about how you saved the presentation and helped him get the VP job. He's proud of you. Complete the circle by grabbing the love you deserve."

"Forget about me," said Krista. "I think you need to concentrate on Steve. Your brother and I understand each other."

"I know I'm butting in where I don't belong. You and Brennan are adults who can make your own decisions. But I love my brother, and I care about you. I can't pretend that I don't see how much you're both hurting. I miss my husband. If Steve's . . ." Liz stopped, swallowed loudly, and gathered her strength. The words quivered on her lips. "If he's dead, then that's what I have to live with. But I won't regret one day of loving him. What would you say if something happened to Brennan? Would you have regrets? Don't let the love for my brother die. I know you'll hate yourself for making this mistake for the rest of your life. Do you want to spend your life with what if?"

No. She didn't.

"Promise me, you'll think about it," Liz begged.

Standing, Krista looked down at her friend, noting the sincerity in her gaze. "I will."

"Good. That's all I can ask." Sighing heavily, Liz scooted up the bed and leaned against the headboard. "I'm tired. I think I'll take a nap."

Nodding, Krista crossed the floor and left the room. She picked up the tray and made her way downstairs. Brennan and Joshua were at the table when she entered the kitchen. Silently, she watched the pair as he fed the baby.

Liz's words rolled around in her head. How do you rebuild trust? Krista wasn't sure she knew how to do it. One thing was for sure: Liz had made several good points. Maybe after things settled down, Krista would ask Brennan to sit down with her, and they could try to address some of their problems. Maybe.

Chapter 35

"I'm on my way," Krista spoke into the telephone. She dropped the receiver into the cradle and picked up a pad and pen before slipping out of her office. Krista tapped on Brennan's door and poked her head inside the room. He sat behind his desk, looking out the window overlooking the Detroit River.

He swiveled the chair, facing the door. "Hi."

"Hi. You wanted to see me?"

Nodding, he waved her inside. "Yeah. Come on in."

A feeling of déjà vu overwhelmed her. This had become their working routine in the five months she'd been with Brennan's team. She'd sit in his office, and they'd brainstorm over an issue until they found a solution.

Krista shut the door, crossed the floor, and slid into a chair at the desk. "Is everything all right?"

Brennan drew in a deep breath and let it out slowly. His features were shadowed with exhaustion and clouded with sadness. Krista fought the urge to comfort him and rush to his side. She ignored her instincts, concentrating on his face. "Did something happen?" she asked.

He shook his head. "Nothing's different. I'm worried about my sister. It's almost Thanksgiving, and we haven't had any news about her husband in two months. I don't know how much longer Lizzie can hold on. She's so fragile right now. I'm afraid for her."

Krista understood completely. As weeks had turned into months, the bruises under Liz's eyes had grown darker. Her small frame had gotten thinner, and the wrinkles at her forehead seemed to be permanently etched into her skin.

"I know," she said. "And Joshua?"

Sadness changed to a giant smile of happiness. "Great! Last night, after you went home, my basketball star rolled over." That spark of happiness quickly faded to sadness. "Steve should be here to see how his son is growing."

Doing her best to quell the little voice in her head, she reached across the desk and placed her hand over his. For a moment, all of their past problems became insignificant. The warmth of his skin took her back to a better time, when they freely touched each other.

Brennan shook off his bad mood and slid his hand from under hers. He ran a finger up and down the bridge of his nose before saying, "Work keeps me focused and chases away the craziness. Speaking of work, let's get back to it. That's why I called you in here." The feelings he'd displayed a few minutes ago were neatly tucked away. Brennan Thomas, the vice president of marketing, sat before her. "Connor Dexter and I met this morning to discuss the Gautier contract. We talked in terms of specifics, including money. Your name came up." He grinned at Krista. "Connor was very pleased and proud of the way you handled the presentation."

"Thank you." That much she already knew. Mr. Dexter had made a point of visiting her office and congratulating her. And that was a big deal. In the three years she'd worked for the agency, Mr. Dexter had never visited before.

"We talked and agreed that if you're interested, we would like you to stay in this department as the special projects manager."

Krista's jaw dropped. Quickly shutting her mouth, she asked cautiously, "Manager?"

"Mm-hmm," he answered.

No more Rachel. Erin would have to complete her own projects. This was sounding really good. Krista still had one more question. "Does this include a raise?"

Chuckling, Brennan named a figure that represented approximately a 25 percent increase in her salary. "Yes. Plus, you'd receive the agency's American Express card."

She frowned. "Why would I need that?"

"You'll be management. As part of this team, you might have to do a small amount of entertaining of clients. Nothing major," he assured.

Entertaining clients still made her feel a bit uneasy. But the anxiety she usually felt faded in comparison to the promotion and raise. Krista could handle herself more effectively then she had a few months ago.

"I know you don't feel real comfortable with that," said Brennan. "But there are additional reasons you will need the card. For example, you might need something computerwise that we don't have, and you can go out and get it."

"Wow!"

He grinned. "Does that mean yes?"

A raise would help with finding a new place to live and moving expenses. Sure, she wanted the job. "Yes."

"Outstanding! I'll sign off on the paperwork so everything will be legal and official. I'm really happy you decided to stay here with us. You'll have better opportunities for career growth here than in IT."

"I th-th-think so, too," Krista responded.

"Let's get back to business. We need to come up with a commercial for the less-expensive line of Gautier cars. You had great data at the presentation. Could you work up a report using that info?"

"Sure."

"Mr. Gautier liked the idea of a simultaneous media and

Web-based campaign. We'll do the same sort of commercial designed for the less-expensive models."

"Smart move."

"Flynn brought up some relevant points at the meeting. We need to explore and refine our proposal." Brennan picked up his coffee cup and sipped from it. Although his tone remained light, Krista could tell that he still didn't like Flynn.

"Okay."

"I'll try to learn—" His next words were cut off by the ringing of the telephone. He reached for the handset, answering, "Brennan Thomas."

There was a pause, and then Brennan's voice went from cool professional to soothing. "Calm down, Lizzie girl."

Liz! Krista gave up all pretense of not listening. She turned to him with an "Is everyone all right?" gleam in her eyes. Rising from the chair, Krista circled the desk and stood in front of him.

"When did they contact you?" said Brennan. His knuckles were white around the handset. "How soon?"

Nervously waiting, Krista snagged her bottom lip between her teeth and tapped her foot against the carpeted floor. *Come on, Brennan. What's going on?*

"I'm on my way," he promised, dropping the phone back into the cradle and jumping to his feet, with a huge grin on his face. "They found him! Steve's alive!"

Without thinking, she threw her arms around Brennan and hugged him close. "Thank God! Thank God!"

The euphoria began to fade, and she recognized other details, like the fact that she was in Brennan's arms. It felt so good and right. She wished she could stay in his arms forever.

Liz's words came back to her. *Do you want to spend the rest of your life wondering what might have been?*

Embarrassed by her response, Krista took a step back, ran a hand over her forehead, and straightened her jacket. "Did Liz give you any info?"

With a slight tremor in his voice, he explained, "Apparently, they raided one of the camps and found him with a group of hostages. He's in Germany right now. They're working on his injuries, and then Steve'll be home in a week."

"Physically, how is he?"

He hunched his shoulders. "Liz said that he's okay. I'll reserve judgment until I see him. Anyway, I'm headed home to be with her. I'd like you to come with me."

The spark of hope in his eyes made her decision easy. She wanted to be with Brennan and Liz. Nodding, she moved around the desk and picked up her pad and pen. "I'm going to close up my office, and I'll meet you at the house," she said.

"See you there."

Krista returned to her office, leaned against the door, and let all the fear and pain ooze out of her body. Steve was okay. That was the best news they had received in weeks.

She was happy for her friend. But the question of her relationship with Brennan still needed an answer. There wouldn't be a reason for her to be around the family anymore. Was she ready to give up Brennan?

Two weeks later Steve Gillis returned to the Harbortown town house. Battered, bruised, and with three broken fingers, several cracked ribs, and a fractured right foot, Steve hobbled into the house.

From the living room entrance, Brennan and Krista watched. Tears sprung to Liz's eyes as she stepped close to her husband. Steve wrapped his arms around Liz and Joshua, holding them tightly in his arms.

Brennan and Krista slowly backed into the living room to give the family a moment of privacy. They heard the couple start up the stairs. Steve stumbled. Brennan rushed into the hallway. Krista followed, standing in the entrance of the living room.

Brennan moved to the right side of Steve and took the baby

and handed him to Krista. Brennan returned to the stairs and wrapped an arm around Steve's midsection, adding support and leverage.

"Now let's go," Brennan commanded, helping the man make it up the stairs. It was slow going: it took almost twenty minutes for them to disappear down the second-floor hallway.

A few minutes later, Brennan reappeared with the baby's diaper bag and a jacket. "They need some time alone. Let's go for a ride," he said to Krista.

"Bottles?"

He poked a finger toward the kitchen. "We'll get them on our way out the door."

Nodding, Krista helped Brennan put on Josh's jacket and followed him through the house to the kitchen. They stopped long enough to pick up three bottles before heading out the door.

"My car," he said, opening the back car door and placing the baby in the car seat.

Krista climbed into the front passenger seat and snapped her seat belt.

Brennan got behind the wheel, fastened his seat belt, started the engine, and backed out of the garage. He put the Saab in drive but didn't hit the gas.

"So where are we going?" Krista asked.

"I don't know." He had this lost and goofy expression on his face.

"You didn't think that far ahead?"

"Nope. They needed time alone. I figured we'd go somewhere else."

Giggling, Krista shook her head. "Let's go to my house." She looked back at Joshua to make sure he was okay. "I've been telling my aunt about this young man since he was born. I think she'd enjoy meeting him."

"Sounds outstanding."

Chapter 36

The sun shone high and bright in the cloudless sky on this November day as Krista, Brennan, and Joshua made their way to her house. For an instant, Krista imagined this was her family, and they were visiting her aunt.

Something deep and primal stirred inside her. Silently, she admitted she wanted all the trappings of a baby and husband of her own. And she wanted Brennan to be part of that life with her.

Brennan parked the Saab in front of Krista's house. Frowning, he turned to her and asked, "Still for sale?"

Shaking her head, Krista grabbed her purse and slung it over her shoulder. She opened the door and climbed out. "Sold."

He got out on the driver's side, ran around the car, and opened the back door, plucking the diaper bag from the Saab's floor. "Why didn't you tell me?"

Krista unhooked the harness securing Joshua in the car seat. Shrugging, she lifted the baby out of the vehicle. Using her hip, she shoved the door shut and started up the driveway. "You had enough on your plate. I didn't want to add anything new."

"You're important to me. I'd like to know what's going on

in your life. Maybe I can help," Brennan offered, following closely behind her.

"There's not much you can do for me," Krista tossed over her shoulder as she continued to the side door. "For almost two months, Liz and Steve stuff has dominated your world. Plus work. Gautier has been demanding a lot of material from us. My problems are the last thing you should be worried about."

He caught her arm and swung her around to face him. "How could you say that?" Pain crossed his handsome face. "It's not true. Krista, you're very important to me. Granted, Liz has monopolized most of my time lately. I care about what happens to you, too."

"We can't discuss this now," she said, resetting the baby on her hip.

"When?"

"Not now. Later."

Krista glanced in Brennan's direction. Their lives seemed so far away from the carefree time they'd spent together last summer. How could they get back to the loving days preceding Erin and her venomous tongue? An apology didn't seem to be enough to smooth the path back to each other.

She removed her keys from her pocket and unlocked the door, calling, "Auntie?"

"In the den," said her aunt.

Standing on the landing, Krista unzipped Joshua's jacket and wiggled him out of it. The scent of baby powder rose from his clothes. She climbed the two stairs leading to the kitchen, dropping Joshua's jacket on a chair en route to the den.

Boxes and crates lined the walls in every room. Paintings, trinkets, and framed photos filled cardboard boxes and wooden crates. Today *Court TV* flashed across the television screen. A man sat on the witness stand, describing a murder.

Auntie glanced up from the magazine in her hands. Her

eyes grew round with surprise and pleasure when she noticed the bundle in Krista's arms. "Who's this little fella?"

Krista sat on the sofa next to her aunt and tickled Josh's cheek. "You know who this is. I talk about him all the time. This is Joshua Gillis."

The older woman held out her hands. Joshua practically leapt from Krista's arms into Auntie Helen's. Laughing, Auntie caught the baby, cuddling him close to her chest. "Hello, Joshua. I've heard all about you."

"Hi, Mrs. Johnson," said Brennan.

Auntie acknowledged the man with a slight tilt of her head. "Brennan. How you doin'?"

"Good, thanks. And you?" he asked, sitting on the love seat across from Krista.

"Fine. Just fine. Krista, I thought you were gonna spend the day with your girlfriend. How come you're here? And with the baby?"

"Steve came home," Krista explained.

"Praise the Lord. I was worried about that boy," Aunt Helen muttered. "Is he okay?"

"Beat-up. Bumps and bruises and a couple of broken bones," said Krista. "But he'll be fine. Liz and Steve needed a little time alone, so we decided to cut out and come see you."

Joshua reached for Auntie's nose. She drew back. "Whoa, little one! Let go!" Grinning at her niece, Auntie Helen said, "He's awfully busy."

Laughing, Krista said, "Tell me about it."

Everyone sat watching the program on the television. After a few minutes, the old girl turned to Brennan, studying him for a beat. Auntie Helen then focused on Krista. Auntie had a sly smile on her face. Krista was shocked by the quick change from passive to devious. What was the old girl up to?

"Why don't you show your friend the rest of the house? Take him up to your place," said Auntie.

Why was her aunt doing this? "Sure," replied Krista. She stood and reached for the baby.

Shaking her head, Auntie Helen held the baby closer. "I'll keep him. We need to get to know each other better. Go on away. If I need you, I'll call."

"Okay." Krista moved through the room to the doorway leading to the front of the house. "Brennan, this way."

Nodding, he rose and followed her out of the den. The tour began in the dining room. Krista led him through to the living room. In the front hall, they took the stairs to the second-floor landing.

"This is where all the bedrooms are."

"Where did your uncle live?"

"Basement apartment," she answered.

"Wow! This is a huge house."

"Yeah. It is." She waved a hand at the bedroom doors. "Auntie Helen has her bedroom on this floor."

Whistling, he stepped around Krista and examined each room. He pointed a finger at a closed door. "Is this one of the bedrooms?"

"No. My place. Attic apartment," she explained.

"This house has a basement and one more floor, right?"

"Yeah."

"No wonder your aunt's thinking of selling. Can I see your place?"

"Sure." She opened the closed door, revealing another set of stairs. "Come on."

They crested the top of the stairs, and Brennan moved between the rooms. "This is nice."

She followed at a slower pace. "It's home."

"I like it." He turned to Krista. "Now that your aunt has sold the place, what do you plan to do?"

"Well, my boss just gave me a great raise," she teased. "I plan to use that money to help me find a new home. I'm leaning toward Canton or Plymouth."

Nodding somberly, Brennan stepped in front of her and dropped his hands on her shoulders. "Have you found anything?"

"Not really. I've been busy with other things."

"Yeah, you have," he muttered softly, massaging her shoulders. Krista found herself leaning into his touch. "It's tough leaving your childhood home, isn't it?"

Tears welled in her eyes as she glanced around the place where she'd had so many good as well as bad memories. She impatiently brushed them away with her hand. This was the only home she'd ever known, and pretty soon, it wouldn't be theirs anymore. Sadly, she dropped onto the sofa and answered, "That's for sure."

"If you need me, I'm here for you."

"I appreciate the offer."

He walked across the living room and glanced out the window facing the street. "You've got a nice view from here."

Talk to him. Tell him, cried the voice in her head. She cleared her throat and called, "Brennan."

Something in her tone must have struck a chord in him. He faced her, with a tiny frown marring his forehead. "Yes?"

"Can we talk?"

"Sure." He strolled back to where she sat and gazed down at her, studying her features. "What about?"

Here goes, she thought, taking a deep breath before answering, "Us."

Hope and surprise lit up his eyes, but he quickly hid it. "What do you mean?"

"You and me. The bet. Our feelings. It's time to put it all out in the open and figure out how to get us back. If we can," Krista whispered sorrowfully before patting the spot next to her. "Please come and sit with me."

Brennan followed her instructions and slipped into the place next to her. "Let me go first," he said. "I'm so, so sorry about the bet. I never meant to hurt you. After the picnic all I could think of was how to make life easier for you. I wanted to get those idiots off your back."

The more he tried to explain, the more uncomfortable Krista became. She didn't want to relive that time in her life. Or think about the way people had treated her before she developed a backbone. "I've heard all of this before. We don't need to replay the tape."

Brennan took her hand. "You do need to hear this. Part of the reason I went along with Flynn is I thought I could help. I figured it was a win-win situation. No one would get hurt."

"You were wrong. I did get hurt."

He dropped his head and muttered softly, "I know."

"Is what we feel for each other real? Do you think it's more than sex? Or were you trying out the new piece of tail?" Krista asked quietly.

"Truthfully, when I agreed to the bet, I didn't think I'd get so involved with you. I thought Liz would help you with your clothes and hair. And you would work in my office. I'd probably see you once or twice while you worked for me." He chuckled. "I was wrong. Everything I feel for you is real. You moved into my heart and became part of my life. Honestly, I don't ever want you to go. I love you."

Krista wanted to laugh and cry at the same time. The way he described things was cute, humorous. But she sympathized and understood how he felt.

"What about you?" he said. He cleared his throat. "Do you still care about me?"

"No."

Pain, deep and piercing, filled Brennan's eyes. He gasped, running a hand over his face. "I see."

"I don't care about you. I love you."

He turned to her, drawing her into his arms. He kissed her deeply, hungrily, and Krista returned his caress. God! How she'd missed him. After a moment of passion, she moved out of his embrace. Panting, she begged, "Please stop. We still have some things to work out."

A muffled curse escaped Brennan. Nodding, he rubbed his hand across his forehead. "What do you want me to do?"

"I want more. When I first went to work for you, all I wanted was for you to like me. Now I'm over that kind of puppy dog, schoolgirl crush. I need a man to love me for the person I am."

"I do."

"Are you sure? Am I your version of Frankenstein's monster?"

"Hell, no," he stated angrily. "And I don't ever want to hear you make that kind of comparison about yourself again. You were never a monster."

"No. I wasn't." She raised a finger in his direction. "Just illustrating a point. I don't know if you can handle it. But I have to say it. When we got out of the car and started up the driveway, all I could think about was having my own family. My husband and my child. I don't want to pretend anymore. I want a commitment. If you're not in this for the long haul, it's time for you to leave."

Smiling down at her, Brennan shook his head. "You are so smart. I want you and a life with you. What Liz has with Steve is where I want to go. The arguments, disagreements, and good times are all part of living and loving together. One big, crazy package. That's the way it's supposed to be."

"I want to stop being embarrassed about the mistakes I make. Everyone makes them. Mine just got amplified because I became a target. Can you take me the way I am?" Krista asked. "Not the way Liz revamped me? I drop food on my clothes and trip over my own feet. Sometimes I can't get a word out without stammering over it. That's the real me."

Brennan smiled.

"What?" she asked.

"I don't care about any of those things. You're fine to me just the way you are."

"Yeah. Right," Krista snorted.

"You are a wonderful person. A few days after you started working for me, we were doing something, I don't remember what, and you smiled at me. It was the most genuine smile I'd ever seen. I was awestruck. Your face lit up, and I couldn't look away. I remember going home and sitting in the living room, trying to figure out what the hell had happened."

Krista remembered that day. At the time she couldn't figure out what was going on with Brennan. It didn't seem real that he had been thinking of her.

"My hair was all over my head. I was dressed by Auntie Helen, and you were attracted to me."

"Yes. And it scared me. But it didn't stop me from spending time with you. If you remember, soon after that, we shared our first kiss."

She did remember that. It was soft and gentle. He gave and took so sweetly, and she had wished for more.

"I don't need you to feel sorry for me. I'm okay with who I am. The real question is, can you live with someone like me?"

"What do you want?" Brennan asked.

Thinking back to Erin's ugly words, Krista captured and held Brennan's gaze. "I don't need or want you to save me. I can take care of myself. What I want is a partner who loves and respects me regardless of whether I can go to the boardroom and dazzle a group of execs. I'm Krista and everything that goes with her. Can you live with that?"

"Absolutely. I want you to be Krista." He tucked a lock of her hair behind her ear and smiled at her. "No one else."

"Brennan, I want it all, a career, marriage, and family. What do you want?"

"You. And everything that goes with you. Whether you're working behind the scenes to snag a client for the agency, or the woman that made love with me on my kitchen floor. You're what I want to come home to at night."

His mention of the kitchen floor made her blush. But she didn't look away. She'd done those things and had enjoyed each and every time they had been together. It was time to own up to them.

"I love you and want you in my life," Brennan stated simply.

"Then what's next?"

"It's time to think about the next step."

"What's that?"

"This isn't the way I planned to do this. But here goes." Brennan slipped to the floor and stood before her on bended knee. He held her hand. "Krista, we love each other. I don't want to waste any more time. I want us to be a family. Will you marry me?"

Smiling at him, she wrapped her arms around his neck and whispered, "Yes!"